THERE'S A
MAN WITH A GUN
OVER THERE

OTHER BOOKS BY R. M. RYAN

Goldilocks in Later Life

The Golden Rules

Vaudeville in the Dark

THERE'S A MAN WITH A GUN OVER THERE

R. M. RYAN

The Permanent Press
Sag Harbor, NY 11963

Hunger Mountain published Chapter Four, in a slightly different version, as "The Veterans."

For information, address:
The Permanent Press
4170 Noyac Road
Sag Harbor, NY 11963
www.thepermanentpress.com

Library of Congress Cataloging-in-Publication Data

Ryan, R. M.—
    There's a man with a gun over there / R.M. Ryan.
        pages ; cm
    ISBN 978-1-57962-385-2 (hardcover)
        1. Vietnam War, 1961–1975—Veterans—Fiction. I. Title.

PS3568.Y393T48 2015
813'.54—dc23   2014048179

Printed in the United States of America.

for Siegfried Lenz,

author of The German Lesson,

and in memory of all those we didn't mean to kill.

What does any of this have to do with Vietnam, Walter?
What the fuck has anything got to do with Vietnam?
What the fuck are you talking about?

THE DUDE
The Big Lebowski

Standing next to me in this lonely crowd
Is a man who swears he's not to blame
All day long I hear him shout so loud
Crying out that he was framed . . .

BOB DYLAN
I Shall Be Released

PROLOGUE.

I t's a dream, but then it isn't.

The yellow 1969 Dodge Charger slams to a stop—squealing, fishtailing, and then blocking my exit from the parking lot beside the Turley Barracks US Army Military Police station in Mannheim, Germany. The Charger takes up a lot of room on Friedrich Ebert Strasse. It's the size of two Volkswagens.

Traffic stalls behind the parked Dodge. A white Citroën flashes its high beams.

I sit there in my Volvo moving the floor shifter back and forth. I want to be ready so I can take off when the Charger moves. I feel so good. Even though I am in the army, I have beaten the system. At the height of the Vietnam War, I am in Germany, thousands of miles away from combat. I wear civilian clothes and drive around in a good car and drink expensive French wines. I have a sexy German girlfriend.

The two of them don't so much get out of the Charger as uncoil themselves from it. They amble toward me. They smile. They have all the time in the world. They don't notice the honking from the stalled traffic behind their Charger. Their teeth seem luminescent in the twilight, their Afros fuller than those normally allowed on the heads of GIs in 1972. Comb handles stick out from the tufts of their hair.

One leans against the passenger door of my car, and the other puts his hands on the door beside me. I try to roll the window up, but I can't. He holds it down with a single thumb. He's stronger than I am, maybe a lot stronger.

He smiles, unconcerned about the Germans coming up behind him who wonder what's going on.

"*Hey, da. Was ist hier los?*" one of the Germans yells.

"No need to anxious yourself, white boy," he says to me, ignoring the Germans. His voice is slurred, liquid. "No need 'tall. We jus' here to speak with you on behalf of Bro Perkins."

He nods toward the Charger, and I can see the shadowed figure of Staff Sergeant Elija Perkins sitting in the backseat. In my job as a plainclothes military policeman, I took his confession and am scheduled to testify at his court-martial next week.

"Bro Perkins—he's a friend of ours, you understand, and we wouldn't want anything bad to happen with him. Understand?"

"Well," I say and wiggle the shift knob rapidly back and forth. "Well, I can't make any promises."

On the passenger seat, I have this new Burgundy I'll sip with Angelika after we make love. I wiggle the shift lever again.

"Bro Perkins is a *good* friend of ours," he says again and points the index finger of his right hand at me as though it were the barrel of a pistol. "A very good friend. We jus' concerned about his welfare. You understand?"

Then he slaps the door of the Volvo, and the two of them get back in the Charger and squeal off down Friedrich Ebert Strasse.

1.

Those men stopped me decades ago, in 1972, in another life, so this story should be long over, shouldn't it?

But it's not, no: it plays, just as I'm falling asleep, night after night, month after month, year after year—a little serial in my brain that won't go away, a loop that keeps spiraling to the same bloody ending.

The story always pauses as I wait to drive my white Volvo out of the MP station parking lot onto Friedrich Ebert Strasse, heading toward Angelika's apartment. The gearshift in neutral, I rev the engine, listening to the throaty sound of the carburetor while I look for an opening in traffic.

This time, I think, as I look at myself in those long-ago days, this time it will all be different. No one will get hurt.

Once again, the story lures me in.

I drive out of the lot and merge into traffic.

I'm thinking, yes, this time things will work out some other way. This time, I hope, the story will change.

This time, I believe, the story won't end with a woman lying bloody on the floor in the Weinheim apartment.

2.

Now you've got to realize that I'm an innocent bystander really. I didn't mean to harm anyone. Not the woman in Weinheim. Not Sergeant Perkins. It was the times. I want to make that clear right from the start. I didn't have a say in the matter. I wasn't in the army by choice. I was just doing what I'd been told to do.

I was in graduate school studying Emerson and Yeats when the army came calling in the spring of 1968. Those were tough times, remember? They started to draft me for the war in Vietnam.

Even now, decades later, those three syllables terrify me. Vi-et-nam. Vi-et-nam.

But maybe you don't remember the war—or maybe you don't care.

Then, in the late sixties, though, the war was everywhere. It was on television every night. A soap opera of death and dying narrated by Walter Cronkite on the evening news. A war with its own box scores—each day's tally of American and enemy dead right there with the baseball standings and the stockmarket close.

Reality television all right: dead bodies face down in rice paddies spinning around, as if they're looking for something lost in the murk; a hand coming out of the ground, frozen in rigor mortis, holding a rifle; a wounded soldier wrapped in bandages until he looks like the *Invisible Man*; corpses tossed in piles like so much garbage.

I was scared of dying. I was terrified of being drafted and ending up dead in Vietnam. That was my dilemma. I had to avoid Vietnam at any cost.

I wanted to stay home and study Emerson, thank you very much, but the government took away my draft deferment. They were coming to get me.

I still can hear the drums from the ROTC drills on campus. I can't get the sound out of my head.

Boom, boom, snare, goes the drum.

Boom, boom, snare.

I took this test at an army recruiting station. It turned out I had an aptitude for learning languages, so I enlisted to get a space in the German language class at the army's language school in Monterey, California, and avoid the draft. Good duty, right? Sunny California. A way to stay out of Vietnam, OK?

I mean, look, I didn't *really* enlist enlist. I enlisted only so that I wouldn't be drafted and sent to the Infantry and then to Vietnam.

The recruiting sergeant told me I'd probably end up in Germany if I behaved myself.

"Do what they tell you to do, Ryan. Don't argue with them or ask questions. Don't make fun of them. Just do what you're told. Lie if you have to."

"Lie?"

He just looked at me.

So I went to the language school, just as they promised me, but then they made me a cop. Sent me to Military Police School after I learned German. I hadn't bargained on that. I was in the same MP unit that trained the shooters at Kent State.

But why should you care? These are my troubles, right? I should work them out in private. They don't affect you, do they? They're not coming after you, are they?

✦ ✦ ✦

I was just doing my job when Goldberg and I arrested Sergeant Perkins. I was an investigator and translator. I worked with these former Nazis in my trade-off to avoid Vietnam. When we arrested Sergeant Perkins for theft and black marketing, he was just a little unexpected roadkill on the road to saving me from combat.

Sergeant Perkins had the bad luck to move in with this blonde German woman and anger the neighbors. You can imagine that, can't you? I mean, there were Germans who still hated Jews. What do you think they thought of their blonde girls living with blacks? So they called the German Customs Police, who came and got me and my colleague Steve Goldberg, and here we were arresting Sergeant Perkins.

Yes, I was a long way from Ralph Waldo Emerson.

Look: Sergeant Perkins made some mistakes. He was married and living with a mistress. He'd stolen ten-pound cans of butter from the mess hall. He had more cartons of Kool cigarettes in his possession than his ration card allowed. He broke some laws. He had, as we MPs liked to say, seriously fucked up and had the even worse luck to get caught.

We MPs *liked* to go around saying, "Oh, man, he seriously fucked up." In fact, we loved to say that. It made what we did seem important.

Of course our judgments were pretty self-serving. To a barber, everyone needs a haircut. To a cop, everyone's a criminal.

As Lance B. Edwards, my MP Customs boss, liked to say, "They're all guilty out there. The world's filled with criminals, except most of them haven't been caught yet."

True enough. Many people—of course including me—cheated on their spouses without having cops knocking at their doors. Mess-hall theft was probably the most common infraction of army rules. And ration cards—who really cared about those silly rules that regulated how many cartons of cigarettes and bottles of alcohol you could have?

So why, then, were we making all this fuss over Sergeant Perkins and some property that couldn't have been worth more than a hundred dollars? Why were Goldberg and I there in Sergeant Perkins's apartment? Why were the German Customs Police there?

Well, Goldberg and I and the Germans were protecting our comfortable little jobs: that's what we were doing. We were also proving how powerful the empire is. The All-Knowing Empire could go anywhere, including Staff Sergeant Elija Perkins's tiny living room.

Of course, our version of the empire didn't want to do anything really dangerous, so we selected low-level criminals who wouldn't fight back. I mean, we didn't want to have any trouble, now did we?

I felt sorry for Sergeant Perkins. I really did. I knew the charges were bullshit. I knew the whole system was just one big charade set up to make someone money. It was part of a racket that must have cost the taxpayers millions and maybe billions. We didn't need all those soldiers and their equipment in Germany. We didn't need all the civilians and dependents and PXs and commissaries: the tons and tons of stuff that traveled with the American army. World War II was long over. Besides, the 500,000 American troops in Germany couldn't really have defended it from the Russians if the Russians had decided to invade. Their army would have had millions of soldiers.

But, hey, if I had let Sergeant Perkins go, my ass would have been on a plane for Saigon faster than you can say, "Don't fuck with the man."

"You've got to draw a line somewhere," Lance B. Edwards was fond of saying and then he would draw a line on a pad and hold it up. "See what I mean?"

I never really did see the meaning of the line between two white spaces, but I took the advice of that recruiting sergeant seriously: I didn't argue with people who outranked me. What's more, I learned to lie.

"That's right," I said. "You've got to draw a line."

✦ ✦ ✦

"Hey, brother," Sergeant Perkins said when I arrested him. "You're kidding, right? You can't bust me for chicken shit stuff like this. This is 1972. I have a family to support."

Me, too, I wanted to say.

But what I said out loud was, "I'm not your brother."

✦ ✦ ✦

"Fuck him," my boss, Lance B. Edwards, said.

Lance was a staff sergeant like Sergeant Perkins, too, but he liked to be called Mr. Mister. Mister Lance B. Edwards.

It had been years since he'd worn a uniform. In fact, none of us in the Mannheim office of the Twenty-Second wore uniforms. We dressed in sport coats and ties. In a world where officers and enlisted men usually wore uniforms—with their ranks prominently displayed, along with the medals of their combat histories—we seemed too mysterious.

And menacing.

All us of were Misters.

In addition, all of us investigators in MP Customs carried leather-framed credentials, which looked like those carried by FBI agents. We called them box tops. The card on one side of the leather case was in German; the card on the other side was in English. A heavy chrome clip held them in our pockets.

"Mr. Edwards," he said, pulling his credentials from his shirt pocket.

"Lance B. Edwards, MP Customs." He snapped the credentials open.

He then snapped the leather case closed, as if that part of the conversation were over.

Lance B. Edwards thought the production and the closing of our credentials was an important moment.

"Got to be decisive. Can't be tentative if you're about to arrest someone."

He sat at his desk practicing how he used his credentials. He made us all practice, so we could do it with one hand.

"Use your index finger."

"You know," Lance B. Edwards told me when I brought Sergeant Perkins back to our office for questioning, "he should have thought about his family before he moved in with the German babe. It's his own goddamned fault, not yours."

Eventually, Sergeant Perkins signed that confession form. Signed it in quadruplicate. I was scrupulous about the way I took confessions. I wanted everyone to know exactly what was going on, so I wouldn't be haunted later on by what I'd done. I paid special attention to the rights we read people.

You have the right to remain silent.

Anything you say can and will be used against you in a court of law.

I paid special attention to those lines. I always repeated them before our suspects signed anything. I repeated the lines three times. Three times. Don't forget that.

No one could possibly misunderstand.

Of course no one ever told our suspects that complete silence would eventually set them free. Simply possessing black-market items was not enough evidence to result in a conviction.

"Get 'em to talk," Lance B. Edwards said. "Guilty people need to have their minds relieved. Besides, the colonel doesn't like it when our cases don't hold."

Twenty-Second MP Customs convictions were based on self-incrimination. And so, if you didn't confess, we would let you go.

But most of our suspects—including Sergeant Perkins—eventually confessed.

✦ ✦ ✦

The raid went the usual way.

The neighbors turned in Sergeant Perkins.

Herr Diener and Herr Hellman, plainclothes investigators from the German Customs Police, came over to our office in Mannheim in their gray-blue suits and their gray-blue, unmarked Opel sedan.

Rudi, their driver, always stayed with the car. He cut quite a figure. Rudi had hands the size and shape of hams; his fingers were as thick as hammer handles. When he adjusted his bowler hat (which was several sizes too small for him), his hands were bigger than the hat. Rudi had to be 100 pounds overweight. He'd outgrown his suit jacket years ago. It was tiny on his bulging chest. Like a doll jacket fitted on a man. He looked like a hulking Oliver Hardy.

Herr Diener and Herr Hellman came into the MP office, where they ceremoniously drank coffee and smoked a couple of our Marlboros. Sometimes Lance B. Edwards gave Herr Diener a whole pack. That was legal, but an entire carton given to a German national was considered black marketing.

Then I got in the backseat of the Opel with Herr Hellman while Herr Diener sat up front with Rudi. Goldberg followed in our unmarked Ford.

"*Ja, hier haben wir die Tickets für das Schauspiel,*" Herr Diener said, holding up the German search warrants.

Here are the tickets for the play.

Herr Hellman polished his little silver revolver with his handkerchief. He wasn't supposed to have one of those. The

Germans had very strict rules forbidding firearms. The gun made all of us nervous, especially Herr Diener.

"Was willst du, Hellman? Was willst du? Du wird uns in Gefängnis bringen."

What are you doing, Hellman? You're going to put us in jail.

✦ ✦ ✦

Goldberg and I often went out with them after one of these raids for a beer and a sausage. Our Germans loved sausages. While we ate, they told stories, but the stories got a little vague when the subject of World War II came up.

"Ach, ich hab im Zweiten Weltkrieg wirklich nichts getan; Papierkrieg, dass war alles," Hellman said.

I really didn't do much in the Second World War. I mostly pushed papers.

And then the subject would get changed, often to the dangers of Communism, and then Diener would explain that Hitler, while a man of many failures, was a staunch anti-Communist, just like, as he said, *"unsere vier."* We four.

"Ja, ja," Hellman would add, *"Hitler hat nur einen Fehler gemacht."*

Hellman smiled as he said this, raising his eyebrows, certain of his wit.

"Hitler only made one mistake," he said and paused for a beat.

"He invaded Russia."

I never knew how to react when Hellman said this—as he often did. I thought, briefly, of mentioning the Jews, but I figured such a comment would get me in trouble somehow, so I said nothing. Goldberg, who was Jewish, looked down at his beer.

Sometimes Hellman would pat my cheek.

"Ach, ja, Herr Ryan, Sie sind einer von uns. Sie würden der Hitlerzeit genossen haben."

Ah, Mister Ryan, you are one of us. You would have enjoyed the Hitler era.

My time in Germany, from 1970 to 1972, was also the time of the Baader-Meinhof Gang, and they were making people pretty nervous.

The Baader-Meinhof Gang was a group of young German anarchists led by Andreas Baader, Ulrike Meinhof, and Gundrun Ensslin. They went around killing German officials and setting off bombs.

Wanted posters with pictures of nineteen Baader-Meinhof gang members were all over Germany in those days. On construction walls, on kiosks, in trains, on power-line poles—all those black-and-white faces of a little anarchist army became wallpaper for the times. The wanted ones stared at those of us who enforced the empire's laws, and their glowering faces made us more than a little worried, as if one of us might be next in the sights of their automatic weapons.

"What kind of bullshit is this?"

Sergeant Perkins keeps shaking his head after we tell him what's going on. "What are we talking about here? Five cartons of cigarettes? I can give my girlfriend a gift, can't I? Ushi here likes to smoke, don't you, baby?"

The blonde woman, sitting in her chair, looks up through the bangs of her hair.

"*Haben Sie vieleicht Taschen?*"

That's Herr Diener, always decorous, a little embarrassed, bowing as he asks for bags to put the evidence in.

"Who the fuck did you say you guys are?"

"Customs police. Twenty-Second MP Customs Unit."

Sergeant Perkins looks at Goldberg and me.

"Customs police? What kind of bullshit is that?"

"This kind of bullshit," Goldberg says and starts reading Sergeant Perkins his rights.

"You have the right to remain silent," he tells him.

Sergeant Perkins looks at me with disgust.

"Five fucking cartons of cigarettes and some butter for Ushi's dad. It was a gift. He's a baker. Come on, man, give me a break."

"Anything you say can and will be used against you in a court of law."

✦ ✦ ✦

We arrested Sergeant Perkins in the spring of 1972.

The *Baader-Meinhof Gruppe* was also pretty busy in those days.

In late 1971, Andreas Baader shot and killed a policeman over a routine traffic stop. A little while later, the gang stole a small fortune in cash from a bank in Kaiserslautern. In May of 1972, about the time of Sergeant Perkins's arrest, the action really heated up. The gang blew up the entrance to the US Army-owned IG Farben building in Frankfurt, killing an American army officer. The next day they set off bombs in the Augsburg Police Department. A few days after that they blew up a judge's car and wounded his wife.

Their violence was so brutal that they made left-wing groups in the United States look like Cub Scouts. Everyone in Germany was both terrified and spellbound by these romantic and murderous criminals. I dreamed of bombs exploding. I could feel the blast cutting off my arms and legs. I lay on the ground, bleeding and helpless.

All of us on US Army bases looked around nervously, scared that we might be their next targets. They might kill us for carrying out an imperialistic war in Vietnam.

A comment of Ulrike Meinhof's, published in *Der Spiegel*, made our culpability perfectly clear.

"We say," she wrote, "the man in uniform's a pig, not a human being."

Imagine, all those good-hearted Americans trying to promote law and order: pigs? Since I was really a uniformed sergeant beneath my Harris Tweed sport coat, was I a pig, too?

Me responsible for the war in Vietnam? Imagine.

Me, the graduate student.

The boy who studied Emerson.

✦ ✦ ✦

"Fuck it," Sergeant Perkins finally said. "Where do I sign those papers?"

It took three hours of sitting in our waiting room for him to ask that question. It usually took just two.

Then I read him his rights. As I said, I was scrupulous about that.

You see. It wasn't my fault. It wasn't my fault at all. He signed the confession form, didn't he?

Boom, boom, snare.

3.

I got to meet Albert Speer in the Heidelberg Post Office. I was with my colleagues from German Customs on our way to their office at the back of the building. They introduced me to Speer.

Remember him? *Reichsminister* Speer? Head of Armaments and Munitions for Hitler. One of the few members of the Nazi High Command not executed by the Americans in Nuremberg at the end of the war. He served twenty years in Spandau Prison and afterward wrote a best-selling book called *Inside the Third Reich*. The day I met him, he had a suntan and wore an expensive wool suit. He looked like a retired bank president or college professor. An elegant man picking up his mail.

"Speer," the postal clerks hissed. They drew the vowels out: Spaaayer.

"Spaaayer, Spaaayer, Spaaayer," they whispered, lingering on the vowels. They sounded like a Greek chorus.

✦ ✦ ✦

"*Ach, Herr* Ryan: *das hört sich wie Rhein an,*" Speer said to me when we were introduced. He bowed when he spoke. A modest-appearing man.

Ah, Mister Ryan, that sounds like "Rhein."

The German word for purity. The fabled river of Wagner and the fairy tales his operas are based on.

"Mit einem Namen wie Rhein, müssen Sie ein Held sein."

With a name like Purity you must be some kind of hero.

I blushed when he said that. He patted me on the arm and smiled.

It never occurred to me that, later on, people would think that I was a war criminal. Me, a criminal—imagine that.

Boom, boom, snare.

Boom, boom, snare.

4.

That meeting with Albert Speer happened decades ago, but I still think about it as if it were yesterday. All the pieces of this story keep repeating in my mind. They won't go away.

Just this afternoon, for instance, when I went out jogging along the California coast, in the stunning light of late afternoon, I found myself chanting the rhymes I learned while marching in army basic training more than forty years ago.

"I want to be an Airborne Ranger," I sang to myself. "I want to lead a life of danger."

I learned that from Drill Sergeant Yankovic in July 1969 as I marched along in the middle of Company B with my M-14 rifle, marched across the sandy, red soil of Fort Polk, Louisiana, in the dawn light.

> *I want to be an Airborne Ranger.*
> *I want to lead a life of danger.*

✦ ✦ ✦

Of course that song's a lie. No one in his right mind would want to be an Airborne Ranger and jump out of airplanes into the dark, shrapnel-filled skies over a battlefield.

"Skies like razors, ground that'll blow your guts out," is how Drill Sergeant Yankovic described the war as he sat on the stoop of the barrack, his uniform soaked with the sweat from a malaria attack. He oozed war.

I didn't want to be an Airborne Ranger. I didn't want to lead a life of danger. I was a coward then, and I am a coward now. The Vietnam War terrified me, but there I was, in July of 1969, marching along in the brightening light of what would become another scorching hot Louisiana morning, affirming just those things I didn't believe. *I want to be an Airborne Ranger. I want to live a life of danger. Airborne! Airborne! Airborne!*

✦ ✦ ✦

How did this happen to me? I keep asking myself this question over and over, and suddenly I'm back in school, walking up the steps of Marshall Junior High in Janesville, Wisconsin.

After Sputnik was launched in 1957, the Russians were on everyone's minds. In 1958, twenty-three of us eighth graders were chosen to learn algebra early.

"You're Janesville's brightest, and you're going to be America's first line of attack against the Russians," Mrs. Downy, the math teacher, told us as she smoothed out the wrinkles in her skirt.

If you look on page twenty-four of the 1958-59 Marshall Junior High *Minor Memories* yearbook, you can see us there.

"Janesville's Algebra Squad," the caption reads.

A little platoon of kids on the steps of the school beside Mrs. Downy in her harlequin glasses. How serious we all look. There we are—Judy Stryker, Roger Polanski, Jane Martin, Ralph Witfield and sixteen others—squinting into the sunlight of the future. Look at the boys in their pressed chinos and the girls in their buttoned-up blouses. We look like extras from *Leave It to Beaver.*

"The future," Mrs. Downy told us, "belongs to you."

But that future also worried us. Would there be enough fallout shelters to protect all of us in the event of a nuclear attack? Would there be enough of those green drums with yellow triangles labeled EMERGENCY SUPPLIES?

At school, we whispered to each other that someone . . . who? . . . someone important . . . *someone* had seen lists of cities the Russians planned on attacking once they built a space station with all the satellites they would shoot into the air, and Janesville was a prime target. We were marked for death.

Janesville, while not the absolute first city to be attacked, was near the top of the list, not far below Chicago. We were, someone told us with authority, the thirty-fourth most important target in the country. I would look out the window of my room before I went to bed and, on clear nights, stare at the stars in their slow circle overhead.

Sputnik was up there, people said, shooting by, night after night, sending its secret signals back to Russia.

In the summer of 1959, Marshall Junior High School offered its first summer-school course in Russian History, and Mrs. Downy recommended that we take it.

"In the future, when we go to war against the Russians, we will understand them first and then blow them to pieces with our superior knowledge of algebra. History and math will be the weapons of the next war."

✦ ✦ ✦

"Russia is a huge, poor country," Mr. Niederman said on the first morning of our summer school Russian History class. "A country with great writers, a country trying to escape itself by moving ever westward."

"So Russia really *is* coming to Janesville," Judy Stryker said, underlining "westward" in her notebook and circling it with stars.

Mr. Niederman was short and harried. His glasses had the gray plastic frames that I would later know as GI glasses. A chain-smoker, he pulled out a pack of Lucky Strikes from his coat pocket and locked himself in the closet of the classroom during the ten-minute breaks between the hours of the class, which lasted all morning. At the end of each break, he emerged in a haze of smoke, as if his enthusiasm had set him on fire.

We had to memorize the dates and the names of Russian leaders in a fat history book, identify cities on a variety of historic and contemporary maps, and read *The Brothers Karamazov*.

"I went into the army when I was eighteen," Mr. Niederman said one day, about halfway through the course. When he spoke he nodded, encouraging people to agree with him. As he did so, his glasses kept slipping down his nose, and he pushed them back up.

"I went to Korea, in the infantry. Oh, how cold it was. You couldn't ever get warm."

His voice floated off in his reverie.

"They shot me. That's why I majored in history when I came back and went to college on the GI Bill. I wanted to find out what happened to me. I wanted to understand why I got shot and why my friends got killed."

That day, Mr. Niederman had brought in a slide projector. He pulled the heavy black window shades down.

"Is Korea part of *Russia?*" Judy Stryker raised her hand and asked. Judy liked to line up her facts.

Mr. Niederman didn't seem to hear the question. Grainy black-and-white images flickered on the wall. Mr. Niederman kept changing the focus on the projector, but the people remained a blur.

"That's Tom Riley there. See. Charpentier is to his right. See the other guy with the BAR? The big gun. That's a Browning Automatic Rifle. See it there? Johnson's holding it. He was my best friend. A mortar shot got him about ten minutes later. See him with that goofy grin, waving—how blurred his hand is."

"Are these *Russian* soldiers?" Judy Stryker asked, as if she were an inspector from the Board of Education.

"There. See," Mr. Niederman said. The slide stuck, and the next slide gave the blurred images of Johnson and the rest a different background. "It's a little bakery just set up along the road by some peasants. We had cakes and tea after Johnson died."

Mr. Niederman sobbed then, his breath came in heaves.

"Mr. Niederman, Mr. Niederman," Judy Stryker asked, "are you all right? Should we take a break now? Do you want to go in the closet and have a cigarette?"

She walked to him. He was bent over, holding on to the podium at the front of the classroom, gagging on his tears. The rest of us looked at our notebooks or walked out of the room.

In the hall, John Rogers said, "What the fuck was that all about?"

"Some war our parents had to fight," Ron Moriarty said.

"Does this mean we're not having a test on that novel about the brothers?" Bill Philippi asked.

"What the fuck was *that* all about?" John Rogers asked again and looked at me.

I didn't know what to say. Mr. Niederman and the Korean War were unknowns in a kind of algebra I wouldn't learn about until I got drafted into the army ten years later.

When Judy Stryker walked him away from the podium, those of us in the hall just stared through the doorway at Mr. Niederman as if he were in another world. The features of his face undone by tears, he looked at us as if he hoped we might throw him a lifeline, but we all began to study the floor.

"This is just too weird," John Rogers whispered.

Yesterday, I looked up Joel Niederman on the Internet and found one in Janesville, at 716 Adams Street, 608-352-2906, so I decided to call him.

The voice that answered was frail, elderly.

"Mr. Niederman?"

"Yes."

"Mr. Niederman, did you teach at Marshall Junior High School in the fifties and sixties?"

"Who is this?"

"Rick Ryan. I was a student of yours. Do you remember a Russian History course you taught in 1959?"

"Who did you say this is?"

"Rick Ryan, Mr. Niederman. I'm calling about the time you cried. It was 1959, Mr. Niederman. Do you remember 1959? Do you remember that, when you were showing us slides from Korea?"

"Korea?"

"Yes, do you remember?"

"Korea was a long time ago. Are you calling from the Veterans?"

"The Veterans . . . yes, I guess I am. I'm calling to tell you I finally understand."

"Who did you say you were?"

5.

I didn't answer him. I didn't say anything. I just stood there holding the phone, listening to his raspy breath, waiting for him to say something.

Neither of us hung up, and pretty soon I realized that we were both waiting for the other to speak, two veterans across the decades.

And then it hit me: what kind of a story did I have to tell? I'd never been in real combat, though maybe I'd killed someone.

I saw the blood stain on the woman's chest and the blood oozing out from underneath her back and then I got scared and rattled the phone into the receiver and stood there breathing in my own raspy way.

Who was I kidding?

This was all getting too close to home.

Who did you say this is? Who? Who?

6.

The truth is, I don't know exactly who I am. I've been living in made-up skin so long I don't know what I look like anymore. I walk around in a permanent Halloween costume.

Look: I can tell you who I'm not.

Maybe that's a good way to start. Yes, let me start there.

I'm not some homeless veteran with his greasy cardboard sign and grocery cart filled with cans and bottles and feces-smeared blankets. I'm not some grimy figure lurking around construction sites to steal pieces of copper.

Not at all. I'm a published poet. I'm a published novelist. I've won prizes and, miracle of miracles, I earn a good living, too, though my employer probably wouldn't enjoy being pulled into this foolish story.

Let's just say that I have a great day job that supports my poetry habit. I earn a damn good living. I have investments and clients. I own Hickey Freeman suits and Allan Edmonds shoes. I counted the other day. I own $3,000 worth of shoes. I drive a BMW.

I've made my dreams come true, but I can't make the nightmare of the army go away. Those days keep sneaking up on me.

Maybe this all started when we moved earlier in the year, and I had to clean all that stuff out of the attic.

It was terrible work: the past had become an inexplicably literal burden. My wife, Carol, and I had been good children and saved so much of our parents' stuff. Old quilts that had belonged to great aunts I'd never met, locks of my great-great-grandmother's hair, deeds to forgotten pieces of property marked CANCELED, my aunt's high school yearbooks with best wishes from people named Berty and Mugsy—and on and on it went that hot summer afternoon in the attic at 332 East Acacia Road until I came across a box with my army uniform inside.

In the upper left-hand corner of the box, hand printed in fat marking-pen ink, are my rank and my last army address. The writing looks new to me, as if, in spite of everything, sergeant continues to be my title, as if Detachment A, Twenty-Second MP Customs Unit remains my permanent address. In the reddish purple ink of the cancellation stamp's circle, US ARMY is at the top, APO 09166 is at the bottom.

"What's this?" my son wonders, looking at the box. He's helping me empty out the attic.

His right index finger taps the date in the middle of the cancellation mark. He taps it. *22 May 72.* Eleven years before he was born.

"That was a long time ago," he says. "Ancient history."

"Is it, now?" my grandmother used to say. "Is it, now?"

My son opens the box.

"You were in the army," he says, surprised. He stares at me, as if I might be a stranger. "Did I know that? How did that happen? You're a poet, right?"

"You're a trained killer," is what Goldberg says when I visit him.

My old army buddy. We've been friends for more than forty years.

"We can makes jokes about it," he says, "but that's the fact of the matter. They taught us how to kill people."

We did make jokes about it until we got to the Military Police School shooting ranges at Fort Gordon, Georgia. When we heard the click of rounds being chambered, the *pop pop pop* of the firing, and the clatter of the expended shell casings hitting the ground, things weren't so funny anymore.

In the dust of the firing, the arm of the paper-target man goes first, and then his head. The human outline is turned to shreds. The army wasn't joking; the army wasn't joking at all. It tore up those human forms; it turned them into confetti.

✦ ✦ ✦

As it happens, though, I'm really not a trained killer. Not at all.

✦ ✦ ✦

"Ryan!" Sergeant Schumacher screams at me. It's a hot August day in 1970 on the pistol range at MP school. He hits me on the top of my steel helmet with his clipboard.

"Fucking A, Ryan, you're not even hitting the target. Get someone else in here wearing your fatigue shirt. I don't want no one flunking this exercise. Ryan, I want you to kill for me!"

"But, Sergeant, I don't know how. I need more training."

"Get someone else the fuck in here, Ryan, or you'll be on KP for the rest of your natural life."

"Yes, Sergeant. Right away, Sergeant."

Pretty soon my friend Peter Everwine, wearing my fatigue shirt, which identifies him as RYAN, easily empties the .45 into the head of the target.

"That's, my boy, Ryan," Sergeant Schumacher says to Peter Everwine and puts his arm around him.

"See that head. That's how those hippies are supposed to look. Blow their brains to little greasy bits. Just remember, Ryan, it was trainees of mine that shot up those Commie college students in Ohio. You know that song they wrote about it? Well, that's a song about me, Ryan. I trained those troops. 'Four dead in O-hio.' You betcha, Ryan. I'm a celebrity."

The next day Drill Sergeant Rodriquez hands me an Expert Pistol Marksman Badge, and my army lies have begun.

7.

It's a dream, and in the gray-blue light of the Rhein-Main Air Base hangar I am doing my job. It's November 1970 and I'm wearing the uniform my son found. This is my first assignment with MP Customs.

One by one, soldiers and civilian contractors stop at my table.

"ID card," I say.

"Show me your orders," I say.

"Open your bag," I say.

"Empty your pockets," I say.

"You can go now," I say.

"Next," I say.

One by one they stand in front of me.

"Harm no one," this black sergeant in the middle of the night says to me.

Diogenes O'Reilly is the name on his ID card. It's two A.M. Sometimes it seems like it's always two A.M. in the army.

Diogenes O'Reilly has flown in from Vietnam. He's wearing his green fatigue pants and a Hawaiian shirt with bright designs of parrots and palm trees.

"You're out of uniform," I say.

"You can't hurt me anymore," Diogenes O'Reilly says. "I've only got three days left to serve."

Corporal Halter, my late-night colleague in the world of MP Customs inspections, stands beside me in the blue-and-white lighted area inside the general darkness of the giant airplane hangar at Rhein-Main Air Base.

"Cool shirt," Corporal Halter says to Diogenes O'Reilly.

"Hurt no one," Diogenes O'Reilly says.

"Go in peace," Diogenes O'Reilly says.

"Walk softly on the earth," Diogenes O'Reilly says.

"Bow low to all the creatures that you meet," Diogenes O'Reilly says.

"Get the fuck out of here," Corporal Halter says.

"Should we just let him go?" I ask.

"Hurt no one," Corporal Halter says as we watch Diogenes O'Reilly shoulder his duffel bag and walk off into the general darkness.

8.

But maybe I'm getting ahead of myself.

Maybe we should linger in 1959, the year of Mr. Niederman and his Korean War slides.

Nineteen fifty-nine was the year that Don McLean, in his famous song, "Bye, Bye, Miss American Pie," said it all went wrong. According to him, the troubles of us Baby Boomers began the morning Buddy Holly went down in a plane crash.

"A Beech Bonanza, N 3794N, crashed at night approximately five miles northwest of the Mason City Municipal Airport, Mason City, Iowa, at approximately 0100, February 3, 1959. The pilot and three passengers were killed and the aircraft was demolished," the anonymous author of the official Civil Aeronautics Board report on the crash explains.

The day the music died was a Tuesday, Mr. Niederman. It was just an ordinary Tuesday when the plane carrying Buddy Holly crashed in that frozen Iowa cornfield. Who would figure that Tuesday for an important day?

Ralph E. Smiley, MD, Acting Coroner, lists the personal effects of Charles Holley as "Cash $193.00 less $11.65 coroner's fees—$181.35. 2 cuff links, silver ½ in. balls having jeweled band. Top portion of ballpoint pen."

Isn't that something, Mr. Niederman, they charged Charles "Buddy" Holley for the coroner's services?

He didn't even spell "Holly" the way Buddy did, but Ralph E. Smiley remembered to charge him $11.65 for . . . for what,

Mr. Niederman? Was Ralph E. Smiley poking beneath Buddy's skin looking for the source of "Maybe Baby"?

Is this what remains of genius in the end—the "top portion of ballpoint pen"?

This is what Buddy had to say:

> *That'll be the day*
> *When you say good-bye*
> *That'll be the day*
> *When you make me cry*

✦ ✦ ✦

In the Civil Aeronautics Board report, we learn that "the airspeed indicator needle was stuck between 165-170 mph." The anonymous author implies that the pilot, who thought he was climbing out of a dark storm cloud, was actually diving toward the harder darkness of the earth.

He misread the signs and was going down when he thought he was going up. Imagine that.

"A generation lost in space" is how Don McLean's song puts it.

✦ ✦ ✦

One afternoon in 1959 when I came home from school I could hear howling and whelping noises, as if a dog were begging to be released from his cage.

I came into the kitchen and could only see the backs of my mother and my aunt. They struggled with something in front of them.

"No!" my aunt commanded.

I was sure they'd brought home a dog. I was excited and squeezed between them.

"No!" my mother said. "He'll see."

"Here," my aunt said, trying to put her hand over my eyes. I thought they had a surprise for me, and I wiggled loose from her hold. I was too big for her. At fourteen, I wasn't a little boy anymore.

It was my father. They were wrestling with my father. Tears, mixed with dirt and sweat, streaked his face. It looked as though deep scars had torn his face up. His right hand gripped a paring knife, and he kept stabbing it at the kitchen table.

"They took my job away from me. My job," he cried. "My job, my job."

"Oh my God," my aunt said, letting go of me. "Grab his hand, Louise. Make him put it down."

"A man without a job is nothing, nothing at all," he sobbed and stabbed the air.

"Get him out of here!" My mother was looking back at me and nodding toward my aunt.

"Get him out of here. I don't want anyone to see this."

Facts were the guide star of Mr. Bauch, the guidance counselor at Marshall Junior High School in 1959.

A thin man with a pursed smile, Mr. Bauch wore these enormous-looking plaid suits with broad shoulders and wide lapels. The creases in his pants were so sharp they puckered the fabric beneath them. His stiff bow ties were too wide for his skinny neck. His clothes were huge on him, as if he lived in a plaid house.

Yes, facts were Mr. Bauch's mantra. He'd take a yellow number-two Ticonderoga pencil from the neat row in the breast pocket of that suit coat, and point it at you. The tips of that row of pencils in his suit-coat pocket looked like a picket fence in front of his heart.

"You must find the facts of the matter," he said, aiming the pencil at us. "The facts of the matter."

How straight the part in his hair was as he nodded, agreeing with himself. The lenses in his wire-rimmed glasses were sometimes opaque in the glare from the fluorescent lighting.

"The facts of the matter. The facts of the matter."

✦ ✦ ✦

Nineteen fifty-nine was the year my father had a nervous breakdown.

Yes, a nervous breakdown was the fact of that matter.

9.

Down in the basement at 863 East Memorial Drive, I had my own world.

There was my dark room, where I loved to watch the images I'd seen weeks ago in my camera viewfinder reemerge on the paper floating in Kodak's Dektol developer beneath the red glow of my safelight.

Here was my father with the reflection of my flash in the lens of his glasses—I remember how he jumped when the flashbulb ignited, as if he were much more agitated than his serious face revealed. Here, too, was my mother blurred as she tried to wave my camera away. My brother with Down syndrome smiled and held up a cracker. My aunt offered a cocktail glass and winked. My uncle turned a steak on the grill. I had images of our house and pictures of our good car and my dad's work car.

I hid out in the darkroom after my father had his nervous breakdown. Unlike the people around me, those appearing in that chemical bath seemed mostly happy. I printed their images over and over, as if that act would keep things from going wrong. I began to cry. It wasn't a very big world in that developing tray, but in there my father wasn't stabbing at imaginary monsters crawling toward him across the kitchen table.

✦ ✦ ✦

In 1959, my mother got a part-time job as a census taker for the US government, and I discovered that I could disguise my voice and call in sick from school on the days when she was out working.

"He's not feeling at all well," I said to Miss Morgenthau, the secretary at Marshall Junior High School. I deepened my voice into that of an adult. "Little Rickie needs to take the day off."

Nineteen fifty-nine was also the year that Charles Van Doren admitted to Congress that he'd been given answers ahead of time on a television quiz show.

But, hey, who cared? It was all good, clean fun on television, right? So what if contestants lie. We all lie, don't we? What's a little fib when entertainment's concerned? The important thing—the really important thing—was that we could be whoever it was we wanted to be. Facts—why, facts were what we said they were. They didn't have to be true, did they?

10.

Just last weekend, I went back to Janesville. My family house on East Memorial Drive is for sale.

"That's quite a place," Patsy Apple, the real estate agent, said when I called to make an appointment to see it. "It's one twenty-four nine."

"That's a big price for a house in Janesville," I said.

"Well, it's a big house," Patsy Apple replied, as if she were reading from a script of real estate agent answers.

While 863 East Memorial Drive was many things, it was never big—no more than 1,000 square feet, but then, they're all tiny, aren't they, the houses of our childhoods when we go back? That's the cliché, sure, but 863 East Memorial was even smaller than that. It hardly had enough room to turn around in. Long ago, four of us and a large dog lived there. That ten-foot-by-ten-foot kitchen barely held the cabinets, the appliances, the kitchen table, and the four of us all at once. When Patsy Apple and I got there one Sunday afternoon to look over the house, Patsy stood where the kitchen table had been. Her full hips took up most of the space. I closed my eyes and saw the paring knife my father held cutting its way through the air and into the table.

"Charming, don't you think," Patsy Apple said. Holding her real estate agent's clipboard, she spun around, like a model on a runway.

"Not exactly what I'm looking for," I said, a discriminating buyer.

"What till you see the upstairs," Patsy Apple said. "That's where the real charm is. Charm squared."

As we go up the stairs to the second floor, the steps creak in exactly the places they did fifty years ago, and there, to the left, is my little room where I told my dreams to the night before drifting off to sleep. I wonder if those dreams are still there, the way the misaligned woodwork is, the way the hardwood floors—with their gray and black sticky residue, probably a mixture of skin oil, tobacco, and dirt—are. The floors have hardly changed after all these years. I kneel down and touch them. The grime has been varnished there by time. It will probably outlive me.

When Patsy Apple walks into another room, I stand up and try to touch my younger self, asleep on the now invisible upper bunk in the empty room with dust witches in the corners.

"Rickie," I whispered. "Get up. Get out of here."

Back there, in 1959, when I stayed home from school, I spent the mornings watching soap operas.

Even in college I seldom missed an episode of *Days of Our Lives.*

"Like sands through the hourglass, so are the *Days of our Lives,*" the show begins, the gentle voice of Macdonald Carey speaking that ominous warning. How seductively he invited us to let our own lives trickle away while we watched television, our real and actual lives evaporating while we wasted our time on illusions.

Back in 1959, I set up this little pretend television studio in the basement, beside my darkroom. I had a stage and a TV camera made out of a shoe box. I sat on the stage and talked into the shoe box camera. I was on stage with my little life, all alone, talking to the wide world. The *Today Show* of 863 East Memorial Drive. I took sips of Mogen David wine my parents had hidden in the basement. Pretending to be an adult, I figured I should have an adult drink by my side.

Hidden in another part of the basement was a box of .22 bullet cartridges, so I decided to incorporate a little gunplay into one of my dramas.

Alcohol and ammunition. That's the stuff of real life, isn't it?

With pliers, I plucked out the lead bullets from two shells and put the gunpowder-filled casings into an empty Maxwell House coffee can. I filled the can with loose pieces of newspaper.

I pretended that I was sitting in a haunted house where dark deeds were afoot and talked my heart out to that shoe box. A minute later, I took a match and lit the newspapers in the coffee can.

Deafening—the explosion was deafening. Literally.

Blam!

All I could hear in my ears was a ringing sound, and the basement filled with smoke and the smell of exploded gunpowder. I went to grab the can, to stop the second explosion. Luckily, it went off before my hand touched it.

Blam!

The second explosion seemed louder than the first, and the shock of it threw me backward, and I knocked over my glass of Mogen David, turning the old rug that was the floor of my TV stage a faded purple, as if from the reign of a kingdom that didn't work out.

"How was your day at school?" my mom asked when she got home.

"Fine," I said.

"Well, you look tired. I think that paper route is wearing you out."

✦ ✦ ✦

I didn't have to pretend. It was a haunted house all right. Some kind of ghost had gotten my father and was now after me as well.

✦ ✦ ✦

I forgot to tell you—I was a paperboy in 1959. Yes, just like the boy in the Don McLean song.

But in those days I didn't know the story of Buddy Holly dying in a plane crash.

Although I probably danced to his songs at those teen dances on Friday nights, I didn't know exactly who Buddy Holly was back then. What's more, plenty of songs still played on WLS in Chicago while I folded the papers for my own paper route. *My* music didn't die.

I sat on the backstairs of 863 East Memorial Drive with the stack of forty-three *Rockford Morning Stars* that Sid Grinker, the route manager, dropped off. He came by seven days a week, at around four A.M., in his old Buick Estate wagon with its back springs collapsed from the weight of all the newspapers he carried. The car's grill pointed upward, as if it were ready to take off, hot fire pouring out of his rocket-like rear taillights, its stubby tail fins ready to guide it through the air.

Sid Grinker had emphysema. I could hear his congested wheezing as he got out of the car and heaved the papers up against our back door. When I went outside to pick up the stack of papers wrapped in string, I could see the hot coal of his cigarette inside the darkened windshield as he backed out of our driveway.

"He's Got the Whole World in His Hands" was the song I remember from that time.

It was fading from the Hit Parade but still played on the radio at four thirty A.M. while I sat folding the papers once across their width and then tucking the ends into each other and stacking them in my white bag soiled with newsprint. The fresh papers smelled vaguely like fish, and the lines of my fingerprints were filled with ink, as if I were marked by the *Rockford Morning Star*.

At five thirty A.M., I slow my bicycle in front of Roger Hartinger's house and toss the *Morning Star* in a looping arc through the still-dark sky toward his porch. My first paper delivered.

"He's got you and me, brother, in His hands," I sing as I ride off to deliver the second one.

11.

"*Ach, ja,* this is just a diversion, this story of yours," Albert Speer says. "A diversion."

He's recently been visiting my dreams. So vivid, in a kind of hypercolor, as if I am more than really there.

In my dream, Albert Speer and I are standing together at the edge of a garden attached to a country house. It's summer. The slow hum of fat bees, and golden butterflies cruising by.

"How do you say, Herr Ryan, you make a diversion? Do I say that correctly? My English is technical but *nicht idiomatisch.*"

In my dreams Albert Speer always worries about his English, and yet he seems to understand everything, even what isn't said.

"*Ja, das habe ich auch getan.*"

"I did that, too, Herr Ryan. I made diversions. I distracted my inquisitors. I kept changing the subject. I told them about my childhood. I showed them pictures of my family. I showed them plans for buildings. I talked about everything except the Hitler time. *Die Hitlerzeit.* I had a soft look in my eyes. Goering was such a fool—all that bluster, as if he believed he could intimidate the Americans. I knew better."

He cups his hands together behind his back and bends into his thought.

"Wars are never our fault, are they, Herr Ryan?"

"But Albert," I say. I always call him Albert in my dreams, as if he's my uncle. "I wasn't in a war. I avoided the war."

Albert Speer's smile is both wise and ironic.

"*Ach*, Herr Ryan, wars could not be fought without people like you. Those who go along with everything, who do what they're told. The Cult of Cooperation. You were the bedrock of Adolf Hitler. We needed you. It was people like you who guarded the prisoners in the concentration camps. Of course you had your doubts. Who wouldn't? But, you: you were a good soldier, weren't you? You got a medal—isn't that what you told me? You did what you were told."

"What choice did I have, Albert? I did the best I could."

"*Ach, ja.* 'What can any of us do?' we say as another box of bullets is shipped to the front."

He shakes his head.

"I always liked that word 'front,'" Speer goes on. "I got so I wondered where the 'back' was. What's behind all this, I wondered as I sat in prison."

He paused, looking at me.

"But, Albert, you were one of the leaders. People followed your orders, didn't they?"

He's not listening to me.

"*Ach ja*," Albert says, "so many wars, and no one's to blame."

12.

I was safe in Janesville, wasn't I? We were an important place, we told ourselves.

In fourth grade, my teacher Miss Soley put up a bulletin-board display: JANESVILLE'S PLACE IN THE WORLD, her cutout letters said, and those were surrounded by pictures of the courthouse and the stores on Milwaukee Avenue and the offices of Parker Pen out on Highway 51 and, of course, the blessed Chevrolet plant, which assembled millions of Chevrolets over the years.

How could Janesville go wrong? General Motors controlled more than 50 percent of the car market. The company was so self-confident that its executives thought about asking President Eisenhower to drop an atomic bomb to commemorate the completion of their Technical Center in 1956.

Janesville was important, that's for sure. I already told you once: we were thirty-fourth on the Russian list of cities to bomb.

But then it all went wrong. The Chevrolet plant closed, perhaps forever, at the end of 2008, and there it stands, an empty shell, the sad memento of an industry based on cheap gas and outrageous styling: there it sits, between the Rock River, where the Black Hawk Indian wars were fought in the 1800s, and the house I lived in. It looks, well, almost as if a neutron bomb had gone off there: the building stands, but the people are gone.

13.

In the summer of 1959, my mother took me aside and asked that I volunteer to be my father's rodman when he worked his new job as a land surveyor. She wanted me to keep an eye on him after his nervous breakdown.

"He still seems sad to me," she said.

It never would have occurred to any of us back then that he was killing himself right in plain sight, and no one lifted a finger.

✦ ✦ ✦

Even though he's been dead for forty years, I can still see him—legs apart, bent at the waist, holding his cap in his left hand, which is, in turn, braced against his thigh. He stares into the telescope of the transit. He squeezes a lit cigarette between the first two fingers of his right hand as he makes small adjustments in the gnarled brass focus knob of the transit lens. I'm standing maybe 100 yards away in a field, my pants legs covered with burrs, holding the flat-sided pole with a row of numbers on it. My dad's trying to get a fix on those numbers in the telescope lens of his transit. He straightens up, puts the cigarette between his lips, and waves his cap at me—signaling that I can relax. Then he writes in his leather surveyor's notebook. When he finishes copying down the number he just saw on my rod, he flips the telescope of the transit straight up. This signal means that I'm to join him for further instructions.

When we get ready to leave the job site, I can see the thick veins on the backs of my dad's hands, his flat fingernails as he unscrews the knobs that hold the transit on its tripod. The instrument is mostly covered in honey-golden-colored brass and looks like a fifteenth-century sextant. He carefully slides it into its green velvet-lined wooden case. Then he pulls out the four-by-six-inch notebook and sketches out the dimensions of the property with one of his beloved green Eberhard 4-H pencils with a pointed red eraser tip. He winds a rubber band around the left-hand side of the pages to keep them from blowing.

The two of us talked about math in those days.

"Math cleans up the world," he told me that summer of 1959 as we rode from surveying job to surveying job in his old Ford work car, with those iron marking stakes rattling around in the trunk. "It puts corners on that mess you see out there."

He waved a hand holding one of the unfiltered Camel cigarettes he chain-smoked, as if he were flicking the messy world away. He had rubber bands looped over the shift lever.

I asked him if Mrs. Downy was right, if we could defeat the Russians with algebra.

"I don't know about that," he said. "I'd choose trigonometry. That's what they use to aim artillery shells. It's called triangulation."

Surveys began with known points, often section markers or those for the US Geological Survey. My father located them with a large magnet in a leather-covered box he held by its strap.

"If you think about it," my dad said, "everything goes back to a known point."

What is the known point for murder?

✦ ✦ ✦

On my birthday in 1959, when I turn fourteen, my aunt gives me the John Gnagy *Learn to Draw* set, which consists of a square of soft plastic that you put on your television screen and a grease pencil for sketching the images that come and go beneath the soft plastic.

Makes Drawing Easy, the box says.

Draw What You See, the goateed John Gnagy says.

I put the plastic on the TV screen. I start with cartoons. Bugs Bunny. I get an eye and part of an ear and then he's gone.

"What's up, Doc?" he asks before he vanishes.

I try for days to capture one—just one—of all the images flitting by: Captain Kangaroo, Tom Terrific, Daffy Duck, The Three Stooges, Beaver Cleaver—but they disappear before I can finish them.

I try the news, but I'm just getting Walter Cronkite's moustache when he turns into a diagram of iron-poor blood being resuscitated by Geritol. I wipe away Walter's moustache and then start copying the man with the microphone standing in the jungle of the Cuban mountains with the rebel soldiers.

"This is a revolution," he says, and I get part of a palm tree, and then here's Eric Sevareid telling me what that means, and I keep ending up with grease-pencil lines connected to nothing.

✦ ✦ ✦

In the movie *Network*, an aging William Holden, playing a broadcast executive, tries to explain the savagely ambitious soul of the youthful Faye Dunaway character, who will stop at nothing to achieve her ends.

"She's from the television generation," Holden says. "She learned life from Bugs Bunny."

✦ ✦ ✦

By the time I was in high school, I wanted to hang around with Brian Jeffrey and Steve Agard. I couldn't have cared less about my dad. While I still worked occasionally with him as a rodman, he would embarrass me by working his tongue beneath the silver bridge that held two false side teeth and sticking out the bridge on the tip of his tongue at café waitresses where we had lunch.

"Oh, Mr. Ryan," the waitresses said.

I have preserved my dad's homemade, leather-covered notebook, its pages filled with sketches of surveys and various coordinates, all done in that fine, gray, almost ghostly penciled printing of an Eberhard 4-H pencil. The entries are like some kind of code about the world.

"SPIKE IN ELM," he writes in neat capital letters followed by "5.55" and "7.89."

I wish now I could ask him what this meant—go back in time, apologize for being such an arrogant shit, and then start from one of those known points and find a better ending for the story.

Yes, if only I could find the known point.

I wish I could find my dad.

I try to hear his voice. I want him to tell me about the lost days, the days I no longer remember.

For Rockland Lot 14 Block 3 1st Hawthorne Park Northerly 57.75 Lot 2 and Southerly 38.50 Lot 3 Block 11 Sumac.

In the pictures of my dad as a young man, he's curly headed and strong but, as the years go by, he becomes more careworn and gaunt.

He wanted me to become a real engineer.

"Engineers solve problems, and the world will never run out of problems," he said. "You'll never lack for work."

He also wanted me to apply for a commission at West Point. He loved the military look. One of the happiest pictures of my father was taken when he was a foreman for the Civilian Conservation Corps. Here he is in a kind of Eisenhower-cut leather jacket and jodhpurs and tall riding boots.

"Jodhpurs," I say to myself. "In Iowa. Jodhpurs in Iowa."

My father had been too old for World War II, and it bothered him that he'd missed it.

"You don't want to miss your generation's war."

Of course, that turned out to be pretty bad advice, but what did my dad know?

Later, when I had a summer job assembling Chevrolets to pay my way through college, one of my workmates, a gray-faced man in a holey T-shirt who installed interior lights, put matters differently. Speaking around the Pall Mall that always dangled from a corner of his mouth, he crawled into the seatless interior of the car, held up the chromed plastic frame of the dome light by one hand, shook the air compressor hose attached to his power screwdriver to straighten it, and said over his shoulder, "Avoid the draft? Are you kidding?" With three zaps of compressed air turning each of the two screws, he mounted the fixture, hopped back out of the car, flicked the ash from his Pall Mall and went on, "You can't avoid the draft! If you don't go in the army, what will you have to talk about in taverns later on?"

Back then, pretty much everyone thought that war was a good idea.

✦ ✦ ✦

One day in the late fall, I went to the city assessor's office in Janesville, and a clerk helped me locate *Rockland Lot 14 Block 3 1*[st] *Hawthorne Park Northerly 57.75 Lot 2 and Southerly 38.50 Lot 3 Block 11 Sumac.* She brought out these enormous three-foot-by-three-foot books covered in gray fabric with red leather spines. In Volume 264, she showed me where Lot 3 Block 11 became 3622 Sumac Street.

I had so little information about my dad, I drove there to see if the place might speak to me.

It was getting dark when I got to the address. At the time my father surveyed it, Lot 3 was part of a farm field owned by Cecil Whitlock. Sometime in the 1960s it got turned into a subdivision. Now a tired rectangular box of a house sits there. The house probably has three small bedrooms and two bathrooms with mildew in the corners of the tile. It and the other houses around it look somehow like coffins.

A MasterCraft waterski boat painted in a silver-flaked purple color that glitters from the light of a nearby mercury-vapor streetlight is parked beside the driveway to Lot 3. I pace back and forth on the sidewalk in front of the house, thinking the place will tell me something when I see . . . is it really possible? . . . a section marker.

A section marker! The term comes unbidden from my subconscious. My father looked for them all the time when he did surveys. The country is gridded with them, I remember suddenly. At the corners of all the 160-acre plots all over the United States. I remember my father talking about them. Little three-inch-by-three-inch square concrete posts with a US Geological Survey emblem centered in the top, a round copper medallion that turns green with the patina of age.

Suddenly, yes, I see one there just under the MasterCraft, and I look around to see if anyone's watching me, and I lift up the boat cover and squat down, studying the ground.

"Hey there, Mister," a voice yells, a little uncertain. "What you doing there under my boat?"

"I'm sorry," I say, "I thought I spotted a section marker here. I actually am looking for my father."

"He's not there."

I stand up, forgetting that I'm beneath the boat's canvas, which now wraps around my head. I breathe in its dusty smell. My speech is muffled. I sound like someone in a tape recording that's running too slow.

"Sorry," I say. "Don't mean any harm."

"You better come out of there."

I go to walk out, but the canvas seems to be holding me. I look down and see feet of the owner pacing back and forth in front of me.

"See there's a section marker here. See."

I bend over, but the section marker turns out to be an old Heileman's Special Export beer can.

"Hey, this is funny, I say. Special Export was the beer when I was in college."

"You and your father better come out of there."

14.

"You told me this book is about Nazis," my wife, Carol, says as she goes over the manuscript. "But here it is, Chapter Fourteen, and I've only met one Nazi, Albert Speer."

Ah, but maybe you've met more than you know.

Nazis didn't start their childhoods in uniform, those lightning bolt Waffen-SS emblems on their collars, Nazis for all the world to see, *Stahlhelme* covering their heads and their ears; their calf-high, polished boots, goose stepping. Look at Goering, see, his fat cheeks, in his school uniform, the little leather knapsack on his back. See, he's singing. Hear him? It's "Heidenröslein." The Schubert song from the Goethe poem. He's his mother's boy. Such a thin, sweet voice, don't you think? Cute in his *lederhosen*. He's not sending the fighters off on another mission. And Goebbels—the little brat: he's arguing with his teacher. Oh, and Hitler's over here doing those watercolors of his. Bormann, so serious as he hits the chalk erasers together, standing ghostlike, haloed by the chalk dust. And Uncle Rudi. Didn't everyone in Germany have an *Onkel* Rudi? *Onkel Rot*, the children called him, because of his red face. Uncle Red. So happy, coming back from camp in that *Hitlerjugend* uniform. Just a boy, really, even though everyone called him *Onkel*. Later he's an SS officer—and look, behind him, come the other boys, legions and legions of boys from all the centuries all over the world, boys who will later go to war, now coming home for supper, and somewhere there I am, too, just a boy—a little boy. See me there: kicking the ball on the playground, going down the slide, at the other end of the teeter-totter from you. I have freckles. I throw my head back when I laugh.

Nazis? Hardly. Little boys on their way.

That's it, you see, the way it just kind of creeps up on you from somewhere. That's what I'm trying to figure out—how that bouncing blue-eyed baby of me ended up working with Nazis. Why, they were the villains, weren't they? Everybody knew that, right? Anyone who'd watched Walter Cronkite narrate *You Are There* knew that.

Me—how did this happen to me? Me, of all people. A pal of the Nazis arresting black soldiers?! Come on. I was a good guy, wasn't I? I had almost worked for the civil rights movement in the sixties. I watched war protests and visited hippies. Me, of all people. Me, my mother's darling young son.

You know those school questionnaires about what you're going to do with your life? Who would answer by saying, "Oh, I'll go to college, study poetry and then I'll go in the army so I can work with old Nazis. Yes, my long-term goal is working with Nazis." Who would say a thing like this?

15.

"We're lucky, Mrs. Ryan—in these modern, scientific days of ours, we can see into things. Atoms and X-rays, Mrs. Ryan— no more mysteries. Atoms and X-rays to make the purchase of a new pair of shoes a matter of science and not of guessing."

This is Mr. Dreyhouse of Dreyhouse Shoes on Main Street in Janesville speaking to my mother. It's still 1959.

He gestures as he speaks, raising up his arms and turning his hands as if he's conducting an orchestra.

"You see, Mrs. Ryan," he says. "Little Rickie will need these feet all his life, and the Adrian X-Ray machine will give him a better fit scientifically. Ah, the lovely Adrian X-Ray machine will allow us to look right into his feet, you see. It's the scientific thing to do."

He holds his hands toward the Adrian and bows. He then walks over and pats it. The wooden exterior of the device is streamlined and edged with aluminum, like a cabinet from the *Normandie*, "The Ship of Light," that's somehow been left off in Janesville.

"Isn't it dangerous to look inside the human body?" my mother asks.

"Why, it's dangerous *not* to. Here, Rickie, step up here and peek at all the secrets you thought were locked away."

He bows again, and I step up on a riser at one side of the Adrian Shoe-Fitting Fluoroscope and tuck my feet into an opening banded with aluminum around its edges. On the top of the machine are three built-in viewfinders that look vaguely like the stereopticons my grandmother had. One viewer on top of the fluoroscope is for the owner of the feet, one is for the companion to the owner, and one is for the shoe salesman.

"Here we go," Mr. Dreyhouse says, throwing a large Bakelite toggle switch. "Let the science begin."

The machine hums beneath my feet, and the black marker needle in a round gauge rises as the electricity warms up the X-ray tube. I make sure my feet are all the way into the opening. The shadowed black outline of the bones in my feet slowly comes into view. The little bones appear to float in a watery green solution. How strange it is to wiggle my toes and see my bones move a moment later. It's like watching a shadow of me with a skeleton inside.

"Yes, Mrs. Ryan, the Adrian Shoe-Fitting Fluoroscope will save your son years of health problems. It's been awarded the famous *Parents Magazine* Seal of Approval, you know. Now *that* should give you confidence."

Unfortunately, *Parents Magazine* didn't have quite enough science to evaluate the Adrian. It didn't know about all those roentgens: the radiation climbing through our three bodies and ricocheting around the shoe store. *Bam* from the penny loafers to the stiletto heels. *Wham* from the bedroom slippers over to the Jack Purcell tennis shoes. *Parents* didn't know that the Adrian Shoe-Fitting Fluoroscope might be more dangerous than Sputnik beeping overhead through our skies. The Adrian might, in fact, be more dangerous than the Communists.

Oh, it was such a dear, sweet era, wasn't it, with those giant cars with their sulfurous exhausts, ruining our lungs, killing us. But we didn't know that. No, we were checking our gas mileage. We studied those instruments in the dashboard. That was all we needed to know, right? The speedometer here in one circle and, in the other circle: TEMP, AMP, OIL, and GAS. All we needed to know, right there. TEMP, AMP, OIL, GAS.

Who could have known? Not Mr. Dreyhouse, surely, standing there in his striped sport coat and tousled hair.

Looking over the glasses at the end of his nose as he answered our questions, he looked like a Norman Rockwell figure. He couldn't have known that his machine was sending out rays sharp as carbon-steel knives. Who could blame him?

Why even Marie Curie, who probably died of radiation poisoning, would go out to her lab at night and see her vials of radioactive material flickering on the shelves in the dark. "The glowing tubes looked like faint, fairy lights," she wrote. She didn't know that these "wonderful compounds" could kill as well as cure.

So strange, isn't it—the way ignorance goes hand in hand with science. My mother, Mr. Dreyhouse, and I there, convinced we were learning something—when really, we were just killing ourselves for no good reason at all.

Nazis? Why, Nazis are always a long way from fourth grade.

My friend, he called me, Albert Speer did. My friend.

Yes, for five minutes, it was Albert Speer and I, the best of friends, but it took me years to get there.

16.

Oh, there it goes in my dreams, floating along, the head of Henry Kissinger, tall as a five-story building, floating sixty feet overhead, filled with gas, a huge Macy's balloon, floating over the marching soldiers. In their gray camouflage uniforms in the gray air, a moving mass.

Thousands of men, marching, marching, marching.

"Go to your left, your right, your left."

The reverberating *clump* of all those boots hitting the ground in unison.

The giant, floating head of Henry Kissinger turning slowly back and forth, his eyeglass lenses becoming opaque when the light hits them.

Millions of men beneath him, marching, marching, marching.

Clump. Clump. Clump.

"Go to your left, your right, your left," marching, marching.

The head of Henry Kissinger nodding.

Clump. Clump. Clump.

He turns to me and smiles, Henry Kissinger does. His teeth are sharp like saw teeth. Brilliant white saw teeth.

"*Sehr schön, nicht wahr?*"

Beautiful, isn't it?

"*Der Krieg ist die Wahrheit.*"

War is the truth.

His voice is like the Arctic wind.

Why is he speaking in German? But then I remember. He is, in fact, German.

The head floats along, nodding, above the marching soldiers.

Clump. Clump. Clump.

The opaque eyes looking in the distance, looking suddenly at me. His face suddenly in front of me, his mouth open, his teeth like a spiked fence, beyond it a dragon howling, hissing fire, howling.

Clump. Clump. Clump.

Millions and millions and millions of men, marching, marching, marching.

17.

I graduated from high school in June of 1963. That summer I worked for Bostwick's, a men's store in Janesville. This was the first of a series of summer jobs that helped pay my way through college.

I secretly believed that good clothes would somehow give me a new family. They would help me escape the haunting of my family. I'd have a sane father with a better car than an old Ford with iron surveying stakes in the trunk and rubber bands on the shift column, and a mother who didn't spend the day in her faded housecoat drinking coffee and discussing how the family fortune had been lost.

"What a man needs," Bill Bostwick, one of the store owners, always said, "is a new Botany 500 suit and a set of matched Samsonite luggage. Those items, along with a half Windsor knot beneath the collar of a new Arrow shirt, will take you to the highest promontories of life."

In August of 1963, when I left for little Cornell College in Iowa, I followed Bill's advice pretty closely. I had that brand-new Botany 500 suit (just like one that Dick Van Dyke wore on his TV show), some Arrow shirts, and a matched pair of Samsonite Ultralite suitcases in Colorado Brown my aunt and uncle gave me. I borrowed a device that made hard plastic label tapes with raised lettering, so my Norelco electric razor was clearly identified as belonging to "Ryan."

"Let me get this straight," my friend Tom Bamberger says. "You graduated from high school in 1963, and you were putting your name on your electric razor because you were worried that someone would steal it?"

"And my alarm clock—oh, and my clothes brush, too. I even put labels on these wooden hangers I had. They had these clamps to hold your pants."

"You had wooden hangers in the fall of 1963? You had a clothes brush?"

"For my Botany 500 suit."

"What's wrong with you? The sixties were just getting started in 1963, and you were worried about creases in your suit. Bob Dylan is writing 'Blowing in the Wind,' and you're suiting up with The Four Freshmen."

Look, Tom: I thought I was keeping up with the times. I thought we were pretty hip there in Mount Vernon, Iowa.

When John Kennedy was assassinated in the fall of my freshman year, I was sitting in my dorm room reading aloud from "The Fable of the Final Hour" by Dan Propper. I thought this was a pretty hip moment.

Of course "The Fable of the Final Hour" hasn't completely stood the test of time. I mean, how many times have you pulled this poem off the shelf in the last few years? How many times has anyone you know read this poem? Have you, in fact, ever *heard* of this poem? With its slightly offbeat spacing and incantatory rhythms, it seemed a piece of early 1960s hip. Now, though, the poem seems almost as earnest as the era it wanted to enlighten.

> *In the 37th minute of the final hour a Bop version of the Star-Spangled Banner was proclaimed official arrangement of the United States Marines*

As I read to my bored roommates from "The Fable of the Final Hour" that chilly November afternoon, I began to feel pretty hip myself, with the syncopated flow of those anapests running along:

> In the 51st minute of the final hour Texas was declared Incapable and assigned a guardian

This was the exact sentence I was reading the afternoon of November 22nd, 1963, when Freddie Sarnack came running into the room.

"The president," he said, out of breath, trying to get enough wind for a full sentence. "The president . . . the president has been shot."

This is probably the one and only moment in my life when I was somehow completely in tune with the subterranean, homesick blues of my time.

"I think you're kidding yourself, Rick," Tom Bamberger tells me. "That isn't a real sixties story. Real sixties stories involve pot or sex or war protests—not reading bad poetry. Did you ever have to wash the smell of tear gas out of your clothes?"

"I was close. There were war protests in Madison. I grew up only forty miles away in Janesville. I visited a lot."

"You visited the sixties," Bamberger tells me. "That's funny."

Oh—and there was the time I was almost a civil rights protester.

18.

In 1965, I can see Dr. Larry Stone, professor of religion, stapling posters to the trees on campus. They announced a trip in March to join a big civil rights march from Selma to Montgomery, Alabama.

Be Part of the History of Your Time.
Join hands with Dr. Martin Luther King Jr.
END
Racial injustice in the South.
We SHALL Overcome

I had my first real girlfriend then, and sex got mixed up in my politics.

Jenny was a folksinger and always talked about how strict her father was and how he would be apoplectic if he discovered his daughter participating in left-wing causes, so she had to be careful, Jenny told me. She wouldn't, therefore, be going to Selma, no—but when I mentioned that I was kind of, sort of thinking about going, her body became electric, and she sang "We Shall Overcome" softly in my ear and let me caress her inner thighs.

At this point, Mr. Cock became involved. While caressing a young lady's thighs covered by the denim of blue jeans wasn't, perhaps, exactly an admission to her inner sanctum, Mr. Cock reasoned that I was on my way.

At this point, Mr. Cock made the decision for me—he was sending himself to Jenny Gleason's vagina via a voter registration program for Negroes in Selma, Alabama.

The information meeting drew a healthy crowd—maybe fifty or sixty students, including one of the conservatives, who sat in the back row holding up a poster that said *SPONGE—Society for the Prevention of Negroes Getting Everything.*

"This is," Dr. Stone said, his voice turned into echoes and screeches by the bad PA system, "one of the profound moments of our time. Years from now, your grandchildren will ask you where you were when Dr. King and his followers joined hands and marched to Montgomery, Alabama. When the histories of the twentieth century are written, these days will have a prominent place. Your grandchildren will ask you where you were that fateful day."

I picked up a schedule and a form I was to have my parents sign. Since I wasn't yet twenty-one, I needed their permission to go. Now this was a problem. My parents—while basically good, kind people—were also white people of their times.

"Those Negroes," my father once told me.

"Yes?"

"Those Negroes have to help themselves out, you know. We can't do it for them."

"This country has brutalized the Negroes," I said, quoting Dr. Stone.

"Well, you'll see. We can't do it for them."

What did that mean, I wondered. When I got angry with him, I yelled it out, "What does that mean? We have to help; it's our duty!"

"You can't sit this game out," Dr. Stone said. "If you don't help the Negro gain the basic rights of citizenship, then the blood of the Negro is on your hands. You are as guilty as some Klansman in a white sheet setting fire to a Negro church. Think about it."

"The government is up to no good," my dad said, picking up a flake of tobacco from his tongue. "No good at all."

"Oh, baby" is what Jenny Gleason said when I told her I was going with Dr. Stone on the trip to Montgomery. Suddenly, in the middle of Iowa, I, who hadn't been out of the Midwest in my life, slurred "Montgomery" as though I were a southerner.

Jenny leaned back on the couch and spread her legs, as if inviting me in, and I began stroking her crotch, which seemed to soften like melting ice cream. I was underneath the bra in no time. Her nipples were as erect as my cock.

"Oh, baby," she said.

✦ ✦ ✦

"Ryan. Rick Ryan," I said to Dr. Stone the next morning, and he checked me off his list, which had thirty or forty names.

Three other people eventually showed up—Wade Leonard, Jeannie Farago, and Mary Rombauer.

We met in front of Lennox Hall, the men's dormitory.

"Wait a minute," Dr. Stone said. "I can't believe we don't have more students than you four. My meeting had ten times that many people, didn't it?"

He said that to Mary Rombauer, who just giggled, unable to answer.

"Look at this. They signed up. Joe Everling, Dawn Moore, Everette Gordon . . . thirty-two people. They all signed up, gave me their parental permission sheets. They were all ready to take freedom south."

He walked up and down the road as if his movement might bring the volunteers in.

"I suppose we won't be needing the school bus," Dr. Stone said after another half an hour. He sighed and then slowly walked over to a yellow Blue Bird bus. The bus drove away, and the five of us got into Wade Leonard's 1959 Ford station wagon, which smelled vaguely like dirty jockstraps. It was a kind of testosterone odor. Wade was a varsity wrestler and wore the purple and white letterman's jacket of the college.

Just as we were about to pull out, Steve Unger, my folk-singer roommate came clomping over in his engineer boots. He carried his big Gibson in a guitar case and wore oversized sunglasses. He looked like a celebrity.

"Did you bring a change of clothes along?" I asked, ever the boy from Janesville.

"I'm a troubadour, man. Got clean underwear and a tooth-brush in my guitar case."

It was a tight fit, but all six of us got into the old Ford.

Wade's car engine turned over slowly, as if it were worried about such a long trip. Once the engine caught, the engine and then the car body and then the six of us vibrated.

Just as we were pulling out of the parking lot, Steve began singing "We Shall Overcome." Only Jenny was there to see us off, and her clear alto voice echoed back to our off-key harmony, and then we were on our way, to save the Negroes in Alabama.

Dr. Stone passed out copies of mimeographed materials with titles like "Tips for Dealing With Racists," "What To Do If You Get Arrested," and "Avoiding Injury and Death."

"Ah, Dr. Stone," Mary Rombauer said, "on the second page of 'Avoiding Injury and Death,' where the specific advice is supposed to be—well, it's empty. I mean the page is blank."

"Oh, my. I was in such a hurry, maybe I forgot."

He began rummaging through a battered leather briefcase.

"Let's see if I have a copy."

I was only halfway listening to this, because I wondered when Dr. Stone would realize that he didn't have an OK from my parents. While he had, as it turned out, forgotten the sheets on avoiding injury and death, he pretty quickly did remember that I hadn't turned in my permission slip.

"Tell you what, Ryan, with so few people on our good pilgrimage, why don't you try calling your parents. A verbal go-ahead would be enough for me."

As Wade Leonard's car drove south on 218, Dr. Stone said we should stop at the first phone booth we saw. It was beside a drive-in restaurant. I went into the phone booth and folded the door closed behind me. I laid out a stack of quarters on the little shelf in the booth, took a deep breath, and rehearsed what I was about to say. I figured my mother would answer.

"Mom," I'd say, a little too brightly. "Mom, I'm going on this field trip."

The phone at the other end kept buzzing, and no one answered.

"She's not home," I said when I came out of the phone booth. "Look. We can keep calling as we go." Maybe we'd get there before I reached her.

"Mom," I'd say, "you'll just never guess where I am."

Just before Mount Pleasant, in the middle of a discussion about how to roll yourself up into a ball if a policeman started whacking you with a billy club, Wade rear-ended a Cadillac. Truth be told, hearing these stories about the ferocity of Southern law enforcement officers had made us all nervous. The car crash seemed inevitable somehow.

The driver of the car we hit got out, carefully arranged a kind of Frank Sinatra straw businessman's hat on his head, walked to the rear of his car, looked at the damage. The car bumpers of the old Ford and the new Cadillac were hooked together like two male deer racks. One of the Ford's headlights was shattered.

The Cadillac driver leaned over the interlocked bumpers and opened his trunk. He pulled out a Speed Graphic camera and began photographing the damage. Done with that, he asked us to step out of the car and photographed all of us.

"Never know just what photographs you might need," the man said with a smile.

Then he did a sketch of the accident on graph paper and told us that he was an insurance agent.

"I always travel equipped for moments like this. It's a life of accidents, you know."

Then we all sat on the bumper of the Ford and bounced it a few times. The two cars, as if done with their business together, pulled apart.

We started south again. The old Ford keep steering to the right, as if the accident had frightened it and now it wanted off the road.

At a gas station outside of Keokuk, just before we left Iowa, my uncle answered the phone at our house.

"Hi, Uncle Gene," I said. "I'm calling about this school civil rights trip."

He heard me out and then said, "Your father's just been diagnosed with lung cancer. You don't have time for civil rights."

When I walked back to the old Ford, I suddenly saw the whole scene—Dr. Stone, Steve Unger, the old Ford, and all the rest—behind a cloudy scrim. I was on one side, and my old life was on the other. I tried to reach across, but my attempt bounced back, as if I had tried to punch a trampoline. The scrim kept me on my side, all by myself.

I hitchhiked back to my little college. When my ride, a retired farmer, heard about my bad news, he drove me all the way to the campus.

"I'm so sorry," he said when he let me off.

That was what Jenny said and what my teachers said and what my uncle said when he came to get me.

19.

It was a simple proposition. The doctor told my mother that if he called her an hour into the surgery, the news wouldn't be good: the tumor would have spread too far, making it inoperable. He would close my father back up. If, on the other hand, he called two or three hours after the surgery began, why, then—then my father had a fighting chance. The doctor would dig the cancer out of his lungs.

I can see my mother in the kitchen the morning of the surgery, wearing an apron and a new dress, baking banana bread and doing dishes, as if becoming a perfect housewife would help my father's chances. My brother is playing with sticks.

The truth is, my mother hardly ever wore an apron or a new dress. Dressed in an old housecoat with a washed-out design that looked like the memory of green-stemmed irises with purple blooms, she liked to sit at the kitchen table smoking Larks and discussing how the family fortune had been lost. She let the dishes pile up. She was really an intellectual who'd been trapped by family life. She'd written a novel—typed it on four-by-six-inch notebook paper and kept it in her little University of Iowa three-ring binder. When I was three or four, I scribbled drawings on the back of her work with my set of giant Crayola crayons, and then the notebook disappeared. She probably threw it away.

Ring. The sound of the phone came an hour into my mother's kitchen chores. After that abrupt first ring, time slowed down. A second seemed to take an hour. The second ring went on forever, its sound broken into separate, jangling tremors, each one of them draining color from my mother's face, as if a faucet slowly closed, turning off her supply of blood.

My brother came over and stood beside me. He held my hand.

"It's probably my friend Brian Jeffrey," I said.

In slow motion, each step covering an infinity of ground in an infinity of time, I went to answer the phone, which was in its own little nook built into the wall, with a dark wood shelf and a dark wood panel underneath that hid the connector for the wires. That nook was one of the few elegant touches in our tiny house.

My mother stands frozen in the kitchen, moving so slowly, as if through the slurry of partly frozen water.

"Hello," I say, picking up the receiver.

The center of the phone dial has our phone number. It begins *PL* in oversized letters. The beginning of *Pleasant*. PL8-7810 is the whole number. When I was little, you didn't have to dial it all—just 7810 was enough. Then it became 8-7810. By the time my father was sick, it was 758-7810. I look at those numbers as if they somehow will save my dad.

"Is Mrs. Ryan there?"

"Who's calling?"

"Dr. Chen."

Yes, Janesville's first Chinese doctor, back there in 1965. I hold the phone out toward my mother in the kitchen. She steps toward me, the film in frame-by-frame slow motion. When I hand her the phone, she drops it, and it spins on the floor, like the turning arrow on *Wheel of Fortune*, pointing at me, my mother, nothing.

"Yes? Oh, I see," my mother says after she picks up the phone. "Yes. Of course. Right away. Yes. Yes."

My mother is taking off her apron as she speaks. She looks at her shoes.

"Right away. Yes. Yes."

She hangs up and stares off into space.

"How is he?" I ask. "How'd the surgery go?"

"We've got to leave now," she says. "Be there when he wakes up."

She wants to drive, and I let her, even though I haven't passed up a chance to drive a car since I got my driver's license.

Traveling Milton Avenue to the Main Street Bridge, we pass through downtown. The stores have been there forever, I think. Forever. Time slows again . . . slower and slower the stores go by. They never change. They'll *never* go away, will they? Not the Clark gas station with its little plaque—*On this spot in 1898, Carrie Jacobs Bond wrote "I Love You Truly."* Not Harrison Chevrolet, Wisconsin Bell, Woolworth's . . . slowly, slowly going by. My mother bent over the steering wheel, looking straight ahead, hypnotized by the vaporous draw of an opaque future.

✦ ✦ ✦

"Where's my watch?" my dad says when he wakes up. "What time is it? Did he get it all?"

"There, there, Earl," my mother says. A nurse propels the gurney my father's lying on through the warren of hallways in the basement of Mercy Hospital. My mother and I trot beside it, trying to keep up. My mother tries to hold my father's hand as we move along, but the nurse keeps pushing him out ahead of us, as if my father is on his way to an urgent meeting somewhere. A second nurse trots along with an IV on wheels. Its tube is hooked to my father's arm. A clear plastic bag sits on the end of his bed, holding dark blood and tissue, the black, oozing detritus of his surgery.

"It's kind of early, isn't it?" my father asks the world, the heavens over him.

I look over at my father. He has fat tears in his eyes. Since he's lying down, they don't drain away. He shakes his head. "No." He seems to be mouthing the word, "No." His mouth quivers with his silent crying. My mother pats his hands as she trots along, saying, "There, there," over and over. My father sobs, gagging on his tears.

20.

Time passed in a dream. Days, I worked in the Janesville Chevrolet assembly plant, earning money to pay for my last years of college. Nights and weekends, I took care of my father.

He never had a chance. He had barely recovered from the surgery when the cancer got him in its final grip. It squeezed the flesh right out of him. He must have lost a pound a day until, by early June, he looked like one of those who's barely survived a concentration camp. He was all bones and tendons and ligaments. His skin hung like a loose-fitting costume over the wires and pulleys of his skeletal system.

We all tried to hope, but the disease just took everything out of him. His head was just this skull with giant eyes on his scrawny body.

We decided to take care of him at home and moved a hospital bed into my bedroom, which had slightly more room than his. By July the cancer was painful, and the doctor showed me how to give him shots of morphine. Even with this instruction, I sometimes missed the vein and hit the bone in his skinny arm or leg, and he whimpered, his large eyes tearing up with love and pity and pain.

He leaned on me as we walked to the bathroom. I could feel his joints rubbing together in his diminished body. I fed him and bathed him and, every couple of days shaved him. Pretty soon, he didn't have the strength to walk, and I reached beneath his body and lifted him out of bed for his trips to the bathroom. He was light to carry. His body felt as though it were made of papier-mâché. The joints in his hips and knees looked huge next to his wasted legs and torso.

These were intimate moments; I'd never been so close to my father. I could have learned so much, but you know what?—I was embarrassed. He creeped me out. He frightened me. His breath smelled rotten, and his face was sunken because he'd quit wearing his tooth bridge. When I carried him, his limp body felt as though it were made out of rubber hoses. I looked at him in horror. I could hardly bear to touch him, afraid that this fierce disease would somehow rub off on me. Never, ever would I be like that, I vowed.

I wanted to be out with my friends drinking beer and howling at the night. I wanted to sit in parked cars with girls, kissing them and feeling their breasts flop loose from their brassieres. But no, I had chores. In the evening, when I got home from work, I had to take care of my dad, while my mother, exhausted from being with him all day, sat downstairs in the living room watching television and smoking and drinking coffee.

I sat inches away from my father's gaunt and yellowed face, pulling his razor through the lather on his sunken cheeks. At first we talked, but then he stared at me as if I were a stranger.

He was like a man slipping down the face of a mountain. I tried to stop his fall, but I could just feel his touch as he slid out of my hands, see the stunned terror in his eyes as he slid farther and farther away.

Every morning I drove off to the Chevrolet assembly plant, where I stood on a riser made of steel grating. I wore a heavy rubber apron and stiff, unwieldy rubber gloves and washed down the passing bodies of Chevy Biscaynes, Bel Airs, and Impalas with dry cleaning fluid so they'd be free of dirt and dust when they went into the spray-paint booth. One primer-gray-covered automobile body a minute jerked by on the squeaking and clanking assembly line.

Arch McConnell, my coworker, caught fire one afternoon. Or the naphtha fumes did. He stood there with his arms out in flames, the fire burning a few inches all around his body, fueled by the chemical fumes. He looked like the painting of Blake's *Glad Day*.

"The fuck . . . the fuck . . . the fuck!" Arch screamed.

He wasn't burned. The fuel somehow protected him; the flames burned a few inches away from his skin and then simply went out.

At the end of my shift, I drove home, listening to WLS in Chicago, where the hit of the summer was "(I Can't Get No) Satisfaction" by The Rolling Stones.

When my father's bowel movements turned black from internal hemorrhaging, we took him to the hospital. The cancer was now eating through his guts. Just before he died, he looked up at the crucifix on the wall of the Catholic hospital and announced, "That's Don Quixote."

My father—incomprehensible as the coordinates he left in his surveyor's notebook—must have known something about Cervantes. And yet he hardly ever read and was not, as far as I knew, a literary man, and I have puzzled over his remark for years. It was so far from what he seemed to know and said so close to his death that his announcement seemed to contain knowledge from beyond the grave.

My father died on July 23rd, 1965, the day after my twentieth birthday. On one day, I left my teenage years behind and on the next I lost my father. The last sight I had of him he was a yellow-green corpse with a slight smile on his face, as if Don Quixote had finally told him the punch line to a joke.

"Daddy dead," my brother said when we told him the next morning. "Daddy dead?"

As if he couldn't quite grasp what we were telling him.

Gary, my brother, died almost exactly a year later in 1966, as if he wanted to search for my father.

✦ ✦ ✦

After we put my father's hospital bed in my room, I moved into his room. I hung my clothes in his closet and slept in his bed. I felt as though I was somehow impersonating him, trying to live in a space that was properly his.

On Saturdays and Sundays, I would quietly go there and try on his clothes, which were exactly my size. They didn't quite fit me, though. The wrinkles and the break points of the fabric were suited to his body, not mine, and the clothes hung on me with the memory of someone else.

The day after my father died, I was so depressed and anxious that I walked quietly upstairs, went into his room, closed the door, and lay on his bed. Even after a month of sleeping there, the smell of the bed, of the pillow, even of the room itself were foreign to me. I lay there that day, rubbing my genitals, and then began masturbating with a furious energy and suddenly was looking up through my tightly closed eyes at the heavens and in a hole between the clouds I could see the faces of the dead I knew—two of my four grandparents and my father. They stared at me, as if they'd opened up a manhole cover in the streets of heaven and now looked down at the subterranean world of the earth below and into the house at 863 East Memorial Drive, where I lay rubbing my cock.

I was so surprised that my left hand stopped its flurried up and down stroking. I let go, and my erect penis waved back and forth as if greeting them.

"Damn," I said aloud, embarrassed, like a kid who's been caught. Then I got annoyed. I wasn't going to give up this therapeutic pleasure.

After a moment, I looked up at them in my dream.

"Get used to it," I said. "Just go on and get used to it. You're going to see this every day I'm alive."

The little halo of their faces vanished.

21.

In the fall of 1965, I went back to college covered by the gauzy folds of my grief. Jenny and I went on dates and held hands as we walked around campus, but I felt as though I was an actor in the staged version of Rick Ryan, reading someone else's lines. Only when Jenny sang some of the folk songs with the anguish of their terrible solitude did the inmost core of my soul reply.

> *Four strong winds that blow lonely . . .*
> *I'll look for you if I'm ever back this way.*

"What ever happened to Eurydice? Who remembers Eurydice?" a professor asked in one of my English literature classes. "The precious stone of her life lost, tumbling down and down. Lost. Irretrievably lost."

✦ ✦ ✦

One strange little bright spot that fall was the Student Talent Show. My God, were we ever so innocent that we put on *a talent* show? Is it possible, living as we did in the eddying streams of irony, that we could take a skinny white boy with an unbuttoned button-down shirt singing "Ol' Man River" seriously? Or how about the pale girl singing "The hills are alive with the sound of music," her fingers grappling with the air in front of her as if she were turning knobs the audience couldn't see. Or maybe this was the beginning of irony—as we recognized how talentless most of us really were, maybe this was the moment when we decided to make fun of everything. Maybe this was the moment when irony became the only value.

But here came this mop-headed boy, his hair dark brown and his grin infectious, playing the Herb Alpert and the Tijuana Brass song, "The Lonely Bull," bending into the notes as if looking for the air of his music in every nook of his body. What pleasure he got from our applause and look at how he spun the trumpet like a six-shooter and then blew across the mouthpiece. A gunfighter, finishing up after shooting. Grimes Poznik, the new gun in town.

22.

By the end of 1965, there were 184,000 American troops in Vietnam, and men were being drafted at the rate of 40,000 a month. But I didn't know any of that then. I don't think I was paying attention.

I don't think I'd recovered yet from the death of my father—maybe, in fact, I've never recovered. I remember walking around in a haze most of the time, only half hearing what my professors and my friends said.

Somewhere in that haze I heard myself asking Jenny to marry me. I thought she could save me from the iron loneliness of my life.

It was a sweet dream, our getting married was. We planned the date for the end of 1967, when, we were sure, the war in Vietnam would be over and the future would be filled with radiant possibilities.

"Are you kidding?" Steve Unger said. "The war's never going to end. It's getting more dangerous every day. I'm quitting school now so they can draft me. It'll be worse than ever in two years."

"That's crazy."

"What—you think you'll escape? We're all going in the army. I just want to get it over with. Get on with my life."

The last I saw of Steve, he was slouched on a bench in the waiting room of the Greyhound Bus Terminal, cradling his guitar, strumming "It Ain't Me, Babe."

Later, somebody heard that Steve was drafted and sent to Vietnam. Someone else said he was performing in a Boston coffeehouse. We also heard that he was a drifter—homeless and living on the streets in Minneapolis. He'd been seen wearing a thin nylon jacket in the middle of winter on a street corner begging, his hands shaking so badly he couldn't hold the change people gave him.

✦ ✦ ✦

Grimes Poznik kept playing. He played everywhere. He'd sit on tree limbs, pop out of bushes.

"All the world's my stage, man," he'd tell you if you asked what he was doing. "I'm giving melodies to the air you breathe."

You'd be walking along, and he'd jump out from behind an acacia tree to play parts from a Mozart horn concerto. He'd be sitting in the far stall of the men's room in the commons playing Miles Davis. The muffled tone of his horn echoed through the whole building. How strange those moments were, how they'd catch you, on your way to your bit of business, there'd be Grimes, that slice of hair down over his forehead, bending into the notes of his song, a reverie right through your day.

"I bring you the night; I bring you the day," he said.

✦ ✦ ✦

Who could guess that Grimes would die, homeless, of alcohol poisoning, on a street in San Francisco in the harder years that came after the 1960s.

✦ ✦ ✦

In spring semester of 1966, I took European history with Professor Kleinholder. I remember the day he brought this ancient record player to class. It had a detachable horn on the top and played these thick 78s.

"*Ja, Ja,*" he said as he put the contraption together. "I am very interested in this American business of powdered foods, of taking water out of things. I think this is how history is— little shiny crystals, and we must put them in water, return them to the life they once had. Here is such a crystal from the past."

His hands shook as he put the record on the machine, cranked the handle to get it going, and set the giant needle on the record. First the sound of spinning static.

"You hear, the way it sounds like the past. Like dust from years ago blowing here into this classroom of our little college."

The blare, then, of a long-ago oompah band began playing a march with a chorus of men singing.

He lifted the needle to pause the playing, and we could still hear a grinding noise as the record went round on its mechanism.

"I have now an experiment. You will get to participate in the old days. The old days for you, but the new days for me. From a time when I was young. History for me, almost yesterday for me. Come stand up. *Ja,* come here. All of you."

Professor Kleinholder became animated as he showed us how to line up in front of the blackboard.

"It is a march song, *ja.* When it plays you will march around in a circle here, to get the feel of it. It is an experiment. We have now a laboratory of history."

Once we were all lined up in the space between the blackboard and the first row of seats, he cranked the handle and put the needle back on the spinning record. The static and then the oom-pah music began again, and a chorus of sturdy male voices sang.

At first awkwardly and then more and more in time to the beat of the music, we marched in a small circle at the front of the classroom. Professor Kleinholder waved his right arm up and down and back and forth as if he were conducting this.

"*Ja*," he said. Actually he yelled over the music, which seemed to get louder. "This is the tune of an old German folk song. We used to sing it in the mountains. It is like the melody of that hymn, 'How Great Thou Art.' I was visiting Berlin in 1932. I was your age, and I heard it playing in the distance. It brought tears to my eyes. Reminded me of when I used to hike in the woods with my friends."

Professor Kleinholder looked off into space.

"When I got closer and heard the song clearly, I could tell that they changed the words. *Ja*. All changed, and these thugs were marching. *Alles verendert*. Do you understand the words? When I first heard this song coming from the streets of Berlin, I knew my innocent days were over. *Vorbei*. Here, let me start the record over. I'll translate for you."

> *The street free for the brown battalions*
> *The street free for the Storm Troopers*
> *Millions, full of hope, look up at the swastika*
> *The day breaks for freedom and for bread.*

We quit marching then and stood there, looking down at our feet, while the scratchy harmonies played themselves out on the cylinder.

"It breaks your heart, what they did to this song, to the country. The country of Beethoven and Schubert. These were the famous Brown Shirts, the precursors to Hitler. You remember this, *ja*? You remember how this goes from sentiment to horror. You remember how easily you marched. You be on your guard. Watch out. *Man muss immer aufpassen*. You must always pay attention. Be careful what you sing, *ja*?"

In his fedora and his elegant suits, Professor Kleinholder was at every war protest that I saw at my little college. I thought about joining in myself, but then it all seemed too complicated. I just watched from across the street, afraid to cross over.

✦ ✦ ✦

"Has anyone noticed," I heard someone in basic training ask, "that our uniform shirts are brown? We're like the Nazis, man. We're Brown Shirts."

"Oh, fuck you," someone else said. "This is the goddamned American army. We're not Nazis. We save the world."

23.

As I look at that army uniform I found in the attic of 332 East Acacia Road, the first image that comes to mind is the little army post office where I mailed the box. It's a single room fronted by a half door with a counter on top.

It was tucked away in a corner of Turley Barracks. Open from ten to noon in the morning and from two to four in the afternoon. Private First Class Ellert the clerk there. Yes, I recall, so clearly now, his name stenciled over the right-hand pocket of his green fatigue shirt, *US Army* printed over the left-hand pocket. The little black stripe on a rocker—the PFC emblem—on each of his collar corners.

He never got promoted in the two years I knew him, and that was odd during the Vietnam War. Even though the combat was a continent away from Germany, promotions fell on us like confetti at a party.

Yes, PFC Ellert and the APO—at the end of my time in the army . . . I was . . . yes . . . oh, now, I remember . . . I was mailing my uniform home so I would have a souvenir of my time in the army.

I actually spent a lot of time with PFC Ellert during the last year of my army service. It began when I started applying to graduate schools. You see, I was trying to get back to where I'd been before the army nabbed me. I was just desperate to be out of the army and go back to studying Emerson and poetry.

In my dreams, though, the army wouldn't let me go.

✦ ✦ ✦

I was riding in a deuce-and-a-half truck with the rest of my platoon. I could see us—both from an overhead viewpoint and also from inside of the truck. You could smell our fear. We wore our steel combat helmets and rested our rifles on the floor of the truck. It was a moonlit night, and one of us quietly sobbed in the dark. Seen from overhead, our helmets lined up like green-gray eggshells, hardly enough protection against what lay in the dark ahead.

I would wake up then, afraid to go back to sleep.

Yes, I wanted out of the army's clutches. While I'd so far managed to stay out of combat, Vietnam was always out there, like a cancer diagnosis. It could always get you.

✦ ✦ ✦

In the fall of 1971, I made almost daily trips to the little post office in Turley Barracks with the applications and the essays required by various graduate school English Departments. I wanted out of the army. Oh how I wanted out.

"Are you sure," I asked PFC Ellert the first time, "that my envelope will arrive on time?"

"Ryan, come on," he said. "You know better than to ask a question like that. You of all people, Mr. Big Shot Customs Inspector. This is, first of all, the army and, second of all, the Postal Service we're talking about here, so there really are no absolutes, are there? What I'd recommend is that you slap one of those pale green Registered Mail forms on the envelope. I'd insure it, as well. That'll make them nervous. They'll think mistakes will be expensive. That way, no one will fuck with it. It's easier to fuck with fourth class mail. Come on, man, you of all people should know that."

✦ ✦ ✦

Yes, of course. He knew that Goldberg and I opened and inspected Parcel Post packages at the Heidelberg Military Post Office, where all the army mail from this area went before being shipped overseas. That was one of my jobs, tearing open mail. Snooping. The other two jobs were doing black-market investigations with the German Customs Police and clearing US soldiers and civilians through customs stations at military transfer points.

Funny, before my army days, I had thought the mail was sacred somehow, untouchable without a search warrant. Part of the castle that was the free man's home.

✦ ✦ ✦

"Forget that chickenshit, good-citizen, social-studies crap, Ryan," Sergeant Dooley said when he was showing me the various Customs inspector routines of my new job in Detachment A of the Twenty-Second MP Customs Unit. "Fourth class mail belongs to the army, and the army can do what it goddamned well pleases. You and me, Ryan, we scare the shit out of fourth class mail. Besides, we're detached here in ole Detachment A. We don't give a howdy goddamn."

That said, Sergeant Dooley walked over to a stack of boxes eight or nine feet high and parried at them with a bayonet he carried.

"Men," he said, imitating a drill sergeant, "this is hand-to-hand combat. Be sure to yell 'Kill!' as you strike your blow for democracy."

He slashed several boxes with the bayonet.

"The poor and dumb have to learn their lesson. This'll teach those fuckers not to pay up for first class postage."

Sergeant Dooley then pulled several of the cut packages out of the stacked pile and shook their contents on the concrete floor of the postal warehouse.

What fell out were the things low-rent people with torn hopes shipped—stiff, crotchless lace panties bought in sex shops; collections of cocktail swizzle sticks; creased, out-of-focus Polaroids of naked women; collections of twigs and rocks; bottles of beer with those European-styled ceramic caps, their contents now slowly leaking and turning their cardboard packing to mush; cracked Hummel figurines, and souvenir cuckoo clocks, their cheap movements broken on the floor.

A bird from one of those clocks, with a misaligned spring in his chest, rapidly puffed himself up and then went through a slow deflation like a blown-out tire. He did this over and over again while making muffled, pleading chirps. Sergeant Dooley's foot flattened him.

"Who buys this crap?" he asked the air.

Later, when Goldberg and I took over the job, we tried to be more careful with these shabby valuables, but after a while we became as callous as Sergeant Dooley.

Who cared about this pitiful stuff?

Goldberg and I were going to graduate school after the army. We were going to be professors: I was English literature, and he was history. We were above this kind of crap, weren't we? We had bigger things on our minds. Goldberg planned to study the beginnings of American imperialism, and I wanted to write about the slow encroachment of evil in Joseph Conrad's *Heart of Darkness*.

Who cared about these stupid army jobs?

We were supposed to be looking for contraband or stolen property, but we never once found anything of consequence. While we heard stories about the Top-Secret Decoder supposedly found by one of our predecessors in a parcel post package, the tale sounded like fiction made up to convince a commander to keep the Twenty-Second MP Customs Unit and all its little perks in business. Usually what Goldberg and I found was just some piece of GI clothing, or a tool, or a piece of camping equipment. The thefts were pathetic, but we recorded them in our LOG OF RECOVERED GOVERNMENT PROPERTY. These numbers, like the body counts in Vietnam, proved that we were doing our jobs, though the army often didn't care if you took your uniforms once your time was up. But we didn't mention that in our reports. If we found a dress uniform, we valued it at $100 because that's what a Penney's suit cost, and Lance B. Edwards, our boss, had a Penney's catalog tucked in his bottom desk drawer that he used to value stolen property.

Once we finished with our inspections, we'd lick the backs of these stickers we had and use them to cover the cuts made by our knives in the packages: *INSPECTED BY THE TWENTY-SECOND MP CUSTOMS.*

"That way," Lance B. Edwards said, "we let everyone know that the Big Green Machine is out there, even reading your love letters to Sally Rottencrotch."

✦ ✦ ✦

After all these years, *my* box is still in good shape. I mailed it first class, so no one from Twenty-Second MP Customs had ripped it open. Instead of turning my uniform in at the end of my time in the army, I stole it. I wanted to have a physical reminder of those years, even though I hardly ever wore that uniform.

Except for ceremonial occasions, I normally worked in civilian clothes. I was an undercover black-market investigator. Pretty cool, eh? I love to haul that line out at parties.

"So what did you do in the army?" people ask.

"Me?" I say. "Oh, just a little police work."

I let a beat go by.

"I was a plainclothes black-market investigator."

"Wow!" they say. Or "Cool!" or "No kidding."

"I worked with old Nazis."

"Really?"

Doing my army time in civilian clothes.

Wearing civvies was, all of us in the unit liked to think, one of the great benefits of the job. Of course there were also some significant disadvantages. Like, for instance, those days when we were ordered to burst into someone's apartment in search of black-market material. With our double-sided credentials held out in front of us as we confronted a startled resident, we'd yell, "Customs Police! *Zoll Polizei!*"

Then, an hour or two later, after tearing the drawers and the closets apart, Herr Hellman and Herr Diener of the German Customs Police, along with Goldberg and me, would load up our unmarked Ford with the evidence we'd confiscated—stolen sacks of rice and flour, all marked PROPERTY OF US ARMY—while occupants of the apartment yelled and cried.

Yes, there was always that, wasn't there?

And that pregnant woman, at the end of the tunnel in my conscience, screaming "Nazi!"

In the army you had what was called a home of record. That was your official hometown address, and I used that of my then-wife Jenny's. That's where she'd grown up: 1648 Bluebell Lane, Rock Hill, MO 63119.

"What a pretty address," the lady clerk at the Armed Forces Entrance and Examination Station in Little Rock, Arkansas, told me while she processed my paperwork on the day I was inducted into the army. She wore white cotton gloves, as if she wanted to avoid the stain of war on her actual flesh.

"I love bluebells," she said, her gloved fingers typing up the papers that took away my civilian rights.

She was horrified when she came to the line on the form called RELIGION. I'd marked the NONE box.

"None," she said. "Don't be silly. You can't choose NONE. What if something happens to you? How will you get to heaven?"

She patted my hand, the glove cool against my skin. I suddenly realized that I was sweating. I picked up the form again and looked down the list of choices.

"I don't see Buddhist or Muslim."

"Well, of course not. Those aren't *real* religions; they can't help you."

I thought about checking OTHER, but I gave in, the way I always did. It just seemed easier.

"OK," I said, and checked METHODIST.

"I'll bet you feel better already. Now you're really in the army."

+ + +

Suit, Man's, Summer, Model 10-16-4, Size 38, the label reads.

My uniform is inside the box, neatly folded there, as if waiting for my return to duty. I set it out on the floor, like one of those paper cutout dolls. Cap on top, shirt inside the coat, the skinny black necktie folded on the front of the shirt. I thread the black belt with the brass buckle through the loops of the pants and lay them out below the coat and then tuck the thin black socks under the cuffless pants bottoms. Even the shoes, with their thick coat of polish and the wrinkle across the top of the right one, are here, ready to go.

Tucked in the pocket of the uniform is a reel of old-time Super 8 film.

A few weeks later I borrow a neighbor's ancient Bell and Howell movie projector and play the film. The machine makes a chattering, meshing noise, and there I am, thirty years ago in the same uniform, a few days after I got home, unsteady in the flicker of the images going through the projector. The colors are murky, as if the past eventually turns into mud. I stare at myself in the past, still trying to make sense of what happened.

I rewind the two or three minutes and watch the scene again. I remember now. I had just gotten out of the army, but my aunt wanted to see me in my uniform.

"There's something about a man in uniform," she'd told me over and over, clinking the ice cubes in her ever-present cocktail glass.

"There's something even better about a man out of uniform," I said to myself, smiling as I remembered what Angelika used to say, but my smile over my little memory went away as I also recalled the day the two German Customs Police and Goldberg and I, all of us wearing civilian clothes, burst into the apartment house at Bruecke Strasse 27 in Weinheim. The pregnant woman stood in the kitchen.

"*Hey da,*" she screamed at us. "*Was ist?*"

Back there in this filmed slice of 1972, in those minutes rescued from the Heraclitean flux, I'm wearing my medals and my fraudulent marksman badge on my pressed green uniform, and it all fits perfectly. It's all a little piece of military artwork, and I don't have to worry about the *Baader-Meinhof Gruppe* blowing up a Ford Capri in my face.

Back there, in 1972, I wanted to get out of that uniform and put the medals away, forget about Bruecke Strasse 27 in Weinheim, but here is my aunt coming over to where I sit in the lawn chair. Her back to the camera (which was held by my uncle), she wobbles a little as she bends over, hands me her glass, grabs my face, and kisses me. It's as though she wants to take my whole face into her mouth.

She takes her glass back, turns then to the camera, and speaks, unaware that this is a silent film, that her address to posterity (which, at the moment, consists of my second wife and my two children) will go forever unheard. Hand on her hip, her breasts cocked, she speaks with confidence to the future and sips from her vodka.

"That's Aunt Margery?" my daughter says, surprised.

"How'd she get so thin?" my son asks.

"By reversing time," my second wife, Carol, says.

"You can do that?" My son smiles.

Don't I wish, I think to myself. Don't I wish.

I go to turn off the projector but put the machine on *Pause* by mistake, and my thirty-year-old image shimmies there on the screen, as if uncertain what to do next. I sit there vibrating in colors, which are both vivid and smudged, my aunt holding both hands toward me, as if she's introducing me to the future.

✦ ✦ ✦

"Yeah, you were a poet," Dennis Martin says when I call him. "I remember that."

Dennis and I were in graduate school together in 1967 and 1968, right before I went in the army.

"Yeah, I also remember you were crazy about Emerson. Went around quoting him all the time. 'The poet is the sayer, the namer, represents beauty.' I always liked that quote, but then you wrote that poem, and all the Emerson stuff came to an end."

"That poem?" At first I can't recall what he's talking about.

"Yeah, that poem. You scared everyone. Creeped us out. Don't you remember? You were channeling murderers."

Of course. Yes. The poem.

THE MAN WHO WASN'T THERE ARRIVES
for the assassins

> My life has been a pretty dull affair,
> Spent in towns you didn't know were there.
> My high-school annual left my picture out,
> And I began to put myself in doubt
> When people said they'd seen me other days
> Walking briskly on the Champs Élysées
> Or throwing pennies in Niagara Falls.
> "But no," they'd say, "it wasn't you at all.
> He had a darker face, a finer nose . . .
> Something in the way he wore his clothes.
> Still I can't help but see him in your face."
> They'd walk away, thinking of another place,
> A man I've never known.

Someday, for a laugh,
I'll tell them "Yes, that was me you saw at Banff,
Hooded face, looking thin and pale,
Or in Kansas stomping through the wheat for quail.
Think . . . I took pictures of your accident;
I cleaned the sickroom for your dying aunt.
I've lived with you like leaves with fall,
You've heard me walk behind you down the hall.
And like the leaves, all my faces mean the same.
They will someday drive you to my name.
Next time you'll know it's me that's come.
When I arrive, there'll be no place to run."

"Look, Dennis," I told him. "That's not me speaking. It's a dramatic monologue—the kind of thing Robert Browning made famous. That poem's in the voice of a killer. It's not my voice."

"Don't give me that literary bullshit. Something dark was running through you. Remember what Whitehead said?"

Jim Whitehead was my poetry teacher.

"You scare the shit out of me" is what Jim said. "You scare the shit out of me."

24.

Remember the old *Twilight Zone* episode—"The Monsters Are Due on Maple Street?" In the voice-over, the show's creator, Rod Serling, said:

"This is Maple Street on a late Saturday afternoon. Maple Street, in the last calm and reflective moments . . . before the monsters came."

My friends and I memorized that when we were kids. We liked to go around growling those sentences, pretending that we were the monsters, scaring ourselves and then laughing.

There weren't any monsters, were there? And if there were monsters, they weren't us, were they?

✦ ✦ ✦

I once lived on one of the world's Maple Streets. 531-A East Maple Street, to be exact. 531-A East Maple Street, Fayetteville, Arkansas, if you want the whole address. I was in graduate school, writing poems and studying for a degree in creative writing.

It was 1968. Just as we'd planned, Jenny and I got married on December 30, 1967. It was a sweet time. We figured the war would end any day. Nineteen sixty-seven was the year of the summer of love. It was an auspicious time. No monsters anywhere, right?

Jenny and I thought seeing John Lennon on the cover of the first issue of *Rolling Stone* was cute. Remember that? He was dressed as a World War I soldier. He had a part in the movie *How I Won the War*. It's all a little period drama. Just a little bit of history. Nothing to do with us, right?

The specifics of the new year slowly come back to me, or at least some of them do.

It's New Year's Day, and I have the flu, an aching, gut-wrenching flu. Oh, I remember now. It's the Hong Kong flu, and then Jenny gets it, and we begin our married life fighting off this attack from Asia, so, OK, there were microscopic monsters and, then, for some reason, the world starts spinning faster. And then it's hard to keep up with 1968, as if we're running to jump on a carnival ride. Faster and faster, it goes. Round and round, and up and down. Nineteen sixty-eight. A Tilt-A-Whirl of a year.

✦ ✦ ✦

It's the year of the Tet Offensive and the Prague Spring, which promises freedom from the Russians until it spins round and becomes the assassination of Martin Luther King on that motel balcony. That baby floating in space at the opening of the movie *2001: A Space Odyssey* falls like innocence abandoned down to where Bobby Kennedy dies on the kitchen floor of a Los Angeles hotel as the crackle of small-arms fire in Chicago at the Democratic presidential convention punctuates the night while the musical *Hair* opens and the Age of Aquarius dawns on Broadway, and Congress repeals the requirement for a gold standard, and Elvis, in his leather suit, makes the girls squeal, as if they're orgasmic, coming right there on network television.

Me, I'm watching much of the year go by in the grainy black-and-white pictures of my little Magnavox thirteen-inch TV.

Hey, hey, LBJ, how many kids did you kill today?

"I shall not seek, and I will not accept, the nomination of my party for another term as your president," Lyndon Johnson solemnly announces as if trying to drown out those chants.

Yes. Nineteen sixty-eight was quite a year. My generation thought that we would save the world. Isn't that what the rock-and-roll lyric says? "We can change the world/Rearrange the world." Mimeograph a list of demands. Take to the streets with some posters, and it's as good as done.

The little, tiny, hardly noticed part of 1968 that barely gets a mention is the end of graduate school deferments.

Hello, Rick, it's Nazi time for you, my friend.

Boom, boom, snare.

It's first two beats on the bass drum and then one on the little snare drum for the army and air force ROTC students every Friday during the school year as they form up and then march in tight formations across the lawn of the university.

Boom, boom, snare.

I am in a classroom on the second floor of a building erected in the decade after the Civil War. The windows of the building must be over ten feet tall. The course is English pros-ody, and we are studying the Robert Browning poem, "How They Brought the Good News from Ghent to Aix":

> I sprang to the stirrup, and Joris, and he;
> I galloped, Dirck galloped, we galloped all three;
> "Good speed!" cried the watch, as the gate-bolts
>   undrew;
> "Speed!" echoed the wall to us galloping through;
> Behind shut the postern, the lights sank to rest,
> And into the midnight we galloped abreast.

"Mostly anapests," Professor Jim Whitehead, with great exu-berance, declaims.

Out there on the spring lawn the ROTC cadets in their blue and green uniforms arrange themselves into ranks and files and then march across the lawn to the tune of the war's booming anapests.

Boom, boom, snare.
Boom, boom, snare.

Yes, the ancient anapests of war. They form squares and rectangles and then single lines that meet and turn.

> I sprang to the stirrup, and Joris, and he;
> I galloped, Dirck galloped, we galloped all three;

The young girls with the snapping flags behind them and the rattle of the drum to their left watch their boys group and regroup. The girls in their tight uniform blouses and ascots. Saluting as the boys pass. Their breasts cinched into pointed brassieres that make their chests look like twin traffic cones.

They're the Angel Flight, but is anyone really thinking of what angels might have to do with the military? Is anyone really thinking of death this spring afternoon?

> I sprang to the stirrup, and Joris, and he;
> I galloped, Dirck galloped, we galloped all three . . .

Boom, boom, snare

✦ ✦ ✦

Ah, yes, 1968. Nineteen sixty-eight is the year of Khe Sanh and the Tet Offensive and the First Battle of Saigon.

Does anyone remember those battles anymore?

"A cold, gray fog lifts on the bodies of American soldiers killed at the perimeter of Khe Sanh, Walter," John Laurence of CBS says on *The Nightly News.*

Those were the monsters, I suppose, but they were a long way from Maple Street, weren't they? They couldn't come here, could they?

✦ ✦ ✦

I don't know that my graduate school draft deferment is coming to an end while I amble along Maple Street toward the university, though I'm sad. Martin Luther King Jr. was shot the night before, and that troubles me a little. Like many other people my age I've sat around singing "We Shall Overcome." I'm in favor of integration, but, truth be told, I haven't done much about civil rights except be sentimental, so I am having an appropriately sentimental moment as I walk along Maple Street toward the university. Vietnam and the struggle for civil rights are a long way off.

Yes, I am walking west from my little apartment, carrying my yellow, college-ruled notebook and a copy of *The Form and Theory of Poetry* by Paul Fussell.

I think I'm going to be a poet, but the world has other plans.

Ah yes, 1968: that Tilt-A-Whirl of a year is stopping to pick me up.

Oh I almost forgot: the Big Mac was introduced nationwide in 1968. America was at war, and it was getting fatter, too.

25.

Ah, graduate school. I'd arrived there in the fall of 1967. I was in the writing program, and that attracted women, so even though I'm engaged to marry Jenny Gleason I began trying to sleep with as many women as I can. Hey, it's right after the Summer of Love, isn't it? I felt like it was my turn.

I also began meeting real poets. Jim Dickey, who would later be famous as the author of the novel *Deliverance,* came to Fayetteville as a visiting writer that fall. He liked my poems, but mostly what we did was get drunk in his hotel room and call various women he knew. Once they came on the line, he would say something like, "There should only be joy, joy, joy in the world," and then he'd shake his head and make a kind of wattling noise.

In 1969, not long before I went in the army, I drove Allen Ginsberg and his friend Peter Orlovsky around. My 1967 Chevelle had something called a reverberator installed under the dash. It changed the sound of the radio with its single control knob. Initially, it produced a crude stereo effect, but, as you turned the knob, it created the sound of an echo chamber. Songs like The Rolling Stones's "(I Can't Get No) Satisfaction" sounded like something sung deep in a cave. The song came out as "I-I-I Ca-Ca-Can't-Can't Ge-ge-ge-get-get-get No-No-No Sat-Sat-sat-satis-satis-satis-satisfaction."

If you turned the unit all the way up, that line—and, in fact, the whole song—became one consonant stuttered out: "N-n-n-n-n-n-n-n-n-n-n."

Peter loved that unit and kept fiddling with it as I drove him and Allen around.

"This is all the poetry we need," Peter said over and over.

Oh yes, did I mention that one of my girlfriends kind of hung around after I got married?

Did I mention that?

I didn't mean to have a girlfriend. It just sort of happened. She was a holdover from my single days. What could I do? She wouldn't go away.

I met her at one of the weekend parties, where girls hung around members of the writing program as if we were football stars. Sarah was sitting in a chair with her legs tucked beneath her, and she kind of raised one up, exposing her panties, and she looked at me and smiled and pretty soon we were rolling around on her bed, and I was coming like I'd never come before and this went on for weeks and then I was married and Jenny was sick and sweaty with the Hong Kong Flu and I made up my mind right then and there that one more time with Sarah would be it—absolutely, for sure *it*—because a marriage vow was a marriage vow. Sickness and health and all that sort of thing, and we only fucked two or three more times after that, Sarah and I—or maybe it was four or five times. It couldn't have been, I swear to God, more than ten times.

And then she moved away, and I was a good boy again.

Yes, 1968, back and forth and round and round.

More than forty years later. I go to the Street View option at Google Maps and type in 531-A East Maple Street, Fayette-ville, Arkansas. What comes up is a leaf-strewn neighborhood on a gray day. Maybe it's fall or late winter. I spin the viewer around, but I can't find the little building of my apartment, which, as I recall, was set back some distance from the street. Maybe it's been torn down. What I remember, after all, happened long ago.

Using the arrows of Google Street View, I move up and down the street, but I don't recognize anything. The scene is far different from the neighborhood I remember. I can't find my old apartment building. Nothing looks the same as it did in 1968.

Google has a white line down the center of Maple Street, and, in the netherland of technology, I follow the line west, crossing College Avenue. The names of the streets I pass sound familiar, but nothing looks familiar.

How frustrating. Should I travel to Fayetteville, get on an actual airplane and see the real place, I wonder, to get the details right? But then, who cares about this story of mine? Do I even care?

And yet, I obsess over it. I can't get it out of my mind. Why?

I sit in front of my computer, my head in my hands, trying to answer that question. I look like a man praying.

What I really wish I could do is travel back to January 1968. That's when my troubles began, though I certainly didn't know it at the time. I wish I could go back there, to those innocent days, to that little one-bedroom apartment and warn my new wife and me that the monsters are definitely coming to Maple Street.

"Look," I'd tell Rick and Jenny, "things are going to get bad. All those promises they made to you—you know, Rickie, back in junior high when you were a bouncing, bright kid on the Algebra Squad—and, Jenny, when you were singing those folk songs and believing that you'd fix the world with love: all those promises they made to you both about how important you would be—those promises are lies. All lies. Things aren't going to work out so well for you. The government's not going to help you. The government might, in fact, be the enemy. The government might just be plotting to kill Little Rickie Ryan."

It's like those green cardboard barrels labeled Emergency Supplies. Remember? The ones with the yellow letters and the round emblem with the triangle in the middle. Civil Defense supplies. Take care of people in trouble, right? Well, the ones I found in the basement of the Janesville Post Office when I had a summer job there in 1967 were empty. Empty. They were a public relations scheme.

And if I were really brave, I'd pull Jenny aside and tell her that Rickie was a two-timing asshole. That Rickie might just, in fact, be one of the monsters.

✦ ✦ ✦

Yes, that little apartment on Maple Street, though I can't find it anywhere on Google Earth. It's gone now, I guess.

But I can see it in my memory: a living room, a bedroom, a kitchen. All tiny. Barely room to move in. My first wife and I there in the soft focus dream of the 1960s. I have a goatee, and Jenny wears bell-bottoms. We're sitting down to *The CBS Evening News with Walter Cronkite*. The iris eye of the CBS logo sees everything, doesn't it?

The CBS Evening News with Walter Cronkite for Tuesday, January 30th, begins, the way it usually does, with an image of the newsroom in New York, a profile shot of Walter Cronkite at the circle desk tapping his papers as if he'd just arrived there, fresh from typing up what he was about to say. Teletypes clatter in the background. Walter looks at the camera. Walter is now facing us.

Jenny and I sit there with our dinner. We eat in the living room, using an old black steamer trunk as a coffee table.

"The United States Embassy in Saigon, South Vietnam, is under attack, bringing the war perilously close to the American high command. Our correspondent Robert Schakne is on the scene."

Our little living room is shaped like a rectangle, television at one end, me at the other, putting a bite of pork chop into my mouth. On one side sits Jenny and on the other is a six-foot bookshelf made from boards and cinder-block bricks. I look over and see the books grouped by genre and alphabetized within each group. Neat. There's *Hamlet* and *New Poets of England and America* and *The Works of Edgar Allen Poe* among the books I've read. Then there are the books for next semester: *Lord Jim* and *In Cold Blood* and *Crime and Punishment*. These are books for the second semester freshman composition course I will teach.

"How crimes happen," the director of the Composition Program tells us. "The slow creep of criminality. The effects of crime on the criminal. The metaphor of crime."

Metaphors, similes—all those techniques of writing. A life of sensitivity. A life of the mind in my little apartment.

"The United States Embassy in Saigon, South Vietnam, is under attack, bringing the war perilously close to the American high command. Our correspondent Robert Schakne is on the scene."

Jenny's mouth is open slightly, her arms are crossed on her chest.

I wish I could walk into this memory and talk to us back then. Warn us.

"You're in danger," I would say, a ghost from the future.

"Walter, this may be one of the worst days in this Vietnamese conflict," Robert Schakne says.

It's comfortable, sitting there, in that tiny apartment at 531-A East Maple Street in Fayetteville.

The books on the wall announcing my brilliance. A man who will soon know about crime and punishment.

I try to close my eyes and hold that moment there, but it flits away, just as it did beneath the soft plastic screen of my John Gnagy Learn-To-Draw set.

I didn't know anything about the war in Vietnam. I didn't, for instance, know the names of the battles I just looked up in the history book. In 1968 I'd never heard of Allelbora and Leatherneck Square and Masher and Double Eagle and White Wing and Dak To and Hill 881 South and Cedar Falls.

So much about the 1960s I didn't know back then. I didn't know that Huey Newton started a jail sentence in January of 1968, that the American Indian Movement was founded in July of 1968, and the Yippie! party in 1967.

I sat at my desk and smoked Winstons ("Taste good, like a cigarette should") and memorized the difference between Italian and Shakespearean sonnets.

"Walter, this may be one of the worst days in this Vietnamese conflict."

Here is the black steamer trunk with its brass rivets. I remember that night. I remember the piece of meat halfway to my mouth as I saw the United States military use a jeep to ram the gates of our own military compound, to retake the place from the Viet Cong. I remember being careful not to set my glass of milk down on the black surface of that trunk. I remember the way the CBS camera scanned the scene, catching images of dead Americans, of bullet holes, and of the fallen embassy seal. I remember sitting frozen there, as if something had changed. I remember looking over at my books, the neat rows of novels and books of poetry in the bookshelf I'd made out of boards and cinder-block brick.

This was different, somehow. Nineteen sixty-eight wasn't going to be like the other years, but I went on with my pork chop, my glass of milk. I went on studying the poetry of William Butler Yeats for my seminar with Professor Ben Kimpel.

The next week we saw Nguyen Ngoc Loan, the chief of the South Vietnamese National Police, shoot a man through the head. Just like that. Poof. A little smoke. The man winces, as though he might have a toothache on his right side. Then he topples over. The moment of the shot is also in newspapers, and so the image reverberates from television to newspapers back to television again.

But the war was a long way away, wasn't it, even though every noon a little cluster of demonstrators stood at the intersection of North Garland and West Maple.

I stood on the other side of the street, watching them, as I sipped from a Coke I just bought at the student union.

"Those fools think the president wants their opinion?" someone in the crowd behind me said.

For Bill Ayers—who was a leader of the Weather Underground, a group that performed all kinds of violent pranks in the late 1960s, including setting off a bomb in a restroom of the Pentagon—"Nineteen sixty-eight began with staccato bursts and gunfire from all sides, the rat-tat-tat of everyday events tattooing the air. I was twenty-three. It was the year of wonder and miracle."

Me, I turned twenty-three that year, too, but there wasn't the rat-tat-tat of much of anything for me, except on television. I was still grieving for the loss of my father, living inside the gauze of that grief, getting fatter from all the heavy meals Jenny prepared.

"Rickie, what are you going to do about the army?" my mother asked in one of her weekly phone calls.

For reasons I can't really explain, I wasn't worried. My fellow students didn't seem too concerned. When I talked to John Freeman and Larry Johnson, they generally said something like, "The army isn't going to want us."

Here's John Laurence on *The CBS Evening News with Walter Cronkite*: "Walter, death is everywhere in the ancient city of Hue—in the mass graves of South Vietnamese soldiers, in the open holes where the bodies of North Vietnamese sprawl, in the women who sit and grieve beside the bodies."

I stayed up late, until one or two in the morning, learning the metrics of poetry, how to scan lines for iambs and trochees and the lovely hoofbeats of those anapests. "I spring to the stirrup, and Joris and he. Dirck galloped, I galloped. We galloped all three."

Tea and cigarettes, a little daytime television, lots of literature—all punctuated by the rat-tat-tat of the war narrated by Walter Cronkite every evening at five thirty.

"Walter, death is everywhere in the ancient city of Hue."

As the days drifted along, the story I missed was this one, from February 17: "Most draft deferments for graduate study and critical jobs were ended by the National Security Council. All graduating seniors at colleges, all first-year graduate students and all men who will receive master's degrees in June will be eligible for the draft."

This was probably Walt Rostow's idea; he was the president's National Security Adviser then.

A few years ago, before he died, I called him in Texas. I wanted to know why he drafted me.

I called the institute where he worked in Austin. He answered his own phone.

"This is Rick Ryan, Mr. Rostow. I want to know why you wanted to draft me in 1968. Why was I so important to you?"

I could hear a scratchy sound. He had put his hand over the mouthpiece of the phone. I could hear a murmured question, probably to his secretary. I guessed he was wondering how my call got through.

But then he couldn't resist, I guess.

"Is this a joke? How can you expect me to remember a single draftee? We had a war to fight."

"Did you really call him?" Carol asks me.

"Look. Those days are over," Walt Rostow says. "You need to get over it. I certainly don't spend much time worrying about that period."

Then the click of the phone hanging up, and the moan of the dial tone.

✦ ✦ ✦

In April of 1968, my mother calls.

"Oh, Rickie," my mother says, crying. "Your number's up."

"What?"

"You have to go."

"To Vietnam?" When I say the three syllables of that country's name, I feel as though a steel hand is squeezing my heart.

"Mom, tell me what happened."

"It's all over for me."

"Mom, come on. Tell me what happened."

"You got this letter from the government, so I opened it. I shouldn't have, but I did."

"What does it say?"

"Here. 'Selective Service System Order to Report for Armed Forces Examination.'"

"Shit. When do I go?"

"June 19th. In Milwaukee. It's a Wednesday."

Time was slowing down for me. Slowing and slowing, like an episode from *Days of Our Lives*. "Like sands through the hourglass, so are the days of our lives." The film running at half or even quarter speed. I could hear my heart beating, as if it were now in my head, filling it with sound. I suddenly remembered the sound of those bullets going off in the basement.

You begin a triangulation from a known point.

"Send me the notice, OK?" I said.

"OK. Rickie?"

"Yes."

"You won't get killed, will you? You're all I have."

What is the known point?

26.

Decades later, when, for the first time, I'm watching the Zapruder film of the Kennedy assassination on the Internet, it occurs to me that I am seeing my era, frame by grainy frame, come apart, just as John Kennedy's head seems to explode when the bullet hits it: yes, that's it. That was the beginning of the end. That was the real "Fable of the Final Hour"—not 1959; not that poem I was reading to my roommates on that Friday in 1963—but here, on Elm Street in Dallas.

I sit there at my desk, in the terrible dark of two A.M. on a day in the twenty-first century, and feel lost and alone as Kennedy slumps over, and I'm frightened and I think I'm wandering around the back of the tapestry, where this piece of yarn connects to that one over there and I hold them and run my fingers along their coarse texture and wonder what the story on the other side is—the story I can't see, the story I probably don't want to know.

27.

"What's the matter?" It's Jenny, and she comes over to me. "Is something wrong with your mother?"

"No. They got me. I'm a goner."

"What do you mean?"

"I have to report for my draft physical."

"What's wrong, Ryan? Ain't life agreeing with you?" Whitehead asks me at one of the writing program parties that seem to be held every weekend.

"I'm getting drafted."

"What's wrong with you, man? You don't see anyone else here getting drafted."

What's happened to me, I wonder. Someone has picked me out, I think. I'm standing in a kind of howling tunnel, being sucked somewhere I don't want to go. Why is this happening to me alone? What have I done?

"What's the matter, man? You don't look so good." It's Rex Harrison. A neat, older guy with carefully ironed button-down collar shirts and an improbable name.

"I'm getting drafted."

"That's too bad. Happened to me once. Once was enough."

"Really."

"I ended up enlisted in the air force. Pushed papers around for four years. It wasn't a bad life, actually. I traveled all over the world."

This is like a shaft of light in the howling tunnel. An escape hatch. A ladder dangling down.

"The only trouble," Rex Harrison tells me, "is that they sometimes ask you to die for them. What a drag that is. You know what, Ryan?"

"No," I say, a little desperate for a clever angle on this.

"I'd be careful if I were you."

He tips his beer bottle toward me, a kind of salute. Then he takes a sip and walks away.

"Yeah, I'd be real careful."

The days passed in the slurry of that cold around me. I went to a draft board in Fayetteville and filled out a form to transfer my physical to Arkansas. That change delayed the date of my physical. It bought me a few more weeks of freedom.

The clerk was about five feet tall and almost as round as he was tall. He had henna-dyed hair and a cigarette dangling from his mouth. He could cough and puff on that cigarette at the same time.

"Going to serve your country, eh, boy?" he said through coughing puffs of smoke. "Not like those hippies out there. Good for you."

My new date was September eleventh. 9/11. It wasn't such an important number back then. Just another Wednesday.

That April, in an announcement I never saw back then, the Defense Department said that 48,000 men would be drafted for military service in April. "Of those drafted, approximately

4,000 will go to the marines corps, which has not been able to fill a higher quota with volunteers."

Once more, I realize that I'm sitting before my computer no longer writing this. No, I've got my elbows on the desk, and my forehead rests on my clasped hands, as if I'm praying again. Sometimes my eyes are closed as I try to remember what happened, sometimes I stare into the slightly flickering white-blue of the computer screen, into some middle distance out there over the heads of Judy Stryker, John Rogers, Ron Moriarty, and little Rickie Ryan. Sometimes I wonder if any of it happened. I'm also looking for another way out of this. Even now, decades later, I don't want to go into the army. Even now, I'm praying that I won't have to go.

"Have you heard any way to get out of this?"

That's me calling my old high school friend Steve Agard in Madison. I didn't know who else to call. When I told my fellow students about the notice for my physical, they looked at their shoes, and John Edwards started crying.

"Aren't you a little late?" Agard asked. "I mean, shouldn't you have done something about this before you got the notice for your physical?"

He was right, of course.

"Look, Ryan. Contact these people. Just a minute."

I could hear him shuffling through papers.

"The Wisconsin Draft Resistance Union. They'll tell you what to do. When's your physical?"

"September."

"You better get on this."

But I didn't get on it, no. The country buried another Kennedy, and Jenny and I drove to her family cottage in Minnesota, outside of Brainerd, on North Long Lake, where I hoped to forget about my pending army physical. Jenny wanted to see her childhood friend John Breitbart. John had dropped out of college and just been drafted into the army, but he seemed almost excited in a strange way, happy that his life would have focus and physical training.

"I'll get in shape and learn to finish things."

We water-skied behind John's red and white speedboat, making circular arcs through the flat and reflective dark water in the hour before sunset. The lake had a glass-like calm. It was perfect skiing water. When I wasn't skiing, I sat in the back of the boat, suddenly noticing the beautiful little pearls of spray thrown up by the boat. It was all a kind of paradise. At night, Jenny and I snuggled away from the chill down under the old cotton blankets that smelled of soap and mildew. Jenny decorated a canoe paddle for me that hung beside the door, and I joined this family tradition of summers at the lake.

The only thing strange about those weeks were the big artillery guns at nearby Camp Ripley—their *boom, boom, boom* echoed all day long. The windows in the cabin vibrated from the shock waves of their explosions. It felt as though a military attack were beginning a few short miles away.

"Are they triangulating those shots?" I asked.

"What's that?" Jenny asked back.

"Oh, it's trigonometry, something my father knew about. It's a way to be accurate. Never mind. I guess I mean those things scare me. It's like they're aimed at us."

"Don't worry. They're just practicing. You'll get used to them," she said.

28.

It was an unusually cool August morning the day I finally drove to Madison for my meeting with the Wisconsin Draft Resistance Union. Puffy clouds, a pale blue sky, the undulating fields broken up by groves of trees.

I had called the day before to make an appointment.

"You already have an appointment," the man's voice on the phone said.

"I do?"

"With death in a rice paddy, my friend. You better get your ass in here if you want to avoid that." He hung up then.

Driving north on Interstate-90, I've got the Delco FM in the Chevelle blasting "(I Can't Get No) Satisfaction" through the reverberator, so "satisfaction" comes out *satisfaction-tion-tion-tion*, the last syllable of the word bouncing up against a wall and coming back. My left arm is out the window, and I pound my hand on the side of the marina blue Chevelle, "Can't get none, no, no, no." I'm going to Madison, fucking A, to find out how to avoid the draft from the people who know how it's done. My buddy Agard has set me up. Madison, oh Madison—Madison will get me out of this.

I parked down near the student union and had a golden beer out on the terrace and watched the sailboats like white thoughts floating over the green-black deep of Lake Mendota. I looked through the window of Paul's Books and saw shelf after shelf of the lovely books I promised myself I'll read once this army business is behind me. I walked up State Street in the sunshine, along with all the lovely, giggling girls in their madras bermuda shorts. The world seemed organized, orderly, and oh so peaceable. Yes, I thought: the Wisconsin Draft Resistance will help me.

Their office was located at 217 South Hamilton Street, down the hill from the Capitol, on a street that seemed suddenly dark after the bright sunshine of State Street. The pillars of the porch were rotted and looked like uncertain exclamation points. I wanted the place to look better—to be businesslike, with crisp cubicles and men in white shirts and narrow ties handing out exemptions to the war—but no, it was a falling-down old house. On its porch was a spongy beige couch without any cushions. Springs stuck out from the seat of its frame.

"The fuck you want, Baby Blue?"

He was incredibly skinny with a curly kind of Afro hairdo, though he wasn't black. Far from it. He was so white he looked like one of those people who spend all their time indoors. He was slug white. He had a hacking, almost tubercular-sounding cough. He stood inside the screened door of the house scratching his stomach under his shirt.

"I suppose you got a draft notice, and now you want some help."

"No, I got my physical notice. I got it moved from Wisconsin to Arkansas. That gave me some extra time. I go in September. Next month." I was so relieved to talk with someone about this that I rushed through the words.

"Believe it or not we have calendars here, too. Even anarchists have to know what day it is. Maybe after the revolution we'll replace calendars with something. Popsicles maybe. April twelfth will be orange. What do you think?"

He opened the door, and I walked into this dark-paneled room with a dusty-smelling carpet. Papers, books, and pamphlets in heaving piles.

"You probably should transfer that physical back to Wisconsin, Baby Blue. They'll be more lenient here than down there in god-and-country land. Fucking rednecks. Still trying to recoup their losses in the Civil War. Taking on the whole fucking world. Just gonna keep losing wars."

I've got a brand-new college-ruled notebook under my arm to write down all the solutions he'll give me to my draft problem. I write down "keep losing wars."

He hands me some forms and says: "Here are the keys to the kingdom, my friend, the trustworthy old SSS Form 150, the special form for conscientious objectors. That's the baby. You fill this out, you're guaranteed at least a year's delay with all the appeals you're going to file, and you might just get out for good."

This is good, I think, yes, the Form 150. I write it down and circle it.

"The SSS on those forms, what does that stand for?"

"Boy in the front row is going to ask questions—bet all your teachers think that you're just the best little scholar, don't they? Selective Service System. Old General Hershey up there in Washington. He always reminds people that it's not a universal draft. Oh no, it's a *selective* system. You'd think, wouldn't you, that he was cherry-picking the nation's youth. Taking just a few of mama's precious little boys."

I write that down, too. "Not a universal system. Mama's precious little boys."

"Funny," I said. "That's what my mother called me. Her precious little . . ."

"What's your name, Baby Blue?"

"Ryan. Rick Ryan."

"Good. They'll like that in the army, the way you start with your last name. Such a good, healthy American name you got there, Rick. Me, I'm Arnie. Rick . . . that'll look good on a tombstone with your service number underneath. Do you know your number?"

"No," I say. Somehow this isn't going the way it should. I don't have anything to write down.

"Yes, you do, Baby Blue. It's your Social Security number. They've just changed the system—made it easy for you. In the old cradle to grave services of the government, the grave's just coming a little sooner than you thought."

He grabs SSS Form 150 out of my hands.

"What am I thinking? It's too late to fill out Form 150. Once you get SSS Form 223, it's a whole new ball game. That changes everything. You had your chance to get out and you threw it away, Baby Blue. Threw it away, you dumb fucking shit."

At that moment in that dark house on that lovely day I felt this strange jerk in my vision, as if a slide changed somewhere, though I wrote down Form 223 in my notebook and then beside it "Changes everything."

"Of course you didn't think anything would happen, did you? You thought if you just lay low, they'd overlook you somehow. You're mama's special little boy, right? Besides, it was too embarrassing to apply for conscientious objector status, wasn't it? You'd been out there in the bushes with your cap gun and your Roy Rogers hat playing cowboys. You were a red-blooded American boy. Didn't want anyone to think you were a coward. Well, they're not dummies, those Selective Service people. They've got the mid-American psyche of yours all figured out."

"What's Form 223?"

"Order to Report For Armed Forces Examination, Bucko. It might as well be your induction notice. It ain't called a Pre-Induction Physical for nothing. They take pretty much everyone."

And now the temperature dropped. It suddenly seemed cold in that room.

"You got medical problems, Baby Blue?"

"As a matter of fact, I have a catch in my back. Had it the other day. Took my breath away."

He laughed—threw his head back and slapped his thighs.

"Vague back problems. I can already see the stamp, Baby Blue. The doctor hits the inkpad and then raises it up a little for dramatic effect. Whap, he hits Form 88. 1-A, Baby Blue, in slightly smeared black ink. 1-A. Ready to go. Old Form 88. Rocket 88, Baby Blue. You're taking off; you're on your way. Now the forms say DD. Know what that is?"

I shake my head. I'm slowly writing "Baby Blue" in my college-ruled notebook and drawing stars around the words.

"Department of Defense. The first of those is DD Form 62, the Certificate of Acceptability. You've made it then. You're in Club Death. He's got another stamp for that. Major Fucker, MD, it'll say, and then he'll sign it. You're on Cemetery Road at last."

A voice I didn't recognize, from somewhere deep inside of me.

"I don't want to go."

"They're smart—take a couple of deer from the herd, and the others just stand there like they think they got a magic wall around them."

"What am I going to do?"

"Here are your choices . . ."

"Wait, let me write them down."

"Such a student. Here they are: Canada or jail. Of course you could injure yourself. Here take a copy of AR 40-501."

"What's that?" I'm writing the title down. It's like some kind of strange Bingo game. Letters and numbers being called off.

"It's got a couple of titles. The one I like best is PROCURE-MENT MEDICAL FITNESS STANDARDS, like you're some kind of part they've ordered, a vehicle they've procured."

"What's it for?"

"Just what it says over and over. 'The causes for rejection are . . .' It gives you a nice list of how to mutilate yourself. Here, see paragraph 2-9, item 2.1: 'Absence (or loss) of distal and middle phalanx of an index, middle, or ring finger of either hand . . .' There you go. Just cut off the two joints, though be sure you cut two. One's not enough. You don't want to screw that one up—cut part of your finger off and still get drafted.

"That's the way I would go, Baby Blue. Shake two of those index finger joints loose. You'll be free, thank God Almighty, free at last, Baby Blue."

He smiled and handed me a copy of the army regulations. "Take this, too."

He gave me a copy of the *Manual for Draft-Age Emigrants to Canada.*

"I'm sorry, Ryan. You're probably a nice, straight American kid. Not like me—got a couple of drug busts, and I think the FBI is on my tail for draft dodging. But I just keep moving around from New York to Madison. Pretty soon I'm headed to Berkeley."

He went over and looked out the window. I wrote down FBI in my notebook.

"You didn't park out there, did you?"

"I'm a few blocks down the street. Why?"

"They're out there."

"Where?"

"They're everywhere."

The afternoon—with its golden glass of beer, its white tufted sailboats, shelves of books, and streets of girls—was gone forever. I could imagine dark-suited men supervising my Chevelle as it was towed away. No more Rolling Stones; no more reverberator.

"You know what I would do if I were you, Ryan?"

He came over and grabbed my hand. The gesture so surprised me that I dropped the notebook on the floor. He began to circle around me, as if we were dancing.

"I'd carve a great big *Fuck You* in my back and let it fester. Get the letters all filled with green pus and let the doctors see that. Green pus and black blood. Oh, that'll freak them out."

We were spinning together, faster and faster.

"The other thing you need to do is get your football helmet and come to Chicago. We're going to have a little jousting match with the Democratic Party. We're bringing the war to their front steps. Be there, baby. Be there with that bloody Fuck You so America can see what it's done to you."

That said, he spun me toward the door.

"Yeah, carve a big *Fuck You* in your back. Let it fester so it turns green. That'll get you out, I guaran-fucking-tee it."

I started out the door.

"You could also cut the end of your trigger finger off. Cut it off, let it dry, and then mail that stiff fucker to the Pentagon. Attach a tag. Write this on it: 'One less finger for the war, motherfuckers.' Now, if you go that route, Baby Blue, be sure you slice the first two joints off. One's not enough."

Then he grabbed me by the front of my shirt and pulled me close. His breath smelled like garlic.

"One more thing, Baby Blue. When you get to your physical, you'll have to fill out this security questionnaire. They have lists of Commie organizations. Check a few of those rascals off. That'll get you an FBI file going. And write on that form *I believe that the war in Vietnam is morally wrong.* Write that a whole bunch of times. In fact, Baby Blue, write that everywhere there's space. Then write *I'm a homo,* too. Whowhee what fun you'll have. You'll be too dangerous to draft."

He pushed me out the door and slammed it shut. The door opened suddenly, and he stood there in an old top hat. He took it off, slowly bowed, and slammed the door again.

As I walked back down State Street, the sunshine and the girls and the books seemed meant for someone else. I wanted to scratch my back where I imagined all the letters of "Fuck You" were festering. I kept crossing and recrossing the street and looking over my shoulder to see if someone in a dark suit was following me. As I got in the Chevelle and pulled away from the curb, I looked in my rearview mirror and saw a man in round sunglasses, a leather vest, and sandals staring at my car.

Of course, I thought, the FBI's incognito these days. They probably followed me the whole way. I turned on the radio.

The FM station was playing cuts from *Sgt. Pepper's Lonely Hearts Club Band*, and I thought the Beatles would cheer me up, but the reverberator got stuck, and final syllables of words sounded like machine-gun fire. *Pepper* turned into *Er-er-er-er.* The last syllable of *lonely* became *Le-le-le-le.* I turned the radio off.

That day in August of 1968—why, that was the day *my* music died.

✦ ✦ ✦

"What'd he say?" my mother asked when I walked in the door of 863 East Memorial Drive. "Can they get you out?"

Suddenly that question seemed so funny. I started to laugh.

"What's so funny?"

I laughed and I laughed until I was making hoarse, barking noises. My mother got me a glass of water.

"My three main options seem to be cutting two joints of my index finger off, carving swear words in my back, or going to Canada."

Then my mother began to pucker up, and her face turned red.

"My little boy," she sobbed. "My precious, little boy. Just like that, they take you away from me. Just like that."

"Funny, that's what Arnie called me. Look, I've heard that Toronto is a pretty nice city."

"I'll never see you again if you go there. You can't do that, Rickie. Can you just tell them I'm a widow? They wouldn't take a widow's only boy, would they?"

She began hiccupping as she sobbed, a pudgy little old lady who'd been a yellow rose in the Rose Parade in Pasadena in 1925.

29.

The fabled 1968 Chicago Democratic Convention began on Monday, August 26th. My mother and I sat with pizzas watching it in the slightly overdone colors of the television set at 863 East Memorial Drive.

Here's Anita Bryant in a blue dress singing "The Battle Hymn of the Republic." She has thick eyelashes on for her part of the battle. The camera pans across the placards with the names of the states held aloft. Up and down, and back and forth go Iowa, Oregon, Massachusetts, Florida, and Arizona like cards in a board game. Bang, goes the gavel. "The chair recognizes . . ." The man doesn't so much speak as rattle the syllables out. "The chair recognizes . . ." The camera cuts to a close-up of Chicago Mayor Richard Daley, fat lipped as he whispers in the ears of men who scurry off. The men wear suits and narrow ties. The women have lacquered hairdos with stiff flips and walk in their high heels as if they don't quite touch the ground.

It's all a great American ritual, sponsored by recessed-filter Parliament cigarettes, Continental Insurance, and Aqua Velva aftershave lotion. "So why be alone?" the announcer asks, and the camera cuts to the minuteman emblem of Continental Insurance. And then: "There's something," a husky-voiced lady says, "about an Aqua Velva man." My mother and I light up cigarettes every time a Parliament commercial comes on.

Oh yes, we do what we're told, out here in America, don't we?

Do you remember the CBS correspondents who covered the floor of the sixty-eight convention while Walter Cronkite sat up above in his glass-windowed booth overlooking everything? They all wore earphones with these antennas on their heads that looked like bent clothes hangers and these matching, tightly fitted gray suits, as if they were crew members in an early version of *Star Trek*, as if the floor of the International Amphitheatre in Chicago were some strange planet that the *Enterprise* had landed on, as if the convention delegates—all those jowly men from Chicago and Mississippi and New York—were aliens from some other planet.

Once in a while, correspondents Dan Rather and Marvin Kalb put their fingers to the earphones connected to the antennas, bent their heads, and listened, as if receiving instructions from some higher plane, perhaps from the booth where Walter Cronkite, that avuncular Oz in the kingdom of CBS News, sat, watching the proceedings below. Perhaps they were getting word about the frenzied confrontations between the police and the student demonstrators outside.

On Wednesday night, August 28th, Walter Cronkite hurriedly interrupts Dan Rather.

"Dan, we have to cut over to Ed Bradley, outside on Michigan Avenue."

The screen fills with gray, blurry images.

"Walter, it's quite a melee out here, with the Chicago police confronting protesters," Ed says, ducking down when something flies past the camera.

The picture is out of focus, as if the cameraman is part of the struggle on the streets. We hear heavy breathing and curses, the thud of nightsticks into bodies, bursts of what sound like gunfire, but the lighting is dim, making the battle something from a hardly seen nightmare. The camera keeps moving around, looking for an image to settle on.

"Is someone shooting?" a bouffant-haired woman in an A-line skirt asks, clutching her purse to her bosom. She's at the edge of the camera shot and nervous as a bird.

"This is Chicago. Chicago for Christ's sake," a voice from somewhere says.

Maybe most frightening is the undigested quality of the film. We're used to television summarizing things after they happen—not puzzling over scenes as they occur.

And, look, there—is it possible?—stopping to pose for the camera, my God, it's Grimes Poznik. He's blowing "Charge!" on his trumpet, as if signaling that now the real chaos of the sixties is underway. Protesters wearing high school football helmets and carrying baseball bats pass the camera in a dark blur. Cops appear, looking back and forth, many of them wearing white helmets.

"What's going on?" my mother asks.

Ed Bradley is coughing. The shots were tear-gas canisters being launched into the crowds of demonstrators.

"Walter, it's chaos out here on Michigan Avenue. It looks more like Vietnam than middle America."

"What's going on?" my mother asks again, her cigarette halfway to her mouth.

✦ ✦ ✦

"We're about talked out," Roger Mudd says to Walter and to America the last night of the convention.

Commentator Eric Sevareid nods. "Yes, Walter, we don't know what else to say."

"We thought about leaving," Walter Cronkite says. "These thugs make it hard to tell America's story . . ."

Thugs? Thugs in America?

How could that be? It must be the war protesters, right? They're the cause of this trouble, not these soldiers in their brown shirts.

✦ ✦ ✦

Esquire magazine hired French novelist Jean Genet, Beat memoirist William Burroughs, and all-around crazy man Terry Southern to cover the Democratic convention.

Southern picked up this observation when he noticed Genet staring at the dashboard of the Ford they were riding in: "What can be in the mind of someone who names an automobile Galaxie?"

I'm reading this quotation now, decades after Terry Southern wrote it down. I think, as I read those long-ago words, of how information can rhyme. I now know (as Terry Southern perhaps didn't) that the overwrought egotism, which put the name Galaxie on an ordinary automobile, took place in the time when none other than Robert McNamara was an executive of the Ford Motor Company.

Mr. McNamara is, of course, one of the chief architects of the war in Vietnam.

✦ ✦ ✦

My first car—my beloved 1961 Ford convertible with the smoky Mileage Maker Six engine and the doors that filled up with water every time it rained—was a Galaxie. I had been living in McNamara's world for years and didn't know it. The Galaxie, in fact, was introduced in 1959, the year Buddy Holly died.

Ah, the lovely years of my youth were just another chapter in the Book of War.

What I didn't know, what Jean Genet doesn't know, is that Robert McNamara is a broken man in 1968. The data he collects add up to one unmistakable total: the war in Vietnam can't be won by the Americans.

✦ ✦ ✦

The day after the Democratic convention ended, I went up to the bathroom where my father had sat shitting black, cancerous blood.

I took off my shirt, studied my back in the mirror, and thought about carving FUCK YOU there. I realized that I would either have to write backward in the reversed image the wall mirror gave me or use a second mirror to guide my hand. It was quite confusing.

I decided to hold a hand mirror in my left hand to check the work of my right hand in the medicine-cabinet mirror. But it was hard going. In the double mirrors, while the letters were in their proper order, everything was confused: up seemed to be down, and left appeared to be right, out was in, and in was out. I kept making mistakes and washed them off, rubbing hard with a brush to get the ink off my skin. My back turned gray from the ink and raw from all the washing.

When I finally had a fairly passable version of FUCK YOU inked on my back, I got a paring knife from the kitchen just to try a cut. I figured healed scars that read FUCK YOU might be even more dramatic than the pus-filled version. I was just drawing blood when I realized that I had no idea if the FUCK YOU I was about to carve was up or down as you actually saw it without the mirrors.

"Oh my God," my mother said when I showed her my back. She began sobbing—big, heaving sobs. "What are you doing? What's happening? What's going on? Everything's getting so strange."

30.

Oh, it was hide and seek for me. Running and running: running as fast as I could to get away. Vi-et-nam. Vi-et-nam. Vi-et-nam. Those three awful syllables. In my brain I was running, running, running. No one could help me, not my dear, gone dad, not my dear, sweet pudgy mother. No one, oh, no one, no.

I think I ran for years and years until it all caught up with me.

By the early 2000s, I had such prosperity: the BMW; the children in private schools; the perfect yuppie life; and there I was in Washington, DC, visiting an old friend, drinking Pinot Grigio at his mansion in Georgetown and spending the night at the Sheraton near the White House, right where presidents got their hair cut.

I have everything, and the next morning—Sunday—I take a cab to the Washington National Cathedral for Easter services and there is Supreme Court Justice Sandra Day O'Connor doing one of the readings and all of us look happy and educated and prosperous and I'm in the cathedral bathroom changing into running gear and putting my dress clothes in a backpack and then jogging down Massachusetts Avenue past the Naval Observatory where the vice president lives.

Lovely, lovely the spring day. It's me and mansions and Al Gore and Sandra Day O'Connor. Lovely, lovely the air as I go running, running, running, just as I have two or three times a week since 1968, and then ahead of me is a line of people walking between two ropes on a sidewalk in a park and people are laughing and talking and suddenly I realize I'm in the line to see the Vietnam Veterans Memorial and people are getting quieter and quieter and I don't know what to do except move along though I don't want to be here and it's kind of like the way I went into the army and then there in the black granite is the first name I see and then the second and the third. Dale R. Buis, the first GI dead in Vietnam, followed by Chester Melvin Ovnard, except I later learn that Chester's name is misspelled on the wall, that it should be Chester Melvin Ovnand, and then I think they can't even get the names right and you and I and all the others are wading deeper and deeper into the dead and it's Maurice Flournoy and Alfons Bankowski and then they're adding up and I remember the box scores on the nightly news with Walter Cronkite and the United States supposedly winning the World Series of War and I'm walk-ing deeper and deeper into the names of the dead. Frederick Garside and Ralph Magee and Glenn Matteson and why, I wonder, am I here and when will this stop and a homeless man wearing a wool blanket—exactly the kind of blanket we had in the military—is pointing at men and saying, "You. You. You're a brother, right? You're my brother aren't you?" and then he's pointing at me, as if some secret thread from the back of the tapestry connects us to each other, "You. You. You're a veteran, right?" and I'm nodding yes and I'm shak-ing my head no and I'm walking deeper and deeper into the names of the dead. Leslie Sampson and Edgar Weitkamp Jr. and Oscar Weston Jr. and I can see my face reflected in the polished black granite among the names and the homeless veteran pointing at me and there is Mr. Niederman and the pregnant woman and we're all there in the vast reflected land of the dead, us and them, us and them, reflected back and forth.

31.

I got back to Maple Street in the fall of 1968 a few weeks before my draft physical.

Now that going to Canada and carving FUCK YOU no longer seemed like good options, I read through AR 40-501 again. I remembered what Arnie told me—cutting off part of my finger was the easiest way to go.

"Though remember," Arnie had warned me, "one joint's not enough. You have to cut off two."

I walked over to Monroe Laner's garage. He was my landlord, and his garage was his woodworking shop. It was filled with flying sawdust and the screech of a saw. Monroe was bent over, pushing a piece of wood into a spinning blade.

"Mr. Laner," I yelled.

He shut off the saw and slid his protective goggles up on his forehead. He smiled.

"About time you came to your senses and started doing some woodworking."

I told him I wanted to even up the legs of my desk chair.

"Why don't you just bring it over here, and I'll do it," he said.

"No, let me try it on my own, Mr. Laner. I'll learn from my mistakes."

"Ain't that the truth," he said and handed me a T-square and a portable circular saw made of dull gray steel.

"Be careful," he said as I hefted the saw. "It's old. The blade guard is missing, and it's a lot heavier than it looks. Sometimes the trigger sticks. Here try it. You've got to snap it hard with your finger to get it to shut off, so be careful. This is a dangerous, old saw. It does good work, but it could cut you up pretty bad, you know."

I squeezed the trigger. It's kind of like a gun, I thought. How funny, but I didn't really feel like laughing.

"Are you sure you don't want my help?"

"I'll be OK," I said.

As I walked back to my little apartment that sunny after-noon in early September, I looked around and started to cry, wishing that I had any life but mine. It all seemed so unfair. Why me?

I set the saw on the little kitchen table. It seemed enor-mous, a tool that could cut up the whole apartment. Sterile and menacing and nasty.

Monroe Laner told me to make sure I braced whatever I cut so the saw wouldn't slip. I put my left hand on the kitchen table. By positioning my left knee on a chair, I brought the weight of my whole body down on my left arm and hand. I set the face of the saw blade along the table's edge. Without turning it on, I pushed the saw along that edge until it barely touched my index finger just below the second joint. I prac-ticed that move a couple of times. The blade was so sharp that it drew a little dot of blood.

The blood surprised me. I hardly felt a thing.

I was starting to sweat, and I sat back down in the chair. Then I went to the refrigerator and popped open a bottle of Coke to calm down. My shirt was wet, soaked through with fear and self-pity.

That gray saw seemed enormous sitting on the tiny kitchen table. I started to cry again. Why was this happening to me? I wondered what Emerson would think. I walked around the apartment sobbing and whapping my left index finger against walls and bookcases and furniture to numb it.

I flipped the silver toggle switch. The saw motor turned on, slowly at first and then faster and faster.

Its handle was curved and indented with the shapes of fingers. I put my right hand on the handle and my right finger in the trigger guard. One last sob came up from my chest, and I tried to steady my breathing.

"There, there," I said aloud, trying to be my own father. "There, there. It'll be over in a second."

I touched the trigger.

Errrrr, the saw screamed.

I felt cold and jerked my hands away. Humped there at the edge of the table, the saw looked like an industrial animal.

"OK, now," I said, whapping my left index finger against the edge of the table. It was really numb. "OK, now."

I set my left index finger on the edge of the table ahead of the saw blade. I put my left knee back on the chair and my weight down, hard, on my left arm and hand.

"OK, now."

I touched the trigger a couple of times with my right hand.

Errrrr, the saw went. *Errrrr.*

I tried to look at what I was doing, but my eyes were filled with sweat and tears. I shook my head to see better.

I gave the trigger a full squeeze. The saw rose up off the table, as if it were alive. The force surprised me. I tried to control it but couldn't, and I started to pull my left hand away.

Rrrrrrr.

The trigger was stuck, I realized. I couldn't stop the blade. Terrified, I dropped the saw. It fell onto the stained carpet of the kitchen floor. With its trigger still stuck, the saw rocked back and forth, an angry little beast getting free. It bounced a couple of times, once with the whirring blade up toward me—grinding teeth, a metal grin of death—then it leaned back toward the carpet, where the blade, propelled by the stuck trigger, got caught in the loops of the old kitchen carpet. The saw began crawling around the kitchen, first away from me toward the wall, but it hit the baseboard a couple of times and turned around, now doing its toothy walk toward my leg, the whine a growl as the carpet slowed the speeding blade and made the whole saw buck like an animal.

Rrrrrr. Rrrrrr.

"Oh my God," I said, fumbling for the heavy rubber plug in the wall socket. "Oh my God."

I pulled hard on the cord, and the saw stopped just as it got to my pants leg, ready to tear me to pieces.

32.

Streamlined, with ribs of aluminum trim on its side, the chartered bus for my physical looked as though it had driven all the way from the 1940s to collect soldiers for yet another war.

I was so nervous I was there an hour early the morning of Wednesday, September 11th, 1968. I started to get on the bus.

"Wouldn't do that if I were you," a driver with a peaked cap said. "No sense being in a hurry for this trip, buddy. Besides, Mr. Bleney from the draft board likes to check the names off before you get on."

He nodded toward a man with a clipboard coming toward us. He had combed over the slick long hairs on one side of his head to mask his baldness on top. When the wind came up, his greasy hair stood straight up, as if a trap door were opening on top of his head.

"You there," the man with the lifted-up hair yelled. "What's your name?"

"Ryan," I said.

"Wait about there," he said. "You're number forty-six. I'm going to line you up alphabetically, make sure you're all here before you get on the bus. Alphabetically by the number, see what I mean? People in Little Rock like to have everyone in order."

As the rest of us arrived, he handed each of us an envelope with a name in the corner and a large number in the middle.

"Got to stay organized, men. This is almost the army, you know. Now listen up. You got vouchers in those envelopes for your meals and for the hotel."

The inside of the bus was dark and smelled vaguely mildewed. The open-faced blond boy sitting next to me said, "Smells like a long time ago, doesn't it?"

His name was Billy Peeler.

Then, a moment later he added, "Is this what it's like to go to war?"

Then, after another moment, "I guess it's always dark when you go to war, right?"

A sergeant at the Armed Forces Examining and Entrance Station in downtown Little Rock met us when the bus arrived that afternoon and walked us over to our hotel. It was a long, erratic line of boys snaking down the sidewalk—boys going off to play war.

Billy Peeler was my roommate.

"You like to party?" Billy asked me after we had thrown our suitcases on our twin beds. "Find some girls. Find some beer."

We were each sitting on the end of our respective beds staring at the wall.

"But I ain't got the heart," Billy said. "My Uncle Wilton says I'm gonna die in Vietnam. Go down in a rice paddy. If the bullet don't get me, the drowning will. Took the starch right out of my pecker, you know."

I nodded. Is this what men talked about before they went to war?

"Got a plan, though, Ryan. Got a good plan. Want to hear it?"

It was his Uncle Wilton's idea, that we could raise our blood sugar level if we skipped supper and drank a six-pack of frozen orange juice concentrate. So we wandered around and bought some Minute Maid at a Piggly Wiggly.

I got through about one and a half of the cardboard canisters. I peeled the packaging back and slurped and chewed on the icy concentrate as if it were a Popsicle. Its taste unbearably sweet at first, the concoction became acidic in my mouth and made me shiver. Little eruptions of vomit came up my esophagus and made the back of my mouth taste sour.

"You know, Ryan," Billy said as he opened his third canister. "I believe I'd rather die in some rice paddy than walk around belching this crap. What a fucking choice you get in America these days, huh. I'm going to bed."

✦ ✦ ✦

The next morning we all gathered in the lobby of the Armed Forces Examining and Entrance Station. A corporal stood on the stairs waiting for us.

"The yellow line, men. You stay on this yellow line all day long. That red and that blue line—they're neither one for you. We designed your line to be the Yellow Brick Road."

He was my first real soldier, a harried, rat-faced corporal in a wrinkled tan uniform. It looked as though he'd slept in it.

"We going to Oz?" someone yelled.

"All right, then, line up!"

"You one of those mean little monkeys that belong to the Wicked Witch of the North?"

"He's not doing such a good job getting us in line, is he?" Billy Peeler said, turning around to whisper.

"You there," the rat-faced corporal said, pointing at Peeler. "Shut up!"

"What about those other guys?" Billy asked.

"You heard me. You're the one that interests me right now. You shut up, or I'll send you to Vietnam this afternoon."

"Can he do that?"

✦ ✦ ✦

The yellow line led us to a room set up with school desks, the kind with paddle tops that folded down the side of the chair.

"All right, now listen up," the rat-faced corporal said. "Look in your envelope and see if you have DD Form 44. Should have your name on it. Keep it close to you until the end. Lose it, and we'll just send you off to war without a name. Where the fuck you think the Unknown Soldier came from? He lost his DD 44. Got it?"

"Boy seems mighty interested in getting everyone on the battlefield," a tall redneck in a ducktail said.

"What you think we're doing here?" the corporal said as he began handing out examination booklets. "This isn't some kind of college entrance examination, you know."

No, it was the Armed Forces Qualification Test. The ole AFQT, as the corporal called it.

"Your Uncle Sam wants to know if you're smart enough to die for him. In case anybody here has the idea of flunking this exam on purpose, you better forget that right away. The flunkers are even more likely to die than the high scorers. They're first in line to die. You want to stay out of combat, you want to get a good score. Maybe they'll make you a typist."

We each got two yellow pencils and a test booklet.

The corporal pulled down a glassine-coated sheet that was coiled up in a long cylinder fastened to the wall. The apparatus looked like one of those pull-down maps above blackboards in schools.

"This is a sample question from the test you're about to take. Read it."

> *Water is an example of a*
> O A. *crystal.*
> O B. *solid.*
> O C. *gas.*
> O D. *liquid.*

"You take your pencil and you black out the correct circle. Got that?"

The redneck got up and started walking toward the front of the room.

"Where you going, troop?"

"Up there—to mark the right answer."

The corporal stared at him.

"You are one dumb motherfucker, troop. I mean, in the test, you mark the right answer by filling in the circle. In the fucking test booklet. The one on your desk."

"Your mama let you talk like that?" the redneck asked as he walked back to his seat.

"Open your test booklets," the corporal said. "Break the seal. See the sample question. It's just like this one. What's the right answer?"

"None of the above."

"Oh, great. We've got college boys here today. I forgot. Funny all right, but the funny boys should fill in the circle for D. D's the answer. Do you have questions?"

"Can't water be a crystal?" someone asked. "Ice, you know. Ice is water, and ice is a crystal."

"A gas," someone else offered. "It evaporates."

The corporal got redder and redder.

"Those aren't the answers the army wants. You got to come up with the answers the army wants. Otherwise you're a dead motherfucker."

The AFQT took two or three hours. When we finished, we were sent into another room to fill out more forms, which were stacked on the classroom desks, waiting for us. I sat down and started filling out DD Form 98, the Armed Forces Security Questionnaire. It had a long list of subversive organizations, some with evocative names like the Cervantes Society, the Military Art Society of Japan, the Dante Alighieri Society (though only between 1935 and 1940), and Everybody's Committee to Outlaw War. I started filling in the "Remarks" section with the sentence Arnie had taught me: "I believe that the war in Vietnam is morally wrong."

"Any Commies here?" a sergeant asked as he walked into the room. He had a handlebar moustache and eyebrows that went up and down when he spoke.

"Let me give you a tip here, gents," the sergeant said. "We can do this easy, or we can do this hard. The hard way is you put down a bunch of Commie organizations and think, oh boy, this'll get me out of Vietnam. What it'll really get you is a lifelong surveillance by the FBI. The government's going to classify you as dangerous. Probably want to kill you off in a firefight. You'll start right here by walking down that blue line to Mr. Rose's FBI office, where you'll get to spend a week getting questioned in one of the little cells he's got in there."

"Oh, pshaw," Billy Peeler said, "you're not going to do that."

"Wanna try me?" the sergeant asked and looked evenly at Billy. "Why don't we look at this form and do things the easy way. No sense in messing up my life, or yours, buddy. You just check the first Yes, meaning you've read the list and then you check all the rest No, meaning you haven't even been in the same town as a Commie. You leave the "Remarks" section empty. Then sign it and you go your way and I'll go mine."

Did I want to be an outlaw for the rest of my life?

I began erasing what I wrote. I really didn't want to get tangled up with the FBI. I felt small and foolish.

"Sergeant," I said as I raised my hand. "May I have two more pencils? I've used up the erasers."

The forms still had the impressionistic outlines of my statement.

"Maybe another form, too. I screwed this one up."

The next room along the yellow line was a kind of locker room with benches and wire baskets. A weary-looking private sat at a table with paper bags.

"One bag per man," he said. "One per man. For your valuables. Take it with you. Take your envelope, too, and wear your undershorts, your shoes, and your socks. The rest of your clothes in the wire basket on a shelf over there."

He was reading *Atlas Shrugged* and didn't look up when he spoke. Every minute or so, he repeated the same message. "One bag per man."

✦ ✦ ✦

Out the door of that room we walked, a little tentatively, each carrying a brown envelope and a paper bag, some of us in stained undershorts, some of us with clean ones, one of us without any undershorts at all. How strange to think that out of this shuffling group of nearly naked men with heavy black and brown shoes and mostly falling-down white tube socks would come the wounded and the dead.

The man without underpants had a giant penis, two or three times the size of the fear-shrunken members owned by the rest of us, but even he, who had literally so much to offer the world, looked as though he'd lost his confidence as he shuffled along, naked except for the tan work boots he wore.

The next room was huge—the size of a couple of basketball courts—with a series of tables arranged in a U-shape. Numbers were affixed to ten-foot poles at each table. Each was a station on the route of the army physical. The pathway started, appropriately enough, with blood. At Station One, four of us at a time sat and had blood drawn. The syringes emptied into tubes that were then racked in neat rows with our names on pieces of masking tape. The deep red of Worley and Adashek and Emory and Ryan. The communion wine of death.

At the next station, the same four were ushered into a room where we put our chests against cold stainless-steel squares on the wall.

"Suck in your chest. Hold your breath for fifteen seconds. We want to make sure there's room for bullets in there. Thank you. Next four step in."

And so the morning went. They examined our eyes, took our blood pressure and looked up our butt holes. Around noon, the line slowed down in front of a table at the last station. A man in a white coat with a stethoscope around his neck studied the paperwork of each man who came up to him.

"Ryan, huh?" he said to me. "That's my wife's maiden name. Let's see. You put down Recurrent Back Pain on this form."

"Yes, it's right back here." I turned to show him.

He got up, came around the table, and began poking my lower back.

"Ouch, yes, that's the pain. Oh, and I've got high blood sugar, too."

"Well, what am I going to do here?" he asked as he sat back down. He rubbed his forehead.

He scribbled on some forms, signed them, and stamped them.

"Here. Hand this in to the clerk after you put on your clothes. Next."

"Am I out?"

"You're done, my friend. You're on your way."

I sat down on the bench in the changing room. Yes, I thought to myself, he liked me; he agreed about my back pain. Can't have any bad backs in the heavy work of war. He did me a favor. Thank you. Thank you. I looked through my paper work, which now was covered by various stamps and initials, and tried to figure out my status, but couldn't make sense of it.

After I changed into my clothes, I handed my envelope to a clerk.

"Am I out?"

"What?" he asked.

"You know—out." I didn't know how to ask the question.

"You're done now. You can go home. Your draft board will get in touch with you."

✦ ✦ ✦

"Out of the way here. Clear a space." A chubby air force captain followed by a marine corps sergeant came down the hallway.

"You're not going home just yet. We need to have everyone line up here, on the red line."

"We're not finished processing them," the clerk said.

"You can get back to that. No one's going anywhere. Get everyone in here on the red line."

Five or ten minutes later we all stood there, some of us still in our baggy underpants and falling-down socks.

"I want you!" the barrel-chested marine sergeant said to the third man as he came down the line behind the air force officer. "And you!" he said to the sixth man. "And you! And you!"

He was picking men who looked to be in good shape.

"Ain't you something," the marine said to our naked man. "That thing of yours already looks like an M-16. I'll take you, that's for sure."

The air force officer was now standing next to me.

"What's going on?" I asked him.

"The marines are drafting. Too many casualties at Khe Sanh. They need men," he whispered. Then in a louder voice: "Straighten up the line, men, so Sergeant O'Brian can see you."

"I'll take you! And you!" the red-faced sergeant said in a gruff voice to the men on either side of me.

After the marine sergeant had taken his conscripts down the hall with him, I went to find the clerk with our paperwork. I was shaking with fear that the marines might take me next.

"What's my classification?" I asked the clerk.

"Let's see." He went through some folders until he found my file. "Here. Item 76. Your P-U-L-H-E-S rating."

"What does that mean?"

"Beats me," the clerk said. "What matters is that you got a 1 in all six categories. You're healthy as a horse. See Item 77. Dr. Medford checked Box A. The 'is qualified box.' Unless you convince them otherwise, your draft board's going to call you I-A, my friend. Ready for the army of the old US of A."

"There's got to be a mistake here. The doctor felt my back. He talked to me. He liked me. He let me out."

The clerk gave me an indifferent smile.

I ran back into the giant room with all the stations. Some of the medics were standing around smoking. Piles of trash were stacked in the corner, including a half-open, blood-smeared box where someone had thrown out the test tubes of our blood, which now was all mixed together with broken glass. It looked like the aftermath of an explosion. The doctor was gone.

"What happened to that doctor who was here?" I asked one of the medics.

"Went home. Gets $200 for a half-day's work and goes home. Not a bad deal."

"There's been a mistake," I said. "I've got a bad back."

"Can't help you here," one of the medics said, stubbing out his cigarette in a coffee cup. "You better see a doctor."

I ran back through the changing room and down the hall-way along the red line. The only open office was that of an army recruiter. I stood in the doorway, puffing. I was so scared I could hardly breathe.

"There's been a mistake," I said to the lanky sergeant, who sat at his desk clipping his fingernails.

"Of course there has, son," he said, pulling a chair out for me to sit in. "Of course there has. You're not just a number, are you? You're a human being. Here. Sit down. You got any college, son?"

33.

But why do I worry? The war's long over, isn't it? They can't come and get me again, can they? It's not dangerous anymore, is it?

Right now, it's a Saturday evening in Milwaukee, Wisconsin. Not a sergeant anywhere. It's May. I've mowed the lawn and pulled some dandelions. My wife is out of town, and I turn on the television to find a little company, and there it is, of all programs, a rerun of the ancient *Lawrence Welk Show* on public television.

"Here's our chorus now to sing a song made popular by Rudy Vallee," Lawrence says. His powder-blue suit is a little too bright, like someone working overtime to stay cheerful. "A-one, an-a-two, an-a-three."

He turns, holding his hand out, and the TV screen cuts to a row of singers. They are elbow to elbow, arrayed in a V, like a chevron, with the tip at the back of the stage. The women are on the left side of the V, the men on the right. Their clothes are all a matching orange, a color that seems vaguely familiar—and then I remember. Of course. Tang. That bright orange, awful-tasting breakfast drink. Tang. It went on the first manned space flight. Ahh, the footprints of the sixties, like the footprints on the moon—they never seem to go away.

How startling is the shift from Lawrence Welk's baby-blue suit to the glowing orange of the chorus. The women's skirts puff out with taffeta. They sway slightly back and forth with the rhythm of their song. The men have middle America's version of the British Mod look, with page-boy haircuts and wide, orange ties and orange shirts with oversized collars. Since most of the men are forty or fifty years old, they look awkward in their costumes, as if they'd drunk from a diluted fountain of youth.

> *We're poor little lambs who have lost our way*
> *Baa, baa, baa.*

How mournful their singing is, how solemn, in spite of all that orange. As if something unspoken has gone wrong that even accordions and bouncy rhythms cannot cure.

> *We're little black sheep who have gone astray*
> *Baa, baa, baa.*

The singers raise their hands ever so slightly, as if pleading with us for understanding. The lovely Lennon Sisters on the left—Dianne, Peggy, Kathy, Janet. There, on the right, is the man with the deep bass voice. Larry Hooper.

> *Gentlemen songsters off on a spree*
> *Doomed from here to eternity*

How odd to see this show nearly forty years after the fact, but I think it was the one my mother and I watched the night before I went in the army.

✦ ✦ ✦

Yes, that day was also a Saturday. It had been hot. I mowed the lawn that day, too.

It's Saturday evening. I am to leave for the army in the morning.

After I mow the lawn, I grill two steaks. My mother and I eat them on TV trays I bring outside. Afterward, we set the trays aside, sitting there in the backyard on East Memorial e, in the webbed lawn chairs, smoking Lark cigarettes.

It is still light. The sky has that sudden clarity you get just before the sun goes down, and I think, I've got to get in shape. My God, I've put this off long enough. I'm going in the army tomorrow, and I've got to get ready. So I stand up, flick away my Lark, do some deep knee bends, and begin running around the backyard in my loafers. I go first along the side of the garage, then north past the sandbox. I turn west by the raspberry bushes and then turn again by the grape arbor and come back along the picket fence. I've run maybe a tenth of a city block.

"Be careful, son," my mother says, lighting another Lark. "Don't hurt yourself."

I go around again. And again. It's easy. My body, my heart feel light.

Oh, this is nothing, I think. Nothing at all. I feel bullet proof as I go along the garage again, turning by the raspberry bushes and then back around the apple tree.

"Don't you think you've exercised enough, Son?" my mother yells. "You don't want to get sick. You shouldn't be running on a full stomach."

The army's probably going to be tough, I think. The army probably won't care if my stomach is full or not, so I head around a fourth time. I'm starting to sweat, but I do another lap, and then a sixth and a seventh. I'm puffing.

"Do you think I've done a mile?" I ask my mother.

In truth, I've probably run a small fraction of a real mile.

"Oh, at least," she says. "Probably more. I lived through World War II, you know, and I never saw anybody run as hard as you have."

I sit back down in the lawn chair with the webbed covering and light up a Lark. The twilight is darkening. When I finish my cigarette, I flick it into the air, where it glows with the fireflies.

I come inside, and my mother and I fix ourselves a pitcher of iced tea, and then we sit in front of the television to watch *The Lawrence Welk Show*.

"Oh, mom," I say. "I hate *The Lawrence Welk Show*."

"Do it for me, son. After all, you're going in the army. These songs will make you feel better."

And there it is, the chevron of singers arrayed across the stage in their Tang orange outfits, singing "The Whiffenpoof Song."

> *Gentleman songsters off on a spree*
> *Doomed from here to eternity*
> *Lord have mercy on such as we*
> *Baa, baa, baa.*

"Wait, mom, isn't that the title of the movie. *From Here To Eternity?*"

"Oh yes," she says, "that movie about World War II. It's too bad—they're just not making good movies like that anymore."

34.

"Ryan," Walt Rostow says to me in a dream, his face coming in close and expanding, as if I'm seeing it in a funhouse mirror. His lips slowly pull back. Cheshire Cat teeth are underneath.

"Ryan," he says, "what a shitty story you're telling us. You don't get it, do you? This isn't about you or your father or your mother. This isn't about irony or drawing lines. We don't care about any of that. We don't have time for that. Get with the fucking program, man. We've got to stop the Commies. It's the domino theory, man. If Vietnam falls, then Asia goes, and pretty soon the rest of the world goes. It's containment. Didn't you pay attention in social studies class?

"Did you really believe that?"

"Oh, Ryan, it's just a dream. I'm just a figment of your imagination."

Cackling, he steps into the car of the Tilt-A-Whirl and spins off into the darkness.

"No one cares, Ryan," he screams at me as he spins back into sight, his Cheshire Cat teeth luminescent. "We took our money and ran. 'Tippecanoe and Tyler Too,' baby."

"Then it was about money?" I yell as he spins this way and that before disappearing back into the dark.

I wait for him to come back into sight, but he doesn't come, at least not this time he doesn't.

"Was it just about the money?" I ask over and over and never get an answer.

35.

"Rick, I don't want to hurt your feelings," my friend Joe Kennedy tells me. "But no one really cares about what you did during the war in Vietnam."

"No one cared back then either," I say. "Look at this Polaroid. See, it says *July 20, 1969*, on the back. Remember that date?"

Joe thinks a minute, and then he smiles.

"Sure. Of course I do," he says. "The moon landing. My wife and I had beer and pizza and invited everyone over to . . ."

"A fucking inspection. That's what I had that day at Fort Polk, Louisiana. Can you believe that? I was in basic training. I'd been a soldier for eleven days. They wouldn't let us watch the moon landing. We were forbidden from going into the dayroom, where the television was. We couldn't join the rest of America because of an inspection.

"Here, Joe. Look at this, at this picture of Drill Sergeant Yankovic sitting on the steps of the dayroom. He was guarding it. That morning, the captain told us we hadn't earned the right to watch men land on the moon."

"Your drill sergeant looks sick, if you ask me," Joe says. "Kind of yellow-looking and skinny."

"True, but that made him scary to us. He was like stretched steel. Tough and sick at the same time. Just like that—his whole uniform would be soaking wet from his malaria. Even his hat. He dripped sweat, fat drops of it. They splattered on the ground. Then his uniform dried pale white from the salt leached out of his body. The army was killing him, and he thrived on it."

✦ ✦ ✦

"This is war, baby. War," Drill Sergeant Yankovic said to a bunch of us trainees late in the evening of July 20, 1969. We stood around the steps to the dayroom hoping the captain would change his mind and let us watch the moon landing. "They don't call it that in Washington, but this is about killing people and breaking things. You're not your mama's little babies anymore. Your mama can't save you."

The sudden flash from Leroy McMaster's Polaroid made us look like ghosts. Leroy wanted to send pictures of Drill Sergeant Yankovic back to his congressman.

"It's un-American not to let us watch the moon landing," Leroy said, waving the pictures he took of the drill sergeant. "Congressman Alsop is a friend of my family. Just wait'll he gets these."

"Take all the pictures you want. No one cares, you moron. No one cares who you send your weenie fucking pictures to," Drill Sergeant Yankovic said. "Send them to Congressman Shit for all I care. Make sure President Turd gets several copies. You dumb fuck—don't you understand? They're the reason you're going to get your asses shot off. They started this war; they don't care about you. Nobody cares about you."

Drill Sergeant Yankovic stood up then, and we moved out of his way. He had long hands, with fingernails like talons. They were stained yellow—perhaps by his malaria or by his unfiltered Camel cigarettes.

He carefully put on his Smokey Bear, drill sergeant hat, pulling down the strap at the back to secure it. Campaign hats, these were called. His seemed to float on his head. He tapped its brim with the yellowed fingernail of his right index finger to make sure it angled down his face.

"We're locking you out of America," he said. "You have to fight your way back in. That dayroom is just the beginning."

He drew himself up to the full six feet of his skinny height, stuck his thumbs in his web belt, and looked at us, a shadow from the tilt of his hat covering up his eyes.

"It's war, baby," he said. "War never goes away. Ole Wernher von Braun shot up the world for the Nazis, and now he's on our side. He's aiming for the moon. We'll start there and then go on to the planets. Shit, the universe is next. You've got to love it. Yessir, ole Wernher's attacking outer space. My man Wernher knows it's war, baby. Don't ever forget that. In the meantime, you keep your soft, civilian asses out of that dayroom."

✦ ✦ ✦

The army training barrack in those days had this large bathroom at one end of the first floor. The head. It was one big, open room with a drain in the middle. It had four toilets at one end, and eight shower nozzles at the other end. Along one side were six sinks and, across from them, six urinals. No stalls enclosed the toilets, the showers, or the urinals.

I suppose this openness was meant to degrade people, to break down their individuality and grease their slide into the gears of the army's Big Green Machine.

Maybe—but Jerry Donenfelter saw this washroom as his studio. Jerry had studied music at the University of Alabama. He was also the drum major in the school's marching band. He loved marching, and he loved choral arrangements.

At first this was a matter of Jerry working up some tight harmonies on "Soldier Boy" while he and some other tenors showered. "Oh, my little soldier boy," four nude men sang to four other guys squatting on the toilets with their green cotton fatigue pants and white undershorts down around their ankles.

Drill Sergeant Yankovic sensed Jerry's talent and made him a squad leader. Squad leaders wore these black felt armbands with corporal stripes pinned around the sleeves of their left arms. They looked like they were in mourning.

Jerry, however, saw his stripes as the first step on a ladder of greatness, and he picked twelve men ("The number Jesus would choose if he went to war," Jerry said) for a close-order drill routine. They rehearsed in the laundry room, and we could hear the muffled cadences of drill commands and the sounds of clumping feet and rifle butts hitting the floor between the washers and the dryers. I think Jerry intended to be the Busby Berkeley of Company B, Fifth Battalion, First Training Brigade.

Jerry, in fact, figured out the customs of the military much faster than the rest of us.

The very first day of our arrival at Company B, First Sergeant Clyde Toler took Jerry along on a trip for supplies. They left in the company jeep. When they came back, they had both the jeep and a deuce-and-a-half truck filled with about a hundred cans of reflective silver paint.

"The man's a genius at scrounging," Toler told Drill Sergeant Yankovic. "A blooming genius."

"Why would anyone want a hundred cans of reflective silver paint?" my friend Joe Kennedy wonders as he listens to my story.

Because real scroungers in the army understood that you should always stockpile any items that come along—you never know when you might need them. And guess what? That paint gave Captain Van Hook an idea about how to impress the colonel.

"Men," Captain Van Hook said to us as we stood in formation on the morning of July 20, 1969. "This is a great day for Company B. This is the day I start to become Major Van Hook. We are going to paint all of the duffel bags with that reflective silver paint Donenfelter found. I'm going to tell the colonel that we plan to shine for our country."

The details of this operation were left to the drill sergeants, who had to figure out a way to get the silver paint on the bags and still have the army-required stenciling of our names and army serial numbers.

While we had plenty of paint, Company B owned but a single paintbrush, which was the size used for house painting, so the drill sergeants set up this duffel-bag painting project the way they set up everything else—by the numbers.

First we stacked all of our empty duffel bags on the parade ground. Then we roughly divided our 200-man company into thirds—one group taking turns painting with the single brush, one group carrying the bags to and from the painters, and one group delivering the paint from Jerry's deuce-and-a-half truck to the painters. We flattened each bag on the ground, painted the top halves, and set the bags in the sun to dry. A few hours later, we turned them over and painted the other halves. Some of the bags had twigs and pieces of gravel stuck in the paint, but removing those imperfections caused the paint to smear, so we left them alone.

Drill Sergeant Yankovic collected a quarter from each of us and went to Leesville, the town next to Fort Polk, where he bought cans of black spray paint. (I've often wondered why no one thought to buy some paintbrushes. Life in the army was filled with these little box canyons of failure.)

Company B had several stencil kits, so in the late afternoon, we divided up again: one group readied the stencils for each bag, one group spray-painted our personal information on the bags, and one group set them out to dry. By seven that night, we were done, though some of the names and serial numbers were wrong. When the men complained, Drill Sergeant Yankovic just laughed.

"Nobody cares about shit like that," he said. "Just make sure your dog tags are in order. Don't want the wrong name on your tombstone."

✦ ✦ ✦

The night our company did its final preparations for the inspection—late the night of July 20, 1969, the night America landed on the moon—was also to be the dress rehearsal of the close-order drill routine Jerry and his men had been practicing.

Around midnight, we finished cleaning up the company area. Captain Van Hook yelled, "Fall in!" We gathered by platoon and stood at parade rest with our rifles at our sides in the dim light of a cloud-covered moon.

That didn't go very well. It was hard to see by the light of that night's half-moon, and we kept stepping on the heels of the men in front of us. Captain Van Hook then ordered that the company trucks and jeeps be placed around the parade area—motors running, lights on. We could see, sort of, and the marching went better, though now we became a shadowy army of the night—the black shapes of helmets and arms and rifles passing back and forth in front of the flickering headlights. Exhaust fumes and the mist from the damp night air made us appear and disappear.

After an hour of this, Captain Van Hook commanded, "In place, march!"

Our boots drummed on the ground, and soon the commands of Jerry Donenfelter rang in time with the cadences of our boots rising and falling and not going anywhere.

What's the future hold in store?

The answer from his squad came back—

Beat the Cong at their own war!

Since I was an *R* and always near the end of the column, it took a minute to see what was happening.

What's the future hold in store?

Jerry repeated the question, and his men answered again with the army's predictable rhetoric—

Beat the Cong at their own war!

To the cadence created by the rise and fall of our boots, Jerry's squad marched along in front of us—dark figures in the blinding light, passing in and out of the fog and the exhaust fumes.

Left, left
Left, right, left

Jerry commanded. He strode beside his men, raising and lowering a huge silver baton like the major at the half-time show for the big game. He'd also painted his boots and his helmet with the reflective silver paint, and his baton, boots, and his helmet glowed in the headlights, leaving behind evanescent trails of light as he marched.

Then the question changed.

What is it that we're fighting for?

The answer—

It's war baby war baby war baby war!

As Jerry's twelve-man squad chanted that, they held out their M-14 rifles with both hands and swung them from left to right in rhythm with their answer.

They turned at the end of our column, did an about-face, and hit the butts of their rifles on the ground in the same rhythm—

It's war baby war baby war baby war!

"Now we're getting somewhere," I heard Drill Sergeant Yankovic mutter. "Now we've really landed on the moon. We own that stony motherfucker."

✦ ✦ ✦

At two or three in the morning—after the jeep and the truck lights were turned off, after the vehicles had been driven away, after our rifles had been stored—a few of us sat on the steps to the locked-up dayroom, hoping that now someone would come and let us in so we could watch the moon landing. Even if it was over, we thought, the networks would surely show reruns of it.

Besides we couldn't go to bed—we weren't allowed to wrinkle our blankets or get dirt on the barrack floor for fear of getting bad marks in our inspection. We had to stay up all night until the colonel came.

We sat in the dark, half-asleep—smoking and talking.

On the other side of the company parade area—like the baggage for a ghostly journey—200 silver duffel bags filled with our clothes were stacked, their reflective paint glowing in the moonlight. Occasionally a twig or a piece of gravel would come loose from the paint and fall off.

"Ain't they pretty," Drill Sergeant Yankovic said from beneath the darkness of his tilted campaign hat when he came up to us. His uniform was dripping wet from his malaria.

We all staggered to our feet.

"Those duffels kind of look like artillery shells, don't they, boys? Just in case you were wondering what the real ammunition of the moon shot is, boys—there it is. All lined up, ready to go. Shoot the moon. Man, they ain't just a kidding."

He walked away, hat tilted, arms out—doing a twirling tap dance across the dark parade field—an imitation of Fred Astaire or Gene Kelly.

"Love that war baby war baby war baby war stuff," he said. "Who'd want to watch television when you can come down here to old Fort Polk and see a *real* show?"

36.

But it didn't end there, no. It took eight weeks, Joe. Eight weeks of humiliation. I fought it; I made fun of it; I was superior to it, but you know what? In the end, the army won. It eventually got me. I did what they told me to do.

Look. There I am on my belly and elbows: crawling across a dusty field screaming, "Drill Sergeant Yankovic loves me more than my Mama ever did." That's me, over here, rifle in front of me, its bayonet fixed, yelling, "Kill! Kill! Kill!" as I attack a target. Now I'm in first-aid class, learning how to close off a sucking chest wound. Look over there: I'm running into a house filled with tear gas, removing my gas mask, and slowly saying my name, rank, and serial number to a training sergeant sitting at a desk with his mask on. The giant plastic eye goggles and twin black canister filters on the mask make him look like an enormous insect in an army uniform. Perhaps this is what really happened to Gregor Samsa in Kafka's novella *The Metamorphosis*.

Oh, Joe, I was smart. I knew so much. I'd read all these books. None of the sergeants could even begin to explain who Gregor Samsa is. I was smarter than they would ever be, and yet there I was, marching along with the rest of my platoon, following their orders, stepping to Drill Sergeant Yankovic's cadence into the post library. In all our battle gear, wearing steel helmets and canteens, my platoon clomped and clattered into that library and stood in formation between the shelves of books. Drill Sergeant Yankovic had us yell, at the top of our lungs, "The Dewey Decimal System will help me find my book! The librarian is my special friend!"

Can irony get me out of here, Joe? Can sarcasm save me?

✦ ✦ ✦

Then there's Peter Peterson.

"Call me Pudgy. Everyone does," Peterson told us, ducking as he spoke, used to being the butt of jokes.

Pudgy must have weighed in at 250 pounds on a five-foot-eight-inch frame. When he ran, his loose gut and floppy breasts jiggled under his white T-shirt. He had a side-to-side, mincing step when he jogged.

"Peterson," Drill Sergeant Yankovic yelled. "When the doctor got to you, did he throw away the baby and keep the afterbirth?"

Pudgy had so many sins that the drill sergeant didn't know where to begin. He just shook his head.

We were all puffing and sweating in the Louisiana heat. Pudgy's face had turned a mottled red.

The drill sergeant, for some reason, didn't sweat at all when he ran. He disdained the T-shirts that we troops wore. He stayed in his campaign hat and his heavy cotton fatigues as he loped easily along beside us, counting out a double-time march cadence. His back and his armpits were dry. Nothing but his malaria made him sweat.

"Peterson, you run like a fucking girl!" the drill sergeant screamed. "How can you stand yourself?"

The drill sergeant halted our platoon and made us stand at attention in the sun. He culled Pudgy from our little herd and forced him to run alone. After a minute of this, the drill sergeant caught up with him and began screaming at him as they went along together.

"Look at them titties of yours, Peterson. If you're going to have titties, at least you should have good ones."

"Suck in that pathetic gut, Peterson."

"You look like Jell-O on legs, Peterson."

Pudgy collapsed, and the drill sergeant assigned two men to walk him back to the company area while the rest of us continued our double-time run.

✦ ✦ ✦

Pudgy couldn't do anything to please the drill sergeant, but at night, in the barrack, during one of those infrequent half hours of the day when no one was yelling at us, Pudgy was hilarious. He did imitations of Jackie Gleason characters—Reginald Van Gleason III going through the barrack doing a white glove inspection; but the one that always ripped us up was the voice of Andy Devine from a long-ago kiddy show. A character called Froggie greeting us, "Hi yah, hi yah, kiddies. Hi yah, hi yah, hi yah." The absurdity of this voice left us doubled over in laughter.

While Pudgy's fat-man humor made us happy, he made Drill Sergeant Yankovic angrier and angrier as the weeks went by. Pudgy was too fat for almost anything requiring physical exertion. He was uncoordinated as well and couldn't master even the simplest marching orders, turning left when he should go right, always on the wrong foot, stumbling, tripping, falling down.

At first Drill Sergeant Yankovic solved the problem by assigning Peterson to the middle of the formation so no one would see him. But Pudgy was such a force of nature that he got everyone beside him out of step, and Drill Sergeant Yankovic's precious formation expanded and contracted like a caterpillar. Drill Sergeant Yankovic then put Pudgy on permanent KP, so he spent his days leaning on a mop in the mess hall, snacking, getting even fatter. The fabric around the buttons of his fatigues first puckered and eventually became unbuttonable.

"Peterson, you're a fucking disgrace to the United States Army. This is a pretty sad lot, but you're the worst of the worst."

✦ ✦ ✦

Drill Sergeant Yankovic had a private room at one end of the barrack. He kept it ready for inspections and seldom used it. Its bed was exactly made to inspection standards. A neat row of spotless uniforms hung there, each hanger the proper two inches from its neighbor. Beneath them, on the floor, was a row of dress shoes and combat boots belonging to some mythic soldier who was always ready for a surprise visit from the battalion commander. The real William Yankovic slept elsewhere—in the woods, we heard; in whorehouses, we heard. He never sleeps, we heard; he crawls the perimeter of Fort Polk all night long, we heard.

One evening, Pudgy discovered that the drill sergeant's room was unlocked. He went in and came out wearing the dress version of the drill sergeant's campaign hat.

"I wouldn't do that if I were you," Phil Danzig said, looking around, but Pudgy was on a roll. He put every stupid officer and sergeant into a single caricature.

"Mens," Pudgy commanded, "listen up. Drop down and gimme ten! Mens, if your brains were paper, there wouldn't be enough to make a Kotex for a flea. Mens, gimme another ten. Mens, I want you to get your hands off your cocks and put on your socks and gimme another ten and tell me who's the commander of your battalion. Gimme ten more. Mens, we're gonna win that war in Vietnam if we have to kill everyone to do it. All at once now, with Drill Sergeant Froggie, 'Hi yah, kiddies, hi yah, hi yah, hi yah.' Drop down and give Drill Sergeant Froggie ten, mens."

No one laughed. No one said a word.

So busy chuckling over his own routine, Pudgy hadn't noticed the silence.

"On a count of three, now—all together, one, two, three. 'Hi yah, kiddies, hi yah, hi yah, hi yah.'"

Then, after another moment of silence, "You so much as get dust on that hat, Peterson, you'll wish you'd never been born."

Pudgy lifted his right hand to his ear, Reginald Van Gleason III listening to the dulcet tones of his girlfriend.

Drill Sergeant Yankovic elbowed his way through the circle gathered around Pudgy. He was wearing a leather gun holster with a .45 inside. A belt holding a couple of grenades went across his chest.

"Here your dumb ole drill sergeant thought he was coming by to give his men a thrill with their cherry guard-duty assignments—up all night long in shacks filled with copperhead snakes, making sure no hippies or other undesirables break into Fort Polk and steal the hearts of your commanding officers. Please. No applause. I have your best interests always in my heart, but what are you doing here? Making fun of poor ole good-hearted Drill Sergeant Yankovic. Wearing Drill Sergeant Yankovic's hat. Drill Sergeant Yankovic, who answered his country's call and killed the yellow man to save us from the Russians. Now you think he's funny."

Drill Sergeant Yankovic was walking round and round Pudgy, clearing a space.

"You fat fucker," Drill Sergeant Yankovic said and grabbed the front of Pudgy's fatigue shirt, ripping the top two buttons off.

"Hey," Pudgy said, his fat fingers chasing the falling buttons through the air. "You can't do this, can you?"

The drill sergeant actually lifted the enormous weight of Pudgy off the ground with his left hand. He pulled out the pistol with his right and let Pudgy drop to the floor, where he tried to pick up his fallen buttons.

"You fat fucker, we got demerits from the post commander because of you. He saw that little dance step you call a march.

Do you know what that means? We don't win the Best-Platoon Award. Now Drill Sergeant Yankovic always wins the Best-Platoon Award. Get that, Peterson?"

He knelt down beside him and held the .45 to Pudgy's head.

"Come on," Pudgy pleaded. "Quit kidding around. Can't one of you guys help me here? I'm in real trouble."

I looked at my feet.

"Hey!" Art Kailas yelled. "That's a gun."

"No, you dumb fucking Greek. That's not a gun. It's a piece. A sidearm. It's a Colt automatic. Designed to quell the yellow man in the Boxer Rebellion."

He stood up and holstered the .45.

"You're so fucking smart, you hold one of these."

Drill Sergeant Yankovic yanked one of the grenades from the strap across his chest and pulled the pin out. The grenade began to hiss. I tried to remember the class we'd had in grenades and what the hiss meant. I closed my eyes and squeezed them shut. I prayed to be transported out of there. When I opened them, we were all still there, and Art Kailas was holding the grenade.

"Here, Kailas, as long as you keep squeezing this handle closed, the grenade's like your hometown softball. You let go of it, though, you're gonna take the whole barrack out. We'll go up like a wet spray of flesh-tinted blood. The wind will give us life's last blow job. Got it, Kailas? You're a strong guy. You should be able to hang on."

Drill Sergeant Yankovic grabbed Pudgy by the fabric of his fatigue shirt.

"Ten, hut, Peterson. We'll start with the basics."

Pudgy pulled himself up and stared off into the middle distance with that blank look all at-attention soldiers had.

"Right face, Peterson."

It was a beat too slow, but he did it. I began to smile. Maybe Pudgy would make it.

"Forward, march, Peterson."

He did that, too. A space opened up, and he marched down toward the other end of the barrack.

"Halt! About face! Forward, march!"

Yes, he was doing it—or no, he did it about halfway back, and then his feet took on a spastic life of their own, wiggling suddenly and changing step and causing Pudgy to trip and then awkwardly right himself. He was sweating and breathing hard.

"You dumb fucker," the Drill Sergeant screamed and walked toward him with the gun out. He pulled the top back, chambering a round. The room was quiet except for the metallic slide and click of the gun. "I should put you out of your misery."

He pointed the gun at Pudgy, who simply bowed his head as if he'd been expecting this for years.

Drill Sergeant Yankovic dropped the gun to his side, and I felt sudden relief. Maybe now he'd quit, but no—no, he fired. And again he fired—into the floor. The sound of the shots ricocheted back and forth through the barrack. A puff of smoke drifted among us.

"They're blanks, right?" someone asked.

Drill Sergeant Yankovic's head snapped toward the speaker, and he briefly pointed the .45 at him.

"You want to find out?"

Kailas dropped the grenade, and we all stood frozen there as it spun on the waxed red floor, which suddenly looked bloody.

A moment later a little smoke oozed from it. I held my face tight, waiting for the concussion from an explosion, but that puff of smoke was it.

"Kailas, if that had been a live grenade, you would have vaporized your buddies. You want to think about that?"

"Drill Sergeant, I'm sorry if I handled your hat. I'm sorry if I mess up your formations."

It was Pudgy speaking in a clear, adult voice.

"I know I'm not much of a soldier, but you can't kill me for being awkward."

I wished we were all sitting around chanting, "Hi yah, kiddies. Hi yah, hi yah, hi yah."

Drill Sergeant Yankovic looked at Pudgy and then walked over to him. He put the muzzle of the gun right under Pudgy's chin and forced him to walk back to his room. He slammed the door. A moment later we heard crashing noises and whimpered yells and a series of commands. "Forward, march. In place, march. Left turn, march."

One of the other drill sergeants marched the rest of us over to post headquarters, where we got our guard-duty assignments.

"Where's Private Peterson?" the NCO in charge asked.

"On sick leave, Sergeant," one of us said.

"Fucking shirker is more like it."

The next morning, after staying up all night, we stumbled back into our barrack. Pudgy's bed was stripped of its sheets and blankets, and his gear was stacked on the floor. When we returned from classes that afternoon, all his stuff was gone. I never saw him or his silver duffel bag again.

"To the moon, Alice!" Pudgy used to scream, running down the aisle in the middle of the barrack with his silver duffel bag as if he were going to hurl it into outer space. He sounded just like Jackie Gleason playing Ralph Kramden on the old *Honeymooners* television show. "To the moon!"

Pudgy's bed, down at the end of the row, stayed empty for the rest of our time in basic training, its striped mattress rolled up and tied, sitting on top of the mattress springs.

We used it once more the day of graduation.

That day, a sinewy colonel, with so many ribbons on his chest they seemed like they climbed over his shoulder and down his back, spoke to us while we stood at attention. How easy this is, I realized. I didn't even have to think about how to stand anymore.

"Men, in life, your first battle is with yourselves. The fact that you're here today means you've given yourself fiber by taking on discipline. You've tasted your first military victory, and your drill sergeants will give you your first medal. Wear it with pride."

We held out our hands, and Drill Sergeant Yankovic slapped a red and yellow National Defense Service Medal ribbon in each of them. He hit my hand so hard, the edge of the medal cut my skin.

"Fucking colonels," Drill Sergeant Yankovic said after the ceremony, "always making morals. Shit, everybody gets this medal."

I was rubbing the scratch in my hand as I stood by Pudgy's bed that evening. Someone had sneaked beer into the barrack. We unrolled the mattress and set Phil Danzig's little record player there.

> Come on, all of you big, strong men,
> Uncle Sam needs your help again.
> He's got himself in a terrible jam
> Way down yonder in Vietnam
> So put down your books and pick up a gun
> We're gonna have a whole lot of fun.

It was just then, in early September 1969, when I first heard Country Joe and the Fish sing the "I-Feel-Like-I'm-Fixin'-To-Die Rag." The other guys and I raised our beer bottles and toasted it. It was funny. We stood around Pudgy's bed with the little rectangles of our National Defense medals centered over the left-hand shirt pockets of our khaki uniforms. They looked like little stains of blood and viscera.

The second time we played the song, no one laughed. No one said a word.

The evening was cool, the first touch of fall. The sun had just gone down. I was a brand-new PFC with a silver duffel bag whose color was already beginning to crack.

> *There ain't no time to wonder why*
> *Whoopee, we're all gonna die*

37.

"All those pockets of crazies," my friend Tom Bamberger says, "but so what? The world is full of crazies."

That's true, I think, so why don't I get over those days? So what if I wound up in the military? It's happened to tens of millions, probably hundreds of millions of men over the years.

"Armies have been around so long no one even notices them anymore," the ghost of Albert Speer says, putting his bony fingers together. "It isn't prostitution that's the oldest business in the world; it's war. Mother Battle and her bloody babies."

But I wasn't really bloodied, was I?

"Let's just wait and see if you tell the truth, Ryan; see if you're willing to tell what really happened to you."

38.

It's a blur, a carnival in the dark. All of us on the Tilt-A-Whirl. Circling and circling.

I can feel the wind on my face as I spin around. Every so often a lurid green and purple light comes on, framing a face across from me.

"Hi yah, kiddies, hi yah, hi yah, hi yah," Pudgy Peterson says and then down he spins around, his head snapping back in his seat. Drill Sergeant Yankovic appears. He's smiling. "I still own you, Ryan. Your soft, civilian ass is mine," and there, look, smiling is Jerry Donenfelter. "Oh, my little solder boy," he sings as he spins around. And then, oh, face after face: Walt Rostow, Albert Speer, Lance B. Edwards, and Sergeant Perkins. Face after face comes into view, in the lurid light, and goes away, round and round.

And then I have this order to obey. Order Number 56, signed by Stanley P. Arthur, Major. SUBJECT: Basic German Course, Defense Language Institute, West Coast. REPORTING DATE: 24 SEP 1969. I don't have time to think about what's going on. I just have to do what I'm told.

"Once you get things figured out, the military's easy," Rex Harrison explained to me at that party back in Fayetteville. "Life will slide along. The military solves all those big identity questions for you. You know who you are. They give you a rank and a job and a place to sleep. They feed you; they clothe you."

"You've got to draw a line somewhere."

Lance B. Edwards's face suddenly appears from the dark. "If you don't, then where are you, Ryan, where are you?" He holds up a blank pad.

"You see, Ryan. It should be perfectly clear."

✦ ✦ ✦

I lost twenty pounds in basic training. My clothes didn't fit anymore. I was a new person; I didn't even look the same. When I got back to Jenny's house in Saint Louis, she handed me a copy of Emerson.

"He's been waiting for you," she said and smiled.

But I didn't have time for Emerson anymore. I wanted to make sure I got to the army's language school on time. I was terrified of making a mistake.

"If you miss that September date," the recruiting sergeant in Little Rock had told me, "you'll be one sorry sack of shit, Ryan. Then it's the army's choice. They'll send you to Vietnam."

Jenny insisted on coming with me to Monterey.

"We're married, you know," she said, and it took me a moment to remember that. I had been so busy folding my uniforms for the trip that I'd forgotten about her.

We loaded the car with our clothes and some household goods. Our baggage weighed so much that the car collapsed the shock absorbers and sat on its frame. We drove across the country on Interstate 80. I have pictures of myself from that time with my butch-cut army hair. I look tentative and baffled. One thing's for sure: I was scared. Those were dangerous days. One wrong move, and I would have ended up in Vietnam.

✦ ✦ ✦

In 1969, the Defense Language Institute was a series of old wooden buildings and newer cinder-block structures sitting on some hilltop acreage between Monterey and Pacific Grove,

California. The site has beautiful views of Monterey Bay. The day I arrived there was warm and sunny. The scenery was so beautiful that I felt as though I were walking through a travel poster.

"Ryan, yup, right here. German class," the charge-of-quarters corporal in the orderly room told me as he looked at a sheet of paper. "We've got you on our list. You're safe from Vietnam right now, buddy. You start next Monday. You got to show up here at seven thirty for formation. Captain Pfloeger likes to start on time."

"What do I do between now and then?"

Corporal Matson looked puzzled.

"Let's see. It's Wednesday. I'd eat some abalone at Fisherman's Wharf. I'd drive down to Big Sur. I don't know."

"Isn't there some kind of duty roster?"

"Please, Ryan. This is about as far from the real army as you can get, and we want to keep it that way. All right? Don't say words like 'duty roster.' You might give somebody ideas."

"My wife's with me. Can I live with her?"

He stared at me.

"Absolutely, unless you want me to move in with her." He paused. "You kind of lost it in basic training, didn't you, buddy? Of course. Just fill out these forms."

An hour later, after completing the paperwork, I was a registered married man, looking for off-post housing.

"Just call me, or whoever's CQ and give them an address and a phone number when you find an apartment."

Maybe my luck was changing. I drove back to the Holiday Inn in Seaside, where Jenny and I were staying. I put on civilian clothes, and Jenny and I stood there in front of the picture window looking at the ocean.

"Can you believe this?" I asked myself. It's all so beautiful. Yes, maybe my luck really was changing. Maybe the dark gods who took my father and put me in the army will leave me alone. I squeezed Jenny's hand.

The only apartment we could afford was a dreary little two-room place at 1075 Third Street. But it was close to the ocean and an inland lagoon. Those seemed like good omens, though the constant *ar, ar, ar* of the sea lions barking at night got a little wearing. In the mornings, fog rolled into the apartment through its uninsulated walls. The first morning I woke up feeling that I was inside a cloudy dream, going from one sleep to another, and I held on to Jenny, terrified.

Then I began sobbing: air-gulping, breath-taking sobs.

"What's the matter, baby?" Jenny asked.

"Maybe I'm not going to die after all," I said between sobs. "Maybe I'll live."

✦ ✦ ✦

"*Guten Tag!*" Herr Schefke, the civilian teacher said that first Monday after the welcoming speeches were over.

I was assigned to Room 250, Nisei Hall. I was so excited to begin. This will be my ticket to Europe, I thought. A foreign language! I was learning a foreign language!

"*Guten Tag!*" our little class of six students said back to Herr Schefke—or tried to.

"*Ja, ja,*" Herr Schefke said, rubbing his hands together as if he were about to begin a gourmet meal.

I still have my notes from that day. We were supposed to memorize the sound of the language. We had no reading material at all, just a bunch of seven-inch, reel-to-reel tapes. Those of us who lived off the base also got our own Wollensak portable tape recorders and a set of green Koss earphones.

I arranged the recorder and my study materials on a wobbly table in a corner of the living room on Third Street. The controls on the tape recorder looked like the keys on an accordion. I went back and forth between PLAY, STOP, REWIND, and PLAY as I listened to the strange syllables and tried to memorize them, repeating the sentences over and over.

Guten Tag! Ist daß hier die Deutschklasse?
Ja, daß ist die Deutschklasse.

That was how the program worked. We had to learn the lines of a spoken dialogue, going by sound alone, and repeat the lines the next morning in Room 250.

In pairs, we would come to the front of the classroom. Each one of us in the duo took first one side in the dialogue and then the other. We did this over and over. The theory of this learning was based on the notion that children learn language this way, by hearing others speak and responding to that.

Amazing. In the midst of the terrible war in Vietnam, the US Army taught me to learn like a child.

Of course there was also the unstated threat that I'd be sent to Vietnam if I didn't do my homework.

On the surface, though, it was all good fun.

"Bitte, machen Sie Fehler!" Herr Scheffke said, waving his hand at us. A blessing from a benevolent spirit. He didn't want us to be nervous. Please, he told us, make all the mistakes you want.

I still have some of the tapes, and I've located an old reel-to-reel tape recorder. The voice comes on a little off-key. The tape is stiff and sticky from a lack of use.

Wer ist der Lehrer?
Herr Neumann ist der Lehrer
Wo ist der Lehrer?
Der Lehrer ist dort.

✦ ✦ ✦

Incredible. The US Army handed me the keys to another culture. If I was lucky, I would go to Germany fluent in its language, getting two years abroad courtesy of the American taxpayer. Wonderful.

Wonderful, too, my classmates Peter Everwine, Eric Lundberg, and Art Schmid from Yale. We had students from Stanford, Penn, and the University of Virginia. Steve Goldberg, who sat beside me in classroom 250 of Nisei Hall, had been accepted into the PhD program in history at Harvard. All these certified bright boys—and yes, I kept up with them. Me, little Rickie Ryan, Louise Ryan's boy from Janesville, smarter than he ever thought.

> *Guten Tag!*
> *Guten Tag!*
> *Ist daß hier die Deutschklasse?*
> *Ja, daß ist die Deutschklasse.*

Those were our first phrases in German. Wonderful. *Wunderbar.*

"*Schönes Wochenende,*" everyone says that first Friday. Have a nice weekend.

Even though we're required to wear our green army suits with their modest little PFC stripes on the sleeves, we were treated like students at an exclusive private college. We were civilized; we discussed restaurants; we went to plays like *Rosencrantz and Guildenstern Are Dead* at the American Conservatory Theater in San Francisco. My assassins poem came out in a Bantam Book anthology. When I felt shaky about my identity, I opened the blue paperback, and there I was, on page 162, a published author.

Jenny got a job at a bakery in Carmel, and that gave us a little financial security. To celebrate, I went to the I. Magnin store and bought a green Harris Tweed sport coat I couldn't really afford and a couple of button-down collar shirts so I could pretend that I went to an Ivy League school.

In the midst of horrific danger, it was a safe little world. I'd never seen the ocean before I got to Monterey and kept inhaling its brisk air, which seemed as though it had been scrubbed clean of all impurities on its long voyage to us.

Es ist interessant.
Auf Wiedersehen!
Auf Wiedersehen!

✦ ✦ ✦

"You have a cagey heart," my second wife, Carol, says to me when I show her my story. "Did you ever let it out for poor Jenny?"

I don't think I did. I was frightened and wanted her comfort, but I also wanted the life of my times, which meant sexual freedom. I wasn't, I don't think, in love with her. I was in love with me.

I can still see her walking into that Carmel bakery wearing her too-large, white nylon uniform. Her slip often got caught by the static electricity in the nylon and hung at odd angles, exposing her panties beneath the semitransparent uniform. The job was belittling, and I felt so sorry for her, a Phi Beta Kappa college graduate, walking into that bakery with her underwear showing. And for what? A life in the army? What a price in human dignity we paid.

Both of us were belittled by our subservient lives. I was probably making less per hour than she was. Me, with my master's degree and my published poem. Surely I was worth more than that. I felt sorry for both of us, but you know what: I mostly felt sorry for me. I couldn't wait to get away from the army life and often drove down to Big Sur on Saturdays after I dropped off Jenny at work. I could walk the beaches there and forget who I was.

Toward the end of October 1969, I sat on a rock and filled my head with sunshine and forgetfulness. Out of nowhere three naked women cartwheeled in front of me. Their pubic hair was at my eye level.

"Groovy, soldier boy," one said after she stood up, her breasts wiggling. The clipped sides of my army haircut gave me away. She bent over, kissed me on the lips, and grabbed my hand, rubbing it against the bristly hair of her crotch. Then she ran away laughing. I wanted to be a longhaired hippie guy with these beautiful women available to me. Why oh why did I ever get married?

I walked south along the beach, scrambling over rock outcroppings, getting my shoes wet in the ocean. I came to a cove behind a rock and found a couple moaning their way through sex. They were both naked, sitting up, perched on a blanket. She sat on his lap, facing him, languidly going up and down.

All of a sudden she opened her eyes and looked at me.

"Nice, huh?" she asked, a remark that seemed to take in the sex, the light, the ocean—the everything of being in California just then.

"Nice," her partner said. He began to thrust harder. His eyes were still closed. "Nice."

I walked back to the car slowly, looking for the cartwheeling girls. They had disappeared, and I drove back to Carmel to pick up Jenny from work. I was depressed. I wasn't sure I wanted a wife. I really wanted to fuck women besides Jenny. My mother had told me: I wasn't ready for marriage.

At the end of the bits of German dialogue, a crisp American voice came on the tape.

> *You will now hear some phrases not contained in the dialogue. You are to repeat the phrases.*

39.

Here is the head of Henry Kissinger again, floating, bobbing this way and that. Once again, his eyeglasses become opaque when he turns toward the light.

"*Ja, ja,*" he says and, occasionally, begins laughing.

In this dream, the head of Henry Kissinger is held in place by three braided stainless steel cables that rise fifty or sixty feet from a normal-sized but headless torso seated at a desk far beneath the head. The body wears an elegant blue suit, white shirt, and silk tie. The collar of the shirt wraps around a dark hole. The cables disappear inside the hole and are anchored there inside the body.

The head nods and speaks in that avuncular Henry Kissinger manner.

"Who'd have thought an immigrant boy like me could rule the world."

Then he laughs again.

The body at the desk aligns and taps some papers and puts them in a neat pile. "*Ja, alles in Ordnung. Alles klar.*"

Everything in order. Everything clear.

Across the front edge of the desk is a row of old-fashioned, wooden-handled stamps.

Occasionally a young man in a Harris Tweed sport coat much like the one I bought at I. Magnin presents himself to the headless body and looks up at the head of Henry Kissinger with a kind of awe.

"You are a fine young man," the head of Henry Kissinger booms. Then he throws his head back and laughs. "Yale is it, young man? Are you a Yale man?"

The head of Henry Kissinger looks down. The lenses of his glasses are opaque.

"Yessir, Mr. Kissinger. Class of 1967. A Yale man, yes."

"Very good," the head of Henry Kissinger says.

His right hand, yards beneath his head, picks up a stamp and stamps the young man's face. The stamp head is circular, a foot across.

CIA, the black letters across the young man's face read. CIA.

"You are one of us now," the head of Henry Kissinger proclaims. "One of us. Yes, yes."

Then I am standing there in my Harris Tweed sport coat.

"You, young man. Where are you from?" the head of Henry Kissinger asks me. The arms of the body in front of me cross on its chest. I can see the head, far above, swaying back and forth on the steel cables.

"Columbia perhaps. You look like you might be a Columbia man."

"Arkansas," I say. "The University of Arkansas."

The right arm of the torso reaches toward the stamps and stops in midgesture.

"I have Harvard," the head of Henry Kissinger booms. "I have Yale and Princeton and Columbia. I have Stanford, but not Arkansas, no. I don't think you're one of us, young man. You're just not smart enough. You'll have to move along."

I back away from the desk and pull out a .45.

Bam. Bam. Bam.

I fire and fire some more. The spent cartridges clatter on the floor, smoking as they fall. I miss him every time. I am sweating and terrified.

"I'm a killer, you fucker," I scream up at the head of Henry Kissinger. "You don't understand. I'm a killer."

"I'm sorry," Henry Kissinger laughs. "You missed. You didn't qualify as a killer. Remember? Peter Everwine did that for you. Peter went to Yale. I'm sorry. You're just not one of us, are you?"

But I want to be, don't I? I want to be one of us. I start to cry.

"I'll try, sir," I say. "I'll do what you tell me to do. I'll do whatever you say. Just give me a chance. Give me a chance."

40.

On Wednesday, October 15th, our German teachers took all four or five classes of their students on a field trip to San Francisco. We went to the German Consulate, where we watched an earnest black-and-white movie about a plot to assassinate Hitler, a movie to prove to us that there were "good" Germans as well as these stock SS villains gleefully exterminating Jews.

What did I care about the difference between "good" and "bad" Germans? The Hitler era was a long time ago. Besides, I had my Harris Tweed sport coat on. I thought I looked pretty elegant. God, I was excited. I just wanted to inhale the wonderful possibility of learning a new language in the company of my bright new friends. I wanted to walk narrow cobblestone streets in Europe in my new green jacket.

After the movie, our teachers took all twenty or thirty of us over to Schroeder's German restaurant on Front Street in our civilian clothes. It was a delicious feeling, being in the army and leaving my uniform behind. Our group included two Green Berets. They were hillbillies, one from Tennessee and the other from West Virginia. They didn't look so good out of uniform, though. They looked diminished in their short-sleeved shirts and out-of-style brogans. One of them had a faded tattoo on his forearm. Shabby, shabby. The rest of us, dressed mostly in tweed coats of some kind, look as though we're on our way to teach a university class. Those tweed clothes are our real uniform, and we look jaunty.

While the dark paneling, the beer steins, the murals, and the buck heads on the wall of the restaurant were Germanic clichés, I didn't care. The place seemed European to me, far more European than anything I'd ever seen. I was so excited about the possibility of going to Europe that I could hardly contain myself.

The streets around the restaurant were crowded that day. It was a national day of protest against the war in Vietnam. Since many of the protesters wore black armbands, it was also a day of mourning.

Most of us PFCs were against the war, but we didn't say or do anything as we walked through the throngs of demonstrators. We didn't want to jinx our chances for assignments in Germany.

Even my euphoria couldn't cover up what a strange day it was. Here we were in the army walking among thousands and thousands of antiwar protesters. In the restaurant, we sat under stuffed boar heads and sang *"Deutschland, Deutschland über alles,"* which is still the anthem of Germany.

"What's a little compromise among friends," Goldberg said. "We're the good Americans, right?"

Out of our group, only Neil Renner, a charming blond kid who wore John Lennon glasses and punctuated his speech with little whistling sounds, had the courage to make his opinions known and showed up at the lunch with a black armband around the sleeve of his tweed sport coat. The rest of us looked away, embarrassed. When Neil tried to make a joke, we studied our plates filled with sauerbraten and spaetzle as if he weren't there.

I still have one of the Zap Comix Neil gave me. He bought it in San Francisco. Mr. Natural *Visits the City.*

WATCH OUT a street sign says in the comic. WATCH OUT.

✦ ✦ ✦

Nisei Hall was a two-story cinder-block building named after the Japanese Americans US officials quarantined in what looked a lot like concentration camps after the start of World War II. Some of the Nisei taught American soldiers the Japanese language to help the United States occupy Japan at the end of the war.

Room 250 wasn't very big. It was actually half a room, divided off from the next classroom by a folding accordion door made by, oddly enough, a firm in Janesville. The classroom probably wouldn't have held more than eight students and a teacher. Even our little class of six felt crowded.

Each classroom door had a window so that the supervisor could check on us and our teachers. That supervisor was generally Frau Schneider, who would sneak up on the classes, her head suddenly appearing in the window like a portrait. The language programs had stringent testing standards imposed by the army, and there simply wasn't time for idle chit chat. We had to memorize, memorize, memorize. It was Frau Schneider's job to keep us on schedule.

She occasionally made a surprise visit inside a classroom and threw her arms up and down for emphasis as she went through a dialogue.

Week after week went by at DLI, and we sat in Room 250 of Nisei Hall repeating aloud the dialogues we memorized every night as we listened to our Wollensak tape recorders. We didn't study Beethoven or Goethe or Nietzsche. No, our guides were military people: our dialogues had characters with names like Captain Quick who guided us around. In German his name was more elegant: Hauptmann Schnell.

So what if all the characters had military ranks? They were teaching us German, weren't they? Did it matter how that happened? We had castles ahead of us, river cruises on the Danube, cobblestone avenues, and tall glasses of beer. Did it matter how we got there? We would get to culture later on, wouldn't we?

Night after night, I sat in the corner of the living room, headphones on, snapping the keys of the controls. PLAY, STOP, REWIND, PLAY. The American voice introduced the German.

Listen carefully,

he said. But eventually the voices were German. A little tired, sometimes thick with cigarette smoke or hangovers, they slowly enunciate basic German sentences. While many people my age are getting stoned and listening to Pink Floyd through their earphones, I'm sitting in a chilly two-room apartment in Monterey repeating German.

Was machen Sie in Monterey?
Ich lerne hier Deutsch.
Wirklich? I lerne auch Deutsch.

Through the heavy green Koss headphones with the big plug attached to the Wollensak came the crisp German syllables.

What are you doing in Monterey?
I am here learning German.
Really? I am also learning German.

Every evening I sat in the corner of that apartment going over and over the dialogues. I occasionally looked up and saw Jenny sitting there reading or staring off into space.

I went back to the Defense Language Institute last fall. The Basic German course is still being taught, though with new materials.

"But Hauptmann Schnell continues to be a man of these new times," Ben de la Silva, president of the DLI alumni group, tells me. "I understand that there are photographs taken in East German bathrooms after the Wall came down. 'Hauptmann Schnell Was Here' was written on the toilet walls, as if good old Captain Quick, famous DLI alumni, had beaten everyone there."

I still have the tapes and the books from my class, but I no longer have Jenny, no. Not Jenny sitting there, her legs folded up beneath her. Jenny sitting there, rocking back and forth, holding on to her legs. I should apologize for what I did to her.

I am so sorry, Jenny. Will you forgive me?

But then, back then I have drills to learn. Idioms to master. I don't have time to apologize.

New pattern,

the flat voice says.

New pattern.
Model.

Jung.
Ich bin jung.

Now you do it.

Yes, I say to myself along with him.

Now you do it, Rick.
You do it.

You're young.

Now you do it.

41.

My mother came to visit for Thanksgiving. She was so excited. She hadn't been away from Janesville in years. Before coming to see us, she spent a day in San Francisco's Chinatown.

"I took a secret trip to San Francisco," she said. "Your grandparents would have worried—me alone in that big city. So I didn't tell anyone." She ate Egg Foo Young in Chinatown and, the next day, flew on to Monterey. Even now, decades after the fact, I smile when I think of my chubby and not very cosmopolitan mother clutching her purse as she gets into a cab outside of her hotel for the trip to the airport.

Later that week, on Saturday probably, I took her down to the Big Sur beach I loved. Sure enough, several women were there, naked and cartwheeling.

"Don't see this kind of thing much in Wisconsin," my mother said.

No, you don't, I thought. Bless my mother's heart and her secret trip to San Francisco, but I'm going to take my own secret trip, I vow in my soul. I'm becoming a cultured person. I'm really leaving Janesville for good, I think. I'm taking off for the good life. A grand tour all courtesy of the United States Army. A life of women and good food—a life in Europe.

It was beginning already in Monterey when Jenny and I and the Goldbergs became friends. Nancy Goldberg knew about food and art and a kind of—what?—joie de vivre.

At the Goldbergs' apartment we ate this strange spiky vegetable I'd never seen before called an artichoke. We had Gouda and Jarlsberg cheese. Little pieces on toothpicks. In Janesville the only cheese I remember is Kraft, and that usually in grilled-cheese sandwiches or melted on a hamburger patty. One weekend Nancy made paella using fresh fish from Fisherman's Wharf. I'd never seen squid or cod before.

"It doesn't taste fishy," I said, remembering what my mother always said about the fish in Janesville.

The four of us went to San Francisco and ordered wine with our lunch at Ghirardelli Square. The restaurant had walls of exposed brick, the kind of thing we covered up in Janesville. I heard the word "Chardonnay" for the first time in my life that day.

On another Saturday, Nancy mixed the insides of another strange California fruit with chopped onions and tomatoes, and we had guacamole to dip in with chips before our Mexican-themed dinner with tortillas. That was the first time I'd seen a tortilla.

✦ ✦ ✦

It was a rich life for me. The weekdays were filled with German. *"Die Hauptgeschäftstrasse von Frankfurt ist die Zeil,"* it says in our army homework. The main business street of Frankfurt is the Zeil. Pretty soon, I thought, I'll be driving there. Me in Europe, I thought. I was giddy with the prospect. Jenny and I studied various Dansk dish patterns. Nancy, who had relatives working for the army in Germany, said we can get them at huge discounts from the PX in Germany.

"We will live like royalty over there," she said, "on nothing at all. It's all so cheap."

Yes, I was giddy thinking of myself there, driving on *die Zeil. Die Hauptgeschäftstrasse von Frankfurt ist die Zeil.* I got so excited, I test drove one of the new Volksporsches, squealing around corners while the car salesman asked, "When are you leaving for Germany, Lieutenant?" I didn't correct him about my rank, nor did I tell him that I probably can't afford a Volksporsche with my meager savings and my PFC's pay.

This wasn't a time for reality. I was inventing a new and cultured Rick Ryan. I read Herb Caen in the *San Francisco Chronicle.* On Mondays, with the graduates of Ivy League schools, I discussed movies and ballet performances. Even though I'm on a military post where a brisk trumpet plays reveille at seven A.M., retreat at five thirty P.M., and taps at ten P.M., even though we all wear the green suit, brown shirt, and black tie of the American army uniform, the real military of drilling and bivouacking and fighting a war in Vietnam seemed like it came from another planet.

Most weekends Neil Renner went to San Francisco in his yellow Fiat 850 Spyder convertible, a car so small it almost looked like one of those cars circus clowns wore around their waists held up by suspenders. Neil came back to class on Mondays looking groggy as he showed us Grateful Dead records, psychedelic tie-dyed T-shirts, and comic books by R. Crumb.

My big counterculture moment was going to hear Jerry Rubin, a founder of the Yippie Party and one of the Chicago Seven, speak in the gym of a local Monterey college.

"Program?!" Jerry sputtered to a question someone asks.

He's short, maybe five feet five. He paced back and forth.

"We have no program. After the revolution, we'll do it as we feel it. The pigs always want to take the magic out of things by demanding programs."

Circling in and out of the crowd were the kids who organized the speech. The boys wore Castro-styled fatigues and Mao caps. The girls had on fringed, peasant-styled clothing, with muslin blouses that show off their breasts. I got a hard-on looking at them, but I imagined what would happen if a guy with a short haircut went up to one of them and asked her out.

"Ha!" I said aloud. People turned to stare at me.

They circled through the crowds with steel cooking pots to take donations. "The judges ought to go to jail and see the reality they're sending people to."

"What is law? Law is any goddamned thing the pigs want it to be."

"Pigs"—that word sounded so inflammatory back then.

"You can't riot every day," Rubin said at the end. "You get tired."

> *It's one, two, three, what are we fighting for?*
> *Don't ask me, I don't give a damn.*
> *Next stop is Vietnam.*

The music was scratchy, played over a sound system the boys in the Castro suits had rigged up.

Man, I think, I know that music. I'm in on the deal.

Jerry bowed his head and raised his arms over his head, his fingers formed the V of the peace symbol.

"OK, everyone," a fat girl in a too-tight blouse said as she came on the stage pulling her hair out of her face. Her belly and breasts flopped as she walked. "OK. OK. Thank you for coming."

Jerry disappeared, and the crowd was leaving the gym. Every so often a door banged.

"OK, people. People?" the fat girl said. "OK, listen up. OK, let's use this energy to let the pigs at Fort Ord know what we think of their stinking, awful war. OK, there's a sign-up sheet in the back of the room. OK, people."

The crowd kept leaving.

"Off the pigs," a man in the audience yelled, but he left, too.

"Far fucking out," another man said, right behind him out the door.

✦ ✦ ✦

The next week, going to the PX at Fort Ord to buy a Bob Dylan record, I passed a scraggly little group set up 100 yards from the main entrance to the post. The heavy girl was there holding up a sign that read, BRING THE TROOPS HOME NOW!

The PX didn't have any Bob Dylan records, but they did have one from Jimi Hendrix with a Dylan song, "All Along the Watchtower":

> *Two riders were approaching*
> *And the wind began to howl*

42.

Herr Engeler, Herr Engeler. A slumping bear of a man in a baggy suit. His ties, unlike those of Herr Schefke, always hung loose and askew. He usually arrived late to Room 250 with papers sticking out of his accordion-like briefcase. He sat down with a sigh, as if the world weighed heavily on him, and his briefcase hit the floor a moment later like a punctuation mark.

"*Na, ja,*" he said most days, his hair falling across his face. Oh dear.

He looked down at the linoleum squares on the floor for a moment, gathering his thoughts. Then he looked up, combing his hair back with his fingers. He looked wistful, with a little smile, as if he shared a secret with us. The other instructors were so brisk, getting our German ready, polishing us for our days in the *Vaterland*, but Herr Engeler seemed like he was preparing us for something else. He seemed to feel sorry for us.

Again, he ran his fingers through his hair, pulling it back over his head. He pointed at one of us.

"*Ach, ja, wir beginnen jetzt mit Ihnen.*"

We begin with you.

He pointed at PFC Chuck Quarles, in the back row. Blushing, Chuck said his part.

Wie heißt die Strasse hier?

Herr Engeler pointed at Renner next.

Die Zeil, die Hauptgeschäftsstraße von Frankfurt.

Sentence by sentence, we went through the dialogue in the first hour, each of us taking a turn. While this is the normal routine of our mornings, Herr Engeler seemed to have his mind elsewhere.

It was the end of April, and our course ended in July. We were all beginning to feel jittery. The bargain we'd made with the army was coming to an end. In July the army could do whatever it wanted with us. Vietnam was always a possibility.

Early on, Lee Rasmussen had reminded us of that. He started with us in September, chattering away during the breaks outside of Nisei Hall.

"Gonna get me one of those Porsche automobiles over there in ole Deutschland," he said. "Gonna drive me up and down those ole autobahns like no one's ever driven them before."

He had the thumb and index finger of his right hand on the knot of his black GI necktie and wiggled it back and forth, as if it were too tight or too loose or too something. A nervous tic.

"Gonna have me some of that good life over there in Germany."

In the mornings, though, when we were supposed to repeat the dialogues, Lee couldn't talk. All he could do was smile and wiggle that tie knot back and forth. It was quite strange, really. Even the career sergeants, who weren't very smart, could sputter out a few phrases, but not Lee. Pretty soon he disappeared from our class and was put on permanent KP while he awaited reassignment.

The last time I saw Lee he was wiping off tables in the company mess hall. Then Lee was gone. We heard he'd been sent to combat radioman's school and, we supposed, to one of the most dangerous jobs of all in the Vietnam War—going through the jungle with fifty pounds of radio on his back. When the radio was set up, it had a giant whip antenna attached that said to the enemy, "Here I am. Come and get me."

✦ ✦ ✦

Years later, I looked up his name on a list of those commemorated by the Vietnam war memorial.

God.

There he was. Specialist Four Lee S. Rasmussen.

Casualty was on May 5, 1970
in BINH THUAN, SOUTH VIETNAM
HOSTILE, GROUND CASUALTY
MULTIPLE FRAGMENTATION WOUNDS

Or maybe it was another Lee S. Rasmussen. The truth is, I'll never know the truth.

Perhaps that's the truth of those terrible times.

We'll never know the truth.

✦ ✦ ✦

We moved through our days at the Defense Language Institute like men walking beneath a long row of swords dangling from threads attached to the ceiling. One could fall at any time, though, God knows, I tried to forget about the army. I went for walks along the coast at Big Sur and camped in the hills. I dreamed of Europe. I imagined myself lounging at sidewalk cafés with a glass of beer, or sitting at a table covered by pristine white linens as I speeded by train across the European countryside.

In all of this I hardly ever thought about Jenny, who trudged off every day in one of her white nylon uniforms to her job in the bakery.

Herr Engeler seemed even more distracted than usual that April. He would lose his place in the dialogue, or begin speaking what we students called real German, the German of our teachers' actual lives. That German, while vaguely familiar, was speeded up and slurred and beyond our powers of recognition.

"Do you think Herr Engeler knows where we're going?" Art Schmid wondered aloud during the break. "Maybe he's seen our orders. Maybe he's afraid to tell us. Maybe we're not going to Germany."

"I think I'm getting assigned to The Grateful Dead as their translator," Neil Renner said and whistled.

"Shhh," Herr Engeler said the next afternoon when he came in the classroom. He clutched his giant briefcase to his chest, as if protecting it. After looking out the window in the classroom door to make sure no one was watching, he set the briefcase on the table at the front of the room.

"Herr Renner, you will stand watch at the door, *bitte schön*, and give us one of your whistles if you see Frau Schneider marching down on us, *verstehen Sie?*"

Renner grinned, probably amused that he would be chosen to guard anything.

Herr Engeler opened the mouth of the briefcase and reached inside, and I shivered. It seemed like he was going to let us in on a secret of some kind.

He set a gray-covered book on the table. *Das Dritte Reich* was the simple title. *The Third Reich*. The Hitler era. Beside it he put an old map, some pictures, and an official-looking document in script.

"*Ich war auch einmal Soldat,*" he said, sitting on the top of the table and brushing the hair out of his face. "*Genau wie Sie.*"

I was also once a soldier. Just like you.

"*Es war einmal ein Krieg . . .*" He looked off in the distance. That's how fairy tales began.

He repeated himself in English: "Once upon a time, *ja,* there was a war."

"*Hier ist das Haus, wo das Knäbchen Albert Engeler wohnt mit seiner Mutter, seinem Vater, und seiner geliebten Schwester Erika.*"

Here is the house where the young boy Albert Engeler lived with his mother, his father, and his beloved sister Erika.

He passed around an old black-and-white photograph of his childhood house. It was faced with stucco and had a series of figures over the door. That family of four stood on the walkway in front of the house, holding on to one another.

"*Guck' mal,*" Herr Engeler said. "*Oben an der Tür, die Engelsfiguren.*" Angel figures above the door. "*Wie mein Familienname. Engeler ist er, der Engel macht.*" An Engeler is one who makes angels.

"Here, look at this photograph, *bitte sehr.* I was lawyer. *Ich war Jurist.*"

Indeed, there was a younger Herr Engeler, mostly just a thinner version of the man sitting in front of us, with his hair falling across his face, in the black gown of someone graduating from law school. He smiled, a face for the good things of the world. The photograph is small and cracked, as if it had been in someone's wallet.

Herr Engeler then handed around a copy of his diploma with the Gothic lettering. It smelled old, like dead hope.

"But *der* Herr Hitler was interested in me, also, you see. He called me, about this war they were having. I tried begging off. I told them I was busy, but no, they insisted. They made me an aide to a general. Here."

In this photograph a dour-looking Albert Engeler stands beside an open-topped Mercedes command car in his over-sized army uniform. Its sleeves almost cover his hands.

"Look at that car," Herr Engeler said. "I was the youngest officer and the chauffer and the car polisher."

He handed around more pictures of himself and his army buddies. He got up then, and glanced out the window of the classroom door.

"*Ja, daß ist das Märchen*," Herr Engeler said and sighed. "That's certainly the fairy tale. *Es war einmal ein Soldat im Krieg gegen Russland*. Once upon a time there was a soldier in the war against Russia. *Daß war ich*. That was me—headed to the Russian front on the general staff. Here. *Sehen Sie*."

He unfolded a yellowed map with blue and red and green routes on top of black details. The way from Germany to Russia. *Kriegskarte* was the heading. War Map. Funny, though, the army just took the highway to Russia. Their route looked like the outline of a vacation trip.

"We left in the summer. I drove. We had the top down. Glorious. The general was in the backseat. The troops were behind us in trucks. Bands along the way. We sang 'Lili Marlene,' and the general saluted those who'd come out to see us off. The onlookers waved flags and shouted 'Heil Hitler!' We commandeered rooms in the finest hotels along the highway. It was a good life, driving to Russia in our open Mercedes."

Herr Engeler smiled at us and, with his hand over his heart, began to sing in a baritone voice.

Vor der Kaserne
Vor dem großen Tor
Steht eine Laterne
Steht sie noch davor.

As he finished the opening of the song, his hand went out, and a trembling finger pointed out Lili Marlene, somewhere beyond where we sat in Room 250.

"Not a gun was fired until we got to some town in Russia. I've forgotten its name. That's where we dug in. We somehow got cut off from the rest of the brigade. Cut off for evermore. It was the fall then. *Kennen Sie diese Geschichte?* Do you know this history?"

Goldberg, our history student, raised his hand to answer "Yes," but Herr Engeler didn't see him. He was talking to some ghostly reality at the back of Room 250 on that sunny afternoon in the spring of 1970, in Monterey, California. The six of us in our brown shirts stared at him, at the colored arrows on the *Kriegskarte*, drawn so boldly across Russia—stared at the smiling young man in his graduation gown—stared at the frowning young man beside the Mercedes-Benz.

"*Ach, ja. Schrecklich.* It got worse and worse. We were so isolated. Our little group—we had our own little war. The big war was on the radio until our batteries went dead. All day long, on the radio, the generals pleaded for artillery. The trucks with the guns were lost somewhere. *So kalt.* Cold, cold. *Ach, die Toten.* So many dead. *Alles verloren.* It's all lost. Winter. So cold, cold. The dead stacked all around us. It was too cold to bury them. The ground broke the tips of the axes. We stacked our *Kameraden.* Made bunkers of them to protect our riflemen. Even in death they could not escape the war."

> Underneath the lantern
> by the barrack gate,
> Darling I remember
> the way you used to wait;

His voice trembled this time. His finger shook as he pointed.

✦ ✦ ✦

"You're not going to believe this," Quarles told someone at the break.

"Shhh," Renner said, as Frau Schneider went by, bowing her head, trying to hear our gossip, nodding, not missing a beat.

43.

Herr Engeler was pacing back and forth when we came back from the break.

"*Ach, ja*," he said and sat back on the table. "*Wo sind wir gewesen?*" Where were we?

"*Im Russland*," Goldberg said.

"Yes, in Russia," Herr Engeler said, starting up again.

In terrible Mother Russia. It was so cold, but then in spring comes the warm weather and all the artillery shells a general could want. Unfortunately they are coming to us from the other side.

My general was quite depressed. He had this headquarters tent and sat at a little table bundled up with four or five coats on, staring at photographs of his wife and children. With each month of the spring, he removed a coat.

For a while, he drank brandy as he sat there. He had one of those windup Victrolas and would play these thick, shellac records. Of course his favorite song was "Lili Marlene." He played it over and over. The record became scratchier and scratchier, and the sound of the woman's voice got farther and farther away from us, as if even she knew that we were losing the war and wanted to get away from our lost little brigade.

In May, he was down to two coats, and he reached into his pants pocket and handed me the keys to the Mercedes and gave me one of these maps you see here.

"Du musst zurück nach Deutchland fahren, Leutnant Enge-ler," he told me. Drive back to Germany. He used the familiar form with me, as if he were my father. *"Wir sind alle tot hier, versteht's du,"* he said. We're all dead here. He wanted to save one of us.

So early the next morning, I took one baked potato. It was my allotment. It was the only kind of food we had.

Oh, that car. We'd arrived at the battle in the bright prom-ise of summer with the top down and the wind in our faces. When they started shooting at us, we forgot about the car. When it started snowing, I covered it with a tarp, and there it sat for the winter. Incredibly, the car started on the first try, though I couldn't get the top up. I didn't care. I put it in gear and headed on down the road.

The guard looked me over as I left the camp. I told him I was reporting back to headquarters. The general had given me a note, like a permission slip to stay home from school, and I showed the guard that.

"I don't care what this note says. You are a traitor to leave us here like this. You should die with your regiment," he said, but he nonetheless waved me on, and I left our doomed camp, the rising sun at my back, driving on this road back to Ger-many. Even with the sun, I was freezing cold because the top was down. Aside from the chill, the big challenge was avoiding all the holes in the road from artillery shells.

I passed soldiers once in a while.

"Hey, da," they yelled.

"Hey, da," I yelled back. Sometimes I gave them rides; sometimes they just looked at me with these gray, starved faces. They were all eyes, shuffling along.

✦ ✦ ✦

I had extra gas in tanks strapped to the running boards, but I ran out of gasoline somewhere in Poland. I started walking. At first, most of the others on the road were soldiers like me fleeing back to Germany, but then people started walking toward us, Poles fleeing the armies coming east from Germany. I knew some Polish and asked a man what the territory was like ahead, in the west toward Germany. It's all crazy they told me—soldiers everywhere—Americans, Russians, everyone shooting at everyone else.

I had some money, German marks—probably worthless by then—but I gave all of it to the man for his clothes, and he took mine. So now he was a German soldier headed back to the front, and I was a Polish peasant headed to Germany. It all made perfect sense then. Funny, those clothes of his smelled like rotten strawberries. I've never forgotten the scent.

I walked and walked. I slept in ditches and drank water from feeding troughs in farm fields. It was still cold there in the east. I have arthritis in my elbow now for all the times I broke the ice on top to get to the water below. When I talk about it, the pain shoots through here.

I was lucky. I could speak some English, some Russian, and some Polish. I'd been an actor at the university. I didn't know it then, but I was about to have my moment. Funny, isn't it, how your moment just slips up on you.

I walked and walked. I'd lost my map, so I never knew exactly where I was. Some nights I could hear the Russians singing around their campfires. Some nights it was the Poles. Less and less often it was the Germans.

After days and days of walking, I was stopped by American soldiers in a Jeep. They had that same haunted look that our soldiers had. All eyes. I spoke to them in Russian. I made quite a show, and they drove me to this German village they'd captured and made the *Bürgermeister* feed me.

I spoke Polish to him. That *Bürgermeister* just fell all over himself bowing and bringing me dishes himself—you know, taking them from the waiters and giving them to me and muttering *"Bitte schön, der Herr."* Thank you sir. *Lebersuppe, sauerbraten, kohl*—liver soup, marinated roast beef, cabbage—a real German meal. I hadn't eaten food like that in months, but I made the mistake of using the German word *Salz*—salt—and the *Bürgermeister* heard my accent from just that one word and knew I was German.

Before I knew it, he threw my coat at me.

"Verräter!" he screamed. Traitor.

I was back on the road. Weeks went by. They seemed like hours. An American truck stopped. A soldier with a gun sat at the back and lifted up a tarp and motioned me up there. All Polish civilians looking at the floor. I thought the game was up, but I didn't say a word. After an hour of driving, the truck stopped.

"Here you are," the soldier at the back says and points to the ground with his gun. When I just sit there, afraid to get out, he says, "Stoppen you-a here-a." I always loved the way the Americans made up words, as if they thought their inventions were a foreign language.

I got down from the back of the truck and walked with the Poles into the American compound. I worked there for several days, digging a trench around the perimeter, cleaning the latrines—peasant work. They fed us hamburgers. Every night hamburgers and ice cream for dessert. Never in my life before had I eaten butter pecan ice cream.

I was homesick for Berlin, so one night I just left. I'd picked up a compass somewhere and started walking through the woods. I had to backtrack. I had come too far west. I had a little knapsack with food and a jar of water in it. I got to this river that was a border somewhere. There was a bridge, but the Russians guarding it wouldn't let me cross, so I went a mile downstream, took off my clothes, and, holding them overhead, swam across. It was so cold my teeth began to chatter halfway across. Then I was shaking all over, and my legs were knocking, one against the other, and all my swimming did was spin me around, naked, in the middle of the river, but the gods were kind, the current, oh sweet God the current lifted me right up to the shore like a sinner God wanted to save. Before I knew it, I was sitting on rocks at the far side of the river, and the morning sun came over the pine trees and warmed me. It took an hour or two, but finally the shivers went out of me.

I lost my compass, and then I lost myself. It was getting more and more dangerous as I walked along, but listen to me, my friends, customs and languages will get you anywhere. You must pay attention. *Immer aufpaßen.*

The first custom I had to learn was that Americans would shoot you if they saw you on the roads, and the Russians would shoot you if they found you in the woods. Figure that one out. It made traveling hard, but somehow I got there, to Berlin. It was late summer by then. The days had gone by as if in a dream. I had lost so much weight from the trip that I had to hold my pants up with my hand, but there I was— wasn't I?—walking into my little town holding up my pants, past the stores, the baker and butcher, and the park with its pond where I sailed my little boats; there I was, thinking the war, thank God was over, walking into my little town, looking for my parents and my sister.

Oh, I remember now. There was this military school at the outskirts of my little town. Inside a fence that looked as though it were made of old sword blades painted black, I saw these French officers in their little round caps and their capes doing marching drills. The school had been turned into a POW camp. I crept around but there wasn't a German soldier in sight. The Berlin area had become a dangerous place for soldier-age Germans by then. It seemed like the war was over. Only Hitler and his comrades didn't yet have the news.

The uniforms of these Frenchmen were ragged and filthy. Their boots were torn, coming apart, but the men had polished them somehow. They carried themselves with style, these men did. They sang as they marched. I don't know why, but for the first time in the awful war, I began to cry. Such lost beauty in the world. The Frenchmen marching round and round. I dabbed my eyes and I walked into the school yard there. French was another language I knew, and I spoke to them.

"Attention! Attention!" I yelled. "You are all free. You can go home now. Go. Go home. The war is over for you."

They were nervous at first, but eventually they got their barrack bags and walked out. As they left, some of them clicked their heels together and saluted me. One man dropped his bag, gripped my shoulders with his hands, and kissed me on both cheeks. I hoped they would make it home. They were so elegant, but who knew what would happen to them—who knew anything back then?

44.

At first my house looked the same—the angels over the front door still protected us. But, on closer inspection, I saw that the bushes were filled with weeds and had grown into a tangled mess. The manicured lawn of my childhood was brown. Likely dead. The only green was a patch or two of weeds. My father had religiously stood there with a hose, watering it. I went to the door. I could see that it was ajar. The lock was broken. I pushed the door all the way open. The hallway was filled with my father's business papers; furniture was thrown around. The paintings were gone; the silverware drawer had been turned over on the counter. Empty. It was all like a dream. The back door was open, and so were many of the windows. It was a warm fall day. I expected to see my sister come down the stairs singing "La-la-lor-la." She did that when she was happy.

I walked around and around in the house, but no one was there. No one had been there for a long time.

I finally stopped at my childhood bedroom, which for some reason had been left untouched. My framed grade school diplomas were still neatly there on the wall. The bed was made with the blanket that had my college medallion on it. I sat on the bed and saw the line of the toes of my old shoes peeking out from under the edge of the blanket. That's where my mother always kept them. I lay down and closed my eyes. I fell asleep and dreamed that I heard the *clitter, clitter* noise my father's push lawn mower made. I could hear the back door slam several times as my sister went in and out with her friends. I opened my eyes and suddenly saw cobwebs stretched across the ceiling of my childhood bedroom. Instead of *clitter, clitter*, I heard the *thud, thud* of artillery shells. The wind blew the back door shut.

I sat up on the bed and thought I should cry. I wanted to cry, but I couldn't. I felt like I was in some absurdist theater production.

✦ ✦ ✦

My little town was filled with children and old people and women. All the men my age had gone to the war. I limped, pretending to have been wounded. The Nazi order was crumbling by then, though its leaders called for "Total War" and put everyone in the military. *Volkssturmsoldaten* they were called. Here, you can see it in this history book of the Third Reich.

He handed the gray book out, and we passed it around.

See, on page 570—the People's Storm Soldiers. It was funny. As someone with military experience, I was made commander of fourteen- and fifteen-year-olds, along with pensioners. I should have told them my main experience was being a coward and a deserter. The guard at my war camp and that *Bürgermeister* were right—I was a traitor.

My *Volkssturmsoldaten* unit only had one weapon—an antitank gun with just one shot. We were supposed to defend the whole town with it. The children took this all so seriously. It was like playing army. Me—I'd had enough of playing army.

And look here, on page 573, Hitler shaking the hands of the boy soldiers. Children being sent to war. They weren't old enough to shave. It was almost over by then. Hitler only had months to go. Why didn't he quit? I ask you now. Why didn't he just stop and save what was left?

The Russians were slowly moving in. They brought food along. Mostly potatoes, but it was food, so I got to be friendly with them. I could speak Russian, remember. They made me a detective, gave me a police badge and some credentials. What they really wanted was a spy, and I made up a few stories to keep them happy so I could keep getting food from them.

The Russians were thugs—or maybe they were just victors. When you lose a war, you have to remember that the enemy gets your stuff. Anyway, these Russians were peasants. Indoor flush toilets fascinated them. They'd never seen anything like them. They kept shitting outside, the way they always did. You'd see them squatting in the ditches. The toilets—why, the toilets they used to wash their potatoes in.

The Russians eventually got tired of me. They didn't like my made-up stories and arrested me one day and locked me in a stadium with a bunch of other ne'er-do-wells. They intended to march us to Siberia or death, whatever came first.

For the second time in the war, a stranger saved me. I was marching with this huge fat man. At night, the guards let us sleep in the grass beside the road. First the fat man gave me his coat to use as a blanket. It was fall and getting cold. He said his fat protected him from the chill night air. Then, one evening, two or three days along the road, he told me that he would die on the march. His health was too frail, he said, so he was willing to risk his life for me. He said he would protect me while I escaped. I left him that extra coat, and he fluffed it up to make it look like I was sleeping beside him. The last sight I had of him came when I climbed up a wall and I could see him in the moonlight with this shape nested beside him like a child or a lover.

There was a ten P.M. curfew then. Anyone out after that time could be shot. Luckily, I had kept my police badge and just banged on the door of an inn yelling "Polizei! Polizei!" That badge turned out to be very handy. I decided to walk along the autobahn back to Frankfurt, and I used the badge to commandeer food and new clothing. I entered the American Sector with a German sausage under my arm.

"I have news, big news," I said as I strolled past the MPs carrying my sausage and speaking my best English. "I've just come from the Russian Front and it's all over for the Germans. The war is over."

Herr Engeler held up his arms like a conductor bringing the music to an end. He bowed his head. His hair fell across his face. A moment later the buzzer sounded announcing the afternoon break.

45.

Frau Schneider could smell that something was up, and there she was, puffing on a cigarette, bent down like Groucho Marx, winding her way among the students taking their ten-minute breaks away from German. She was listening for gossip.

Herr Porzig was our next instructor. *Ach, ja.* Herr Porzig. Giant glasses that looked like goggles, his right arm gone somewhere above the elbow. A vigorous man who strode into the classroom like the tank commander he'd been in the Second World War. He strode in and shoved a couple of the desks out of the way with his good left hand. He was a powerful man.

"*Jetzt beginnen wir,*" he said.

"*Jawohl, Mein Herr!*" Renner said and saluted.

Herr Porzig grabbed Renner by the front of his shirt.

"*Und Sie, mein Freund,*" Herr Porzig said, putting his face with its big glasses right in front of Neil Renner, "*wenn Sie leben wollen, dann müssen Sie aufpassen.*"

And you, my friend, if you will live, then you must pay attention.

One day, I asked Herr Porzig about the dictionaries. The army had issued us Langenscheidt's dictionaries with their yellow plastic covers.

"*Die beste Wörterbücher sind von Cassels herausgegaben,*" Herr Porzig told us, folding his arms across his chest. He scowled and nodded his head. How could anyone possibly disagree? The best dictionaries are published by Cassels.

"Then why," I asked in English, "doesn't the army buy us the best if they want us to fight for them?" I don't think I really cared. I just wanted to annoy him.

"*Warum?*" Herr Porzig asked, his neck getting long and longer as his head came up. Why? "*Warum, Sie fragen. Warum?*"

The neck and the head came higher and higher as if he were back in the turret. He turned back and forth, searching out the enemy.

"*Warum ist Krieg?* The war is why."

His big glasses were like goggles, like those a tank commander wore.

"In war you give everything. You must sacrifice. It takes all you have to fight the Communists. It takes blood and bones. *Blut und Bienen. Der Krieg kommt niemals zu Ende kommt.* The war, *ja*, the war never ends. *Niemals kommt er zu einem Ende.*"

The stub of his arm went up and down. It waved back and forth like a warning of the blood and bones we would lose. He started shoving desks against the walls. *Blam. Blam.*

"The Communists took over everything. *Die sogenannte Volksrepublik Deutschland.* The so-called People's Republic of Germany. They took my house, my land. *Scheisse.* Shit. You give up blood and bones to win. *Blut und Knochen. Jawohl, mein Herr. Jawohl.* You must sacrifice."

Blam a desk went this way. *Blam* a desk went that way. *Blam. Blam. Blam.*

46.

Blam, all right. I stayed out of the way of those desks until the bell rang.

A few days later, soldiers in the Ohio National Guard shot and killed four students during the war protests at Kent State in Ohio. *Blam. Blam. Blam. Blam.* The day after that, my orders finally came. I saved them. The orders, I mean. I wasn't thinking about the dead at Kent State back then. I was too worried about me. I hardly noticed what happened at Kent State.

I have the orders right here: "5 MAY 1970. SPECIAL ORDER NUMBER 100. PERMANENT CHANGE OF STATION. RYAN, RICHARD M., PFC, Co. C, DLIWC, Assigned to: Fourth Regt (MPC) Fort Gordon, GA 30905 to attend course 830-95B10 for approx 8 wks."

Eighteen of us listed there for Military Police School.

"What does that mean?" Jim Eastlake asked.

"Maybe they'll send you to Kent State," Neil Renner said and whistled one of his trilling little tunes. It sounded like birdsong. "Vietnam wasn't enough; they're starting a war against the hippies."

As I write this, I realize now that I was passing through the famous and the horrible moments of my time on the wrong side.

"See. I told you," my friend Tom Bamberger says.

"I thought I was getting away with something," I say.

"Nah. You were just kidding yourself, walking around in that uniform with one of those short haircuts thinking you were some kind of hippie and you were really just a guy in the army with a gun. The man over there with a gun."

✦ ✦ ✦

Oh yes, I almost forgot: the army got even with Neil Renner for the black armband he wore to the lunch in San Francisco. Unlike the rest of us, Neil was sent to Vietnam.

After the orders were handed out, one of the Green Berets came up to Neil while he stood in a circle of us, telling one of his stories.

"Fuck with us," the Green Beret said and shoved Neil in the chest, "fuck with us, Renner, and you'll never get out alive. You understand that, Renner? Do the rest of you understand that, too?"

He pointed his finger like a pistol at each of the rest of us standing there.

"Fuck with us, and you'll never get out alive."

✦ ✦ ✦

I didn't want to look him up, but I had to, my eyes half-closed as my finger went down the names. He wasn't all that far from Rasmussen:

NEIL P. RENNER
Casualty was on Sep 20, 1970
In QUANG TIN, SOUTH VIETNAM
HOSTILE, GROUND CASUALTY
GUN, SMALL ARMS FIRE

47.

"We trained those boys at Kent State," the sergeant said, strutting back and forth in front of us, his thumbs tucked in his utility belt. Goldberg and I and Eastlake and fifteen others are sitting in a classroom at Military Police School, Fort Gordon, Georgia.

"We trained them in how to shoot those hippies. You're not going to read this in any of those Commie newspapers that fool the public, but that was some damn fine shooting. Even got a song out of it. You've heard it, haven't you, all you guys that used to be hippies. 'For What It's Worth.' Buffalo Springfield recorded it. I always figured that group was named after the Springfield rifle that killed all the buffalo. Anyway, I fixed that song up for you."

He flicked on the overhead projector.

> There's a man with a gun over there
> Telling me I got to beware
> That man is one badass MP.
> That MP is going to be me.

"I'll bet all you hippie assholes know the tune to this one, so I'm going to divide you up into a little MP chorus."

With that he roughly separated the classroom into quarters, and, at the tops of our lungs, we each shouted out a line of the song:

There's a man with a gun over there
Telling me I got to beware.
That man is one badass MP.
That MP is going to be me.

"I am," I said to myself, "a long way from Ralph Waldo Emerson."

✦ ✦ ✦

"The Colt .45, men. The storied Colt .45," Sergeant Schumacher said. We trainees sat in bleachers in front of the pistol range.

"The gun was invented to kill Moro tribesmen in the Philippines. Used in close combat it could stop a man cold. The exit wound could tear half your back off."

He put on his yellow Ray-Ban Aviator sunglasses.

"You." Sergeant Schumacher pointed at Jim Eastlake. "Come here."

Jim had this mincing kind of walk, and his head moved back and forth as if he were saying no to each step.

"Good. Now stand there and hold this."

The sergeant pulled a large, beat-up doll out of a bag sitting at his feet. It was about three feet long. One arm was missing, and its eyeballs were gone. It looked like a battered child, but it had been dressed in an embroidered nightgown, with colored stitching around the top and back.

Sergeant Schumacher handed it to Eastlake.

"Here," he said, straightening Eastlake's arm so he held the doll away from his body. "Just hold it out like this. Don't move."

The last sentence made Eastlake jerk his head, but he held the doll away from his body as if it were putrid.

Sergeant Schumacher picked up a .45—and then, in one quick motion, rammed an ammunition clip into the grip, chambered a round, and fired into the chest of the doll.

A fine red mist sprayed out from the back of the doll, some of it hitting Eastlake.

This all happened so fast it had the quality of a dream.

"Oh, how awful," Eastlake yelled and flipped the doll on the ground and jumped back, trying to wipe away the red spray on his fatigue shirt.

He looked stunned and shook his hands, trying to get the fine red dots off.

"I can't take this," he sobbed.

"You're all right, son. Just a little close-quarter shooting. Nothing to worry about. Why don't you sit down now."

"Oh, oh, oh," Eastlake whimpered. He kept shaking his hands.

Eastlake stumbled back to join the rest of us on the bleachers.

"See this?" Sergeant Schumacher held the chest of the doll toward us. It had a small, powder-circled hole in the night-gown. "Now see this." The back of the doll was a tangle of clothing and plastic, all colored blood red. "The back is gone."

Eastlake began vomiting, and we moved away from him.

"Come on, son," Schumacher said, crouching down by where Eastlake bent over throwing up. "Don't take this so seriously."

He held out the battered doll toward Eastlake. I was several feet away and could smell how rotten the doll was.

"It's just ketchup, son. A freezer bag full of ketchup."

Eastlake was shivering.

"But it's the army," Eastlake stuttered. "All this killing."

"Come on, son. Get in the spirit of things here. It's just cowboys and Indians like you used to play, but now the guns are real."

Eastlake was gasping.

"Son, it was just a demonstration. Badass MPs don't get upset like this."

A few days later, Peter Everwine qualified for me on the .45, and my days as an untrained killer began.

Boom. Boom. Snare.

48.

"You thought you were a Jew," Albert Speer says to me in a dream. "It never occurred to you that you might be a Nazi."

He's standing there in a high-collared gray overcoat. He wears the peaked hat of a German officer. The wind howls. Snow swirls around us. All the color of the scene is washed out except the pale flesh of Albert Speer's face.

"So romantic, the Nazis chasing you. Just like in the movies." He smiles.

"How could I be a Jew?" I say. "I'm Scotch-Irish. A Methodist from Wisconsin."

"*Ach, ja,*" he says and shakes his right index finger at me. "I know what happens. The American tourists arrive at Dachau. A short drive from Munich. An afternoon's—how do you say?—getaway. They stand in the one barrack that's left and pronounce it all 'Unbelievable. Cruel—how could they.' *Ja, ja.* I know. They, of course, would never do anything like this. As they sit down for dinner, they can almost feel the starvation—feel how the Jews must have felt."

His voice trails off.

"But we know," he says. "We know about the Indians. We know about the Vietnamese. Now the Iraqis. Who's next? Millions and millions dead. We're watching. You're catching up with us. If I am guilty, you are guilty, too."

He shakes his index finger in the wind. In the snow.

"*Ja, ja,* you think you're innocent. We'll see, Herr Ryan. We'll see."

He pulls the tall collar of his gray coat up around his ears to protect them from the snow, which the wind is driving faster and faster.

"Herr Ryan, you must know the novel *Herz der Finsternis,* yes. By Joseph Conrad. How do you say in English: *Heart of Darkness?* A novel about evil. In that book, the people go upriver in Africa and find evil. That is the story. Well, in my story, we were the evil. We were the evil people journeyed to, Herr Ryan. People came to us. We were the heart of darkness. People like you, Herr Ryan, came to Adolf and Hermann and me and the others. We were already there, waiting, and now perhaps you've joined us, yes, in the heart of darkness."

He grabbed my hand. His touch felt cold, like refrigeration piping. So cold. Sticky cold. He held my hand to his heart. I could feel it. Beating cold sludge. A heart of slurried ice.

49.

Then we got our orders for Germany. The Twenty-Second
MP Group (Customs). Nobody at MP School knew much
about the unit, except that it had plainclothes investigators.
No uniforms. That sounded so great, so exciting—the idea that
I might be a civilian in Germany, traveling around—my uniform and the army forgotten. I'd get there first and then Jenny
would join me once I got settled. A little tour of Europe for
the two of us.

I divided my good luck into manila folders and labeled them
and filled them with brochures. SKIING. TRAVEL. DISHES. It
was going to be my grand tour. I'd be a long, long way from
Janesville. I cut out articles on the great French skier Jean-
Claude Killy. I had brochures on Paris and London. I picked
out the Dansk dishes I liked. SKIING. TRAVEL. DISHES. I
said those words over and over. In the world of Jean-Claude
Killy and Paris and Dansk there were no guns or dirty wars.

"I'm going to Europe," I said over and over to myself.

The word sounded ancient and lovely.

Slowly the word "Vietnam" was leaving my brain.

I'd done it: by God, I'd done it. I'd escaped the fucking
war. The army—can you believe it?—was making my dreams
come true.

Goldberg and I and a bunch of others showed up at Fort
Jackson, South Carolina. We slept in a barrack full of trans-
ferees. Most of our temporary roommates were on their way

to Vietnam, but not us, by God, not us. A few days later we boarded a chartered airliner and flew to Europe, almost the way civilians did.

Once we were seated, I pulled out the manila folders from my briefcase and fingered the titles. SKIING. TRAVEL. DISHES. I could see myself sitting at outdoor cafés. I was smoking Gauloises instead of my usual Winstons. I was drinking a crisp Chablis. It was amazing. I had turned a problem into a solution.

Yes, the army was doing all that for me, for free. For fucking free. I had beaten the system. It was all a nightmare that had turned into a dream.

50.

Gutleut *Kaserne*. The US Army Transfer Station in Frank-furt. It roughly translated as Fort Good People. An old German fortress built of red bricks. Oh, look, here it is, a couple of clicks away, on Wikipedia. See it? If you didn't know better, you'd think it was a university. A place of learning.

Clang. Clang. Clang.

It's six a. m. Someone is walking up and down the aisles of the Tenth Replacement Battalion barrack with a steel pot and spoon.

Clang. Clang. Clang.

"Fuckers think you're special," the buck sergeant says as we fall into formation on the cobblestone parade ground in the center of the *Kaserne*. "I want you back out here in two minutes with your toothbrushes."

Ten minutes later, and we're on our hands and knees scrubbing the cobblestones with our Crest toothpaste.

"I want those stones to shine," the sergeant yells.

"The Nazis used to make the Jews do this," a PFC next to me mutters.

No, that part is not on Wikipedia.

51.

Pretty soon, though, I'm done with *Gutleut Kaserne*. A corporal walks me and another GI over to the Frankfurt *Hauptbahnhof*, where we are to catch a train for Heidelberg. The headquarters of the Twenty-Second MP Group is located there.

"Listen up," a corporal says to me and the other soldier as he leaves us on the train platform. "You're not to speak with any German civilians. Got that? You might give away some secret information. And you, Ryan, no translating, OK?"

I wanted to tell him that I didn't know any secrets, but I kept my opinions to myself.

So we didn't answer the questions of the two German men who also had tickets for our compartment. They began talking about us as if we weren't there.

"*Ist es möglich, daß das Dritte Reich von Soldaten wie diesen zuende gebracht wurde? Dumme wie die, müssen Helfer gehabt haben.*"

They begin to laugh.

"What do you think he's saying, Ryan?"

That they don't think soldiers as dumb as us could have defeated the Third Reich is what he said, but I don't say that. I just shrug.

One of the Germans comes over to look at my name tag and my pistol medal.

"*Ah, der Herr Ryan hier hat ein Eisernes Kreuz, Dritter Klasse. Ich habe auch so was gehabt im Zweiten Weltkrieg. Genau wie er.*"

"What's he talking about?"

"That he was a soldier, just like me, in the Second World War and wore a medal like mine."

"Well you can just tell him that we won that war and we're not like him."

But I don't say anything. I look out the window at the backs of the stucco houses streaming by.

"People just don't realize how powerful we are," the soldier goes on. "We win all of our wars."

"*Soldaten wie diese haben den Krieg nicht gewonnen. Die Russen haben den Krieg gewonnen.*"

It takes me a minute to translate this, and I keep being thrilled at how much German I know. It's sort of like having money I can spend.

But I decided not to tell my train-car colleague what the Germans actually said.

Soldiers like these didn't win the war. The Russians won the war.

✦ ✦ ✦

"Did you tell the German that you cheated to get the medal?" Carol asked me.

"No. By then I figured I'd really earned it. By then I was a fraud who didn't know he was a fraud."

✦ ✦ ✦

Pretty soon ten of us who'd graduated from the Defense Language Institute and Military Police School were together in a temporary billet at Campbell Barracks in Heidelberg.

I was so excited about being in Germany I put on civilian clothes and headed toward town.

"I think you should stay here," my friend Steve Goldberg said. "I've heard this unit has some really nice jobs where you don't have to wear a uniform. There's a rumor that someone from headquarters is coming over here to interview us. Don't you think you should hang around?"

"Goldberg," I said, "I've been waiting to see Europe ever since I read Hemingway. I'm out the door."

Goldberg, as usual, was right. When I got back in the early evening, after having wandered around the old part of Heidelberg, I learned that the NCO in change of personnel for the Twenty-Second MP Group had, in fact, stopped by the billet on his way home from work just to meet people. Between belches from the beer I'd drunk and sausages I'd eaten, I discovered that the people who weren't there were slated to be assigned to the unit's sole uniformed job—doing customs clearances at Rhein-Main Air Base outside of Frankfurt. My little dream of having an office job was over. I'd missed my chance to work in civilian clothes.

"Shit," I said.

"Too bad," Goldberg told me as he packed his duffel bag, preparing for his new job in Mannheim. "I'll see what I can do."

"Shit."

And then Goldberg was gone.

✦ ✦ ✦

I was depressed and a little drunk from the beer. It was warm in the barrack, and we were staying in an attic room, which made the day even warmer. I took a nap.

I woke up a little after sunset, just as the room was getting cool, and saw one other soldier in the area. He was lying on his bunk smoking a cigarette. I could see a shadowed area on the sleeve of his khaki uniform shirt where a Specialist Four emblem had been. I could see the old marks from the stitching. Someone had just ripped the rank marking off the sleeve. I guessed he'd been demoted.

"How's it going?" I said across the room. He went on smoking, ritually bringing his hand back and forth to his mouth. He didn't answer me.

"My name's Ryan," I said a moment later. "I'm new here. Going to the Twenty-Second MPs, at Rhein-Main. Do you know the unit?"

His arm stopped moving for a moment. The cigarette stayed in midair.

"Oh, yeah," he said and started smoking again.

"What can you tell me about it?"

"Watch out for Corporal Kravitz, my friend. Corporal Leon Kravitz." He stubbed out the cigarette on the floor. "Tell him he's a fucking asshole. Tell him Don said so."

The next morning he was gone, but Corporal Kravitz was there.

"Come on, Ryan, get your ass in gear. You've got a real army job, and you don't want to be late for your future."

We drove on the autobahn from Heidelberg to Frankfurt in an AMC Ambassador painted army green, a color that resembled algae-green pond scum.

The army seemed to buy the cars the rest of America didn't want, cars that were great going forty miles an hour but terrifying to ride in at autobahn speeds of eighty and ninety miles per hour. Their soft, ship-like suspensions and squishy brakes made them seem like fumble-fingered fat men trying to lace their shoes.

"I want to make something clear, Ryan," Corporal Kravitz told me on the ride. "I'm making a career of the army, so

I want to do a good job. Got that? This isn't some kind of joke. Maybe you met Don Bruzzard at Campbell Barracks. He thought stealing the pornography we confiscated was funny.

"'Who cares if I keep some of these pictures? I'm not hurting anyone,' he told me," Corporal Kravitz said. "Well, I cared. I got him busted. He broke the rules. He's going to face the rest of his life with a dishonorable discharge."

"Yes, Corporal," I said, coming to a kind of attention while sitting in the passenger seat.

"Oh, Ryan, just remember 'Filter, Flavor, Flip-Top Box.'"

"Pardon me."

"You know, the ad for Marlboro cigarettes. I like to say that. It keeps my mind centered."

Floating simultaneously back and forth and side to side in that pond-scum green AMC, I held on tight to my manila folders. The stuff in there no longer seemed so close at hand. Jean-Claude Killy, Paris, and Dansk: that's what I say to keep myself focused.

✦ ✦ ✦

For my job checking people through customs, I was given a white plastic MP hat and a Sam Browne belt covered with black plastic that always looked a little too shiny. I was issued a .45 by the air force MP station at the beginning of my shift, and I turned it back in when I was done. If you've gone through customs anywhere in the world, you've experienced the work I did at Detachment C of the Twenty-Second MP Customs Unit. We looked at faces for lies and at baggage for contraband. We mostly looked for narcotics, pornography, and weapons.

I worked for nine days followed by three days off.

My working colleague was a man named Dmitri Halter—Corporal Halter. Now Corporal Kravitz had, as the army liked to say, more time in grade as a corporal, so he slightly outranked Corporal Halter and me, but Corporal Halter's favorite book was a paperback copy of the Constitution of the United States. When he disagreed with Corporal Kravitz, he would quote from the Constitution. Corporal Kravitz didn't know much of anything except what his own opinions were, so the Constitution-quoting made him nervous, and he usually dropped any complaint he had against Dmitri and went on to harass someone else. Since Dmitri and I worked together, Dmitri's umbrella of protection included me as well. I kept my mouth shut.

One time, during one of Corporal Kravitz's needless and harassing barrack inspections, Dmitri pulled out his thumb-worn Constitution and said, a man's home is free of unreasonable search and seizures.

"That's in there, in the laws of the United States?" Corporal Kravitz asked. He seemed stunned. The whole moral underpinning of tearing somebody's footlocker apart had just been called into question. "You mean, I'm not supposed to go through your stuff?"

"Not if you want to obey the fundamental laws of the land."

"Then how can the army exist, if high-ranking people can't harass low-ranking people? Explain that to me."

For a moment there, Corporal Kravitz thought he had an edge.

"That's a very good question, Leon. You might want to think it over. In the meantime, I've got to go. I have errands to run. Come on, Ryan. You've got errands, too."

"I hate it when people call me Leon. It just doesn't sound tough enough, you know?"

I looked back just as we left the area, and there was Corporal Kravitz carefully putting the items in Dmitri's footlocker back in order.

"Now I've got the army where I want it," Dmitri said as we walked outside.

✦ ✦ ✦

With most of my savings, I bought a white Volvo 122-S with a four-speed. On my days off, I drove it around the countryside, delighting as I shifted its gears. The days were warm and sunny. The nights were crisp. I found a small apartment in Mörfelden not too far from the air base. I was getting ready for Jenny's arrival.

An attic apartment: its walls were the roof, and the only windows were skylights filled with blue. When I first moved in with the few pieces of furniture I'd bought at a house sale, I felt as though I were floating through space.

I was so lucky, I told myself.

✦ ✦ ✦

At Rhein-Main, the passengers from incoming flights were processed through a giant hangar big enough to hold several airplanes. Offices were built inside the hangar, and they resembled one-room, slat-sided houses, complete with windows and venetian blinds. There was one house for the Twenty-Second MP Group and one for various air force offices.

When the door to the giant hangar was closed (as it mostly was), the interior was dark and lit virtually around the clock by rows of flickering, blue-tinted bulbs in fixtures hanging high overhead. The lights left deep shadows in the corners, and the ambience of the lighted areas was gray, even when it was sunny outside. Day or night, it never really changed. The place seemed darkly hallucinogenic. Because the nine-day shifts were slowly destroying my sense of ordinary time, the days and nights in that hangar seemed the same, the only difference being the feel of the air temperature, as winter came on. What made matters even worse was the division of the nine-day workweek into blocks of three days, so I worked three days of day shifts, three days of swing shifts, and three days of night shifts. I soon was always tired because I couldn't get used to the shifting sleep schedule. Worse, I lost sense of what a normal day was.

Day after day, night after night, in the flickering gray-blue light, the incoming passengers went through two rooms created by walls made of heavy drapes. They were meant to intimidate people. One by one they came into Room One, where we had the amnesty barrel. CONTRABAND HERE. NO QUESTIONS ASKED, the crude sign read. In the next room Halter and I waited, standing before the inspection table, our MP white hats down low over our eyes, our thumbs stuck in our Sam Browne belts.

"Anything I should know about?" I asked.

"Next!" Halter yelled.

And so it went, one passenger at a time, day after day, night after night. We sorted through luggage; we poked our fingers into uniforms and underwear; we squirted out bits of toothpaste and tasted them.

"You want to tell me something?"

"Next!"

"What's in there?"

"Next!"

"Why are you so nervous?"

"Next!"

And then one night, this sergeant pulled out a mortar from his duffel bag and set it up on my table. He lit something and threw it in the barrel and stepped back and cupped his hands over his ears and yelled, "Fire in the hole," and it all happened so fast and something exploded except the explosion was like a firecracker and not a weapon and the man laughed and said that war is one comedy show after another and I got Halter, who said, "So what?" and "Who wants to fill out the arrest paperwork?" and we sent the soldier on his way and there was Corporal Kravitz standing in front of us.

"You motherfuckers let that guy go!?"

"Well, what was his crime, Leon?"

"Illegal possession of an army weapon to start with."

"Shit," Halter said, "you got hundreds of thousands of men walking around with weapons and you're worried about some dumb prankster in the middle of the night. Besides, he was a short-timer. He's probably home by now."

"Where we're going to read about him killing someone."

"Leon, you could say that about half the people here, including you. Here, read the Second Amendment of the Constitution, Leon."

Dmitri handed him the book.

"Read it to us, Leon. It's on page twenty-two."

"A well regulated Militia, being necessary to the security of a free State, the right of the people to keep and bear Arms, shall not be infringed."

Corporal Kravitz was not used to reading and stumbled on some of the wording.

"See, Leon? It's perfectly legal to carry a mortar or two. Fact is, I'm thinking of getting one for myself."

Corporal Kravitz stomped off then. He was afraid of Halter.

"Look, Ryan," Halter told me on another shift. "I've been around dickheads all my life. Remember I grew up in the Bronx. You can't give these fuckers space enough to breathe. You let those bastards get going, pretty soon you won't have a place to live."

52.

This is now November of 1970. I have been in the army for sixteen months. For all these hours and days and weeks I have been able to kid myself—to believe that the boy who writes poetry and reads Ralph Waldo Emerson is still inside my soul. I brought a volume of Emerson with me to Germany and have a new notebook and I sit in the apartment at the used table I bought and try to read and write on one of my days off but I sit there staring up at the skylight and turgid gray sky beyond. I haven't seen a blue sky for weeks. Jenny is coming in December, and I try to get excited about her arrival, but I just can't. Instead I get more and more depressed thinking of the time I'm wasting in the army.

I pace around the apartment, trying to jog my brain out of its funk, but the floor is covered with a rubberized tile that keeps causing me to trip and fall. One night, by accident, I bring my .45 pistol home from work. I take it out of my holster, trying to think of a safe place to store it as I walk into my bedroom. I trip, and the gun goes spinning into the air, and I watch it in slow motion, thinking this might be the end of me if it hits the floor and fires. I close my eyes in terror, but it lands, and the clip of shells pops out, and I fall to the floor weeping.

I go to work and sit in the gray, blue light of the hangar and feel my creative juices leak away. It gets easier and easier to yell at the stupid GIs standing in front of me than write poetry.

"Your duffel bag," I scream at a PFC in the middle of the night. "Empty your fucking duffel bag on the floor: that's what I want you to do."

I poke through his dirty clothes with my billy club and scatter them around.

"Now pick up this shit and get out of here. Now. I said. Now."

I follow him as he walks away, toward the exit. I follow him and scream "Now" over and over at his back. He pulls the duffel bag along by the strap with one hand and holds batches of his clothes with the other hand. He keeps dropping shirts and socks and underwear.

"Get that crap out of my inspection area," I yell as he walks out of the hangar.

"Be careful," Halter says to me later. "You're starting to sound like Leon. Relax, Ryan. This isn't your show, buddy. You just want to get out of here alive with your soul intact."

It seems like the sunshine went away forever that November. Day after day, low-hanging clouds give the world the look of hard iron. I get more depressed. Day after slow-moving day, night after slow-moving night I live in the gray of my work followed by the gray of the apartment, which now depresses me to no end. Gray despair hangs in the chambers of my head the way the smells of boiled cabbage and fried liver linger in the hallways of that Mörfelden apartment building. I keep tripping on the rubberized floor. When I come home from the air base, I sit in the one chair I'd bought and stare at the wall, watching the gray daylight come and go. I don't go anywhere on my days off.

✦ ✦ ✦

Corporal Leon Kravitz, though, is cheerful, and his good cheer rubs on my psyche like fingernails on a chalkboard.

Corporal Kravitz loves the army. When he isn't threatening us, he tries to sell us on its many benefits. He even likes our nine-on-and-three-off schedule.

"The great thing about the army," Corporal Kravitz explains, sitting with his shiny boots up on the desk in the Twenty-Second MP house, "is that we make your week nine days long. You go in the army, and you'll live two days longer every week. Think about it. That's a hundred days a year. Two thousand days over a twenty-year career. Shit, you get 2,000 extra days, a pension, and lifetime medical benefits. The army's the greatest thing since sliced bread."

"I never liked sliced bread all that much," Halter says. "Sliced bread is way overrated if you ask me."

"Nobody's asking you Halter," Corporal Kravitz says. "Even the army can't save you from being an idiot."

"Well, I might be an idiot, but I can do math. I'm afraid no one can add days to the calendar."

Jenny arrived in early December. The air had turned chilly, and it was still gray.

As a joke, Halter suggested that we pick her up at the civilian airport in our MP uniforms. We'd pretend to take her into custody.

"Shit, man, we're pretend cops, so we might as well do a pretend custody," he said. "Come on, man, it'll be funny. Two cute little cops like us."

Yes, that's right. Underneath it all I still thought it was some kind of joke. The sensitive poet, playing policeman. Yes, it would be funny, and there we were in the American Airlines waiting area with our white hats and Sam Browne belts, our billy clubs and our sidearms, waiting for Jenny to land.

Of course people were whispering and pointing at us, and they left a big circle around us.

And there was Jenny coming out of the airplane wearing a floppy leather hat and Italian-looking sunglasses with huge round lenses. She was carrying her guitar. She looked like a model, a model dressed up as a hippie.

"Pretty cool," Halter said. "Pretty fucking cool, man."

"You'll have to come this way, ma'am," I said, and slowly her whole moment of being a cool-looking hippie just evaporated. She stared in disbelief at this new person I'd become.

✦ ✦ ✦

"Please, Steve, you've got to get me out of here."

I called Goldberg in Mannheim.

"Maybe I can get you a job here. Give me a few days."

"Steve," I pleaded a week later.

And a week after that, a few days before Christmas, I was in my green sport coat driving the Volvo to Mannheim for my new job.

"Yes," I said, pumping the air with my fist. Goldberg had rescued me.

✦ ✦ ✦

"Just remember," Corporal Kravitz told me at the end of my last Rhein-Main shift, "'Filter, Flavor, Flip-Top Box.' That's what you'll be protecting, Ryan. Keep those Marlboro cigarettes out of enemy hands. 'Filter, Flavor, Flip-Top Box.'"

53.

"This is big, Ryan," Lance B. Edwards said just after I came to work that first morning at Turley Barracks in Mannheim. "We found tools in a mail inspection. We think it's some kind of ring. They're stealing tools and sending them back to the States. Their commanding officer brought them here for questioning. Here, Ryan, you talk to Clarence. He's waiting in the storeroom. You take him down to the other office in the basement. No one will bother you there."

My new boss, Lance B. Edwards, handed me some affidavit forms.

"Take Clarence down to the basement office and see if he will talk."

He opened the door to the storeroom, and this giant, oafish-looking man stood up. He must have been six five, but he had a stooped posture. With his thick hands and heavy shoes, he looked like the monster in some drawing from a fairy tale. His face was pale, with the color and texture of mashed potatoes.

"Clarence, this is Mr. Ryan. Mr. Ryan has some questions he'd like to ask you."

Clarence's hand enveloped mine when we shook. It was limp. It felt like the hand of the Pillsbury Doughboy.

✦ ✦ ✦

Turley Barracks had probably been built to withstand artillery attacks. Its walls were three or four feet thick. The basement had massive cast-iron bars over its deeply recessed windows, and our office there had the look of an ancient prison. Large metal hooks were fastened on the basement walls outside our office. They looked like places to hang meat carcasses or bodies. I learned later they were hooks to store the workers' bicycles, but that morning, they looked like something from a torture scheme, grim reminders on the way to the abattoir.

I was scared to death. I had never interrogated anyone before. My hand trembled when I held the lighter up to my Winston. I offered Clarence a cigarette. He shook his head and stared at the floor.

We sat down at an old oak desk with a recessed place in the middle for the typewriter. I put carbons between three MP statement forms, tapped them on the desk to align them, and then rolled them into the giant Underwood. Drops of sweat formed a little rivulet down my spine.

"Clarence," I said. He looked up from where he sat. He seemed surprised to see me there. "What's your last name?"

"Kindler," he said. "Clarence Kindler."

I wrote it down on a pad. I wanted to think before typing anything.

"Your middle initial?"

"R for Roger. My mama named me after my grandfather."

"Well, Clarence," I said, taking a deep breath, "may I ask you some questions?"

"You're the boss, Mr. Ryan."

Hearing my name put that way again surprised me and, for the briefest second, I felt as though I should look around for this mysterious Mr. Ryan.

I paused then, trying to think of what my first question should be, but Clarence got there first.

"Mr. Ryan, will there be bars like that where I'm going?"

I was so worried about getting the paperwork right that I didn't hear him at first.

"Bars like what?" I asked back.

I was trying to remember which parts of the form were to be filled out in capital letters. I had to know what he was supposed to initial and what he should sign.

Clarence turned around in his chair and looked at the far wall. He began farting. Big, methane gas farts—a rotten, foul smell. Carrion dead for several days. I felt nauseous.

"Bars like those, over there."

He pointed to the cast-iron bars on the small basement windows. Bars to keep the enemies out of the old *kaserne*—the enemies out, and the soldiers in.

Clarence stood up then. He raised his arms and began circling them, as if he might lift off and fly away from there.

"We stole them, sir. Mr. Ryan, sir," he said. "Yessir, we stole them and mailed them back to Meyers Home."

"What?" I asked. I finally had the forms aligned and scrolled into the Underwood. "Stole what, Clarence?"

"Started with those crescent wrenches. A couple of those, and then we started ordering cases of stuff. That expensive Sun diagnostic equipment, you know. Complete snap-on tool sets in carts on wheels. We mailed the stuff we stole back to Meyers Home."

Clarence kept farting, and I wrote down what he said with a pen first, so I wouldn't make any mistakes when I typed it up.

We were down there in that basement, Clarence and I, writing up the story of what would turn out to be a million dollar tool theft ring.

"Meyers Home, Clarence?" I asked.

"My granny, sir, Mr. Ryan, sir. That's where my granny lived. Meyers Home, North Carolina. We sent them to her, and she put them in her garage, the boxes of tools we sent her."

Clarence and his little mountain family were the patsies for this. The real crooks were a couple of master sergeants who organized everything but let Clarence be the front. I tried to help Clarence and give those sergeants a prominent role in Clarence's confession. I spent an hour writing the whole story out in long hand and then began typing. The whap of the typewriter keys into the depth of those forms sounded final.

On or about 10 APRIL 1969 MSG Elliot KASNER and MSG Robert BLEY ordered me to mail three (3) CRAFTSMAN eighty (80) piece socket-wrench sets owned by the US Army back to my grandmother's house in North Carolina for the purpose of selling same . . .

It was as close as I could come to the voice of Jack Webb.

"Clarence," I said after a couple of pages of confession, "let me show these to Mr. Edwards upstairs. OK?"

The basement hallway of Turley Barracks, lit by fluorescent bulbs, was quite bright. When I got to that dim lobby, which, in the last of that weak December sunshine and in the mist and the fog, was barely lit at all, I had trouble seeing the way ahead. I felt as though I were moving through a dirty aquarium.

Lance B. Edwards's white shirt stood out in the shadows. As I got closer I could see that he was talking to a mountainous black man—one of those people who seem both fat and muscular. He towered over Edwards.

"You've got to read this," I said to Edwards. "Here."

"You," the black man said to me. He grabbed the front of my shirt and put his fist, hard, against my chest. It was hard to breathe. "You the one with that white Volvo?"

Major Arthur. Goldberg had told me about him. The new Mannheim provost marshal. He'd been in charge of the infamous Long Binh Jail in Vietnam. He was reputed to be tough and corrupt. He'd beat you with his bare hands and accept a bribe to stop.

"You, soldier, you parked in the PM's slot. That's me, son. The provost marshal. I rule here, son. You park in my slot again, that'll be a short way to some long hard time, soldier."

Here I was about to break open one of the largest cases ever handled by the Twenty-Second, and I was in big trouble over a parking violation.

"Mr. Edwards," I said, trying to keep a little of the moment's glory. "I've got a signed confession. Read this."

The major stared at me from atop that mountain of flesh. When you stood close to him, his head looked too small and far away to run such a large body.

"Hard time, boy. You remember that, OK? You got an hour to move that car." He shoved me away from him.

Edwards and I walked into the main office of Detachment. Plenty of lights in there.

"Ryan, we've got to stay out of his way. Where he came from, they just beat the crap out of everybody. He's a tough son of a bitch."

Edwards sat down then at his desk. Holding his head in his hands, the way he always did when he read, he studied Clarence's confession. When he was finished, he looked up and smiled.

"Nice work, Ryan. Not bad for the first day on the job. Now get down and put some cuffs on Clarence. It's funny, but I've learned when someone confesses, you want to get those cuffs on him right away. It sort of wraps everything up, you know, professor, like putting a period at the end of a sentence. Oh, and move that fucking car. All right?"

"All right."

"Oh, Ryan."

"Yes."

"Merry Christmas. Merry fucking Christmas."

54.

*J*ean-Claude Killy, Paris, and Dansk.

The Good Life. The Dreams-Coming-True Part. It's happening, yes: we get a wonderful apartment in the small village of Ladenburg on the Neckar River. It has a balcony and hip-looking gray carpeting. We sign up for a Learn-To-Ski Week at the army's resort in Berchtesgaden. We go to Paris for four days. We order our Dansk dishes from the PX, and Jenny gets a job at a base library and brings home stacks of books to read. We lie around on Saturdays listening to an Armed Forces Radio show called *Weekend World*, which is usually about the current music scene. I put on my green sport coat and go to work in the Volvo, often stopping on the way home in the evening to buy some gourmet cheese or wine or chocolate or other treat. We buy skis; we buy European clothes. Jenny gets her guitar fixed and starts playing folk tunes in the evenings. We take weekend trips to Rothenburg and Munich. On my longer leaves, we drive the Volvo to catch the ferry to England.

It's a great life, punctuated by these police episodes. Maybe an arrest a week keeps us out of trouble with headquarters.

Meanwhile, I run into DuWayne Leonard. I knew him in Fayetteville. He's now evidence custodian for the army's Criminal Investigation Division, which is the army's version of the FBI.

"I want to show you something," he says late one afternoon. I've stopped by his office to pick him up. He's coming over to our apartment in Ladenburg for dinner. Afterward we'll listen to the new Santana album: "Abraxas."

"Here," he says as he opens the door of a tall green safe with a crinkled metal finish. "What's your pleasure?"

Inside the safe are shelves holding four- or five-inch balls, some brown, some tar black, some with both colors like a vanilla and chocolate cake.

"I don't know what you mean."

DuWayne laughs.

"I'll choose," he says and slices off a small piece from one of the balls and wraps it in white paper like a piece of cheese.

After dinner, he produces a small brass pipe, and Jenny and I have our first taste of drugs—of, in fact, opiated hash.

Let me take you down, and down the lane we skipping go, bouncing around in the landscape of our heads, rainbows connecting everything. What other word is there but, you guessed it: Wow. Yes, wow and wow and wow.

DuWayne sleeps on our couch, and, after breakfast the next morning, we take a couple of more puffs on the hash and walk to a nearby park. My footsteps seem to have springs in them, and I make a tinkling sound as I walk. The ground is covered with vibrant blue and green patterns that look as though Peter Max designed them. Yellow birds fly out from under my feet as I walk.

Cool, I think. This is so cool.

Do I also think about the fact that I'm smoking evidence that sent someone to jail? Do I think about my hypocrisy?

Boom. Boom. Snare.

Boom. Boom. Snare.

55.

Ah, yes, the good life, all courtesy of the US Army. And, oh, Angelika. I musn't forget my Angelika, my little German revolutionary.

She was the administrator at a University of Maryland office in Turley Barracks. Her office was right across the hall from mine. It was a place where the soldiers from the tank corps, who made up most of Turley's population, could sign up for classes. Perhaps because the office was in a military police station, she didn't get much business, so she spent most of her time reading or hanging out in a nearby army snack bar drinking Cokes. When Lance B. Edwards was gone, she took to visiting me.

Slightly buck-toothed, Angelika exuded a simple sexuality. She wore very short skirts and would occasionally bend over in front me, showing me the crotch of her pink panties. She wore translucent blouses, and you could see the dark outlines of her puffy nipples. When we talked, she would sometimes run her index finger down my arm, and I would often be in a state of half tumescence when I spoke with her, unsure of what we said.

Even though she was German, we had oddly similar backgrounds—both of us were the children of unhappy government workers. We'd both majored in English literature and believed we were intellectuals. We were both working for the US Army and thought of ourselves as subversives, though

Angelika, if her pictures were to be believed, was a little more serious than I was.

She showed me a snapshot of her standing before a Che Guevara poster holding some kind of automatic weapon. She also loved the Baader-Meinhof Gang and had a scrapbook filled with newspaper articles about them. She told me she knew many of the gang members.

Since what mostly interested me about Angelika was her sexuality, I didn't pay much attention to the political stuff. I didn't care about politics.

One morning, she came into my office, gave me a lingering French kiss, and sat down on the top of my desk. Her legs straddled my chest; her crotch was right there in front of me. Without thinking, I began caressing it. She closed her eyes and began humming a tune.

"Oh, my little soldier boy, such fingers *du hast*. My. Yes. My. My."

The next thing she was sitting on my lap rocking back and forth, trying to unzip me.

Even now, decades later, I have to close my eyes when I think of the waves of longing that came over me.

"Your place," I said, breathing hard. "I'll take you home from work. Three thirty. I'll leave early. We can't do this here."

She got up, pulled her tiny skirt down over her exposed panties, blew me a kiss, and left.

I looked down at my crotch. It had blotches of her wetness there.

✦ ✦ ✦

I ached looking at the slow passage of time on my watch but then we were out the door and into the Volvo and she was unzipping my pants and sucking on my cock and I was driving to her little apartment in Neckargmünd. It was really just a large room with a sink and a hot plate and a bathroom to one side and then we were out of our clothes and making love on her squeaky bed.

I get dizzy thinking about the months we were together. I usually stayed until six or seven. I told Angelika I had to leave because I had to check in at my barrack because of my security clearance. When I got home to Jenny, I told her we'd been having special military exercises and that I'd be coming home late for the foreseeable future.

I led this delicious double life. I was having it all. Saint Moritz and Paris and London. A cool apartment. New Dansk dishes. Two women to fuck. All brought to me courtesy of the United States Army. Wonderful.

Sometimes Angelika and I would sneak away from work in the middle of the day and lie around her apartment making love and drinking Riesling. Other times we would have sex standing up in the storage closet at the back of her University of Maryland office.

Angelika wanted me to be her boyfriend, and I didn't have the courage to tell her I was already married. I just kept making up stories about my security clearance when she asked me to go out in public with her.

"We've got to keep this a secret," I said. "I'm not allowed to be seen with a German national. It would compromise my job."

She wanted my picture, and I let her photocopy the one in my customs police identification wallet. She had the photo framed and put it on her dresser.

"I've got my own soldier who will take me to live in America," she kept saying and French kissing me afterward.

I'm not sure why Angelika liked me so much. She probably could have had any soldier she wanted. Maybe she was in love with me.

Her apartment was filled with anti-American political tracts and posters promoting—along with Che and Mao and Ho Chi Minh—the *Baader-Meinhof Gruppe*. She told me she was just a pal of the gang's, though not really a member. I suppose this confession should have triggered an alarm, but I was so interested in the next blow job that I didn't pay it any mind.

As Sergeant Dooley once explained, "You don't want the truth to interfere with your fucking."

Angelika just kept telling me that she and I would go to America together and be revolutionaries together when I got out of the army.

She told me she loved me. She gave me a key to her apartment. How delicious it was when I would get there before she did, undress, crawl under the cool sheets, and wait to surprise her.

"*Ach, ja,*" she would say, stepping out of her skirt as she came toward me. "Here is my American soldier defending his little bit of Deutschland."

Jean-Claude Killy, Paris. Dansk. And, now, add Angelika to that. My lovely Angelika.

56.

The last time I saw Angelika I was lying there, naked in her bed, waiting for her to come back to the apartment.

The door banged open when she arrived. She was furious.

"How could you do this?"

She picked up a broom and began hitting me.

"What are you doing?" I tried to roll away from her blows.

"You've made me have adultery, you asshole."

"What?"

"I saw that woman you rode with yesterday."

Jenny had picked me up at the office. She'd needed the car for an errand.

"I asked that man in your office, that Lance, who the woman is, and he tells me she's your wife. You're married. Because of you I make adultery. I am Catholic. I cannot make adultery and go to heaven."

She started hitting me again with a broom.

"What kind of a man are you? What do you stand for? You stand for nothing. You are interested in nothing but yourself. What have you done to me?"

I grabbed my clothes and ran downstairs naked. I could hear her thumping down the steps behind me.

"*Du Arschloch!*" she yelled. You asshole.

I was trying to get my pants on in this little vestibule at the bottom of the stairs. I stared at the window in the door. It had these gauzy curtains, and I remember wondering whether they were handmade or store-bought and I was trying to get a leg into my pants, but the fabric was twisted somehow and turned inside out and it was as if the pants leg had been sewn shut, and suddenly there she was in that vestibule with the broom raised up over her head to hit me, and I ran outside bare-assed naked like some character in an old silent comedy, and she followed me.

We stood there in the courtyard of the apartment building, facing each other, making moves, then backing off. She held the broom over her head, but I could tell her heart wasn't in it anymore. Her face was smeared with tears.

"I will get you for this. I fix you good. I will call my Baader-Meinhof friends, and they will take care of you. Imperialist pig. Fucking American imperialist pig."

Still naked, I ran for the Volvo and, luckily, found the keys in the pocket of my pants. I tossed my clothes in the backseat and jumped in the car and drove off. I could see her in my rearview mirror, shaking that broom over her head. I can see her to this very day.

"What have you done to me?" she yells. "What have you done?"

57.

And then I was sitting in the witness chair at Sergeant Perkins's court-martial.

"So, Mister Ryan, here is what I want to know," the major prosecuting the case asks me. "You brought Sergeant Perkins to your office for questioning. Is that correct?"

Remember Sergeant Perkins, who started this story off?

"Yessir. Correct."

"Very good. Do you recognize this document?"

The major hands me Sergeant Perkins's confession.

"Yessir. It's a confession form."

"Yes, of course, Mr. Ryan, but who's the confession *from*?"

"I don't know. I'd have to read it, sir."

"You don't recognize it? I mean, don't you recognize Sergeant Perkins's signature here at the end?"

"Major, I've taken a lot of these. They kind of run together. We want to be sure, don't we?"

"Of course. Of course. Look it over. Take your time."

I glanced through it.

"Yes, it was signed by a Sergeant Perkins, sir."

"A Sergeant Perkins?!" the captain defending Sergeant Perkins says, jumping up. "Don't you remember, Mister Ryan?"

"Well, as I said, we do this a lot."

"OK, Mister Ryan," the major interjects. "Let's talk about the rights of Sergeant Perkins. Did you read him his rights?"

The captain sits back down. I'm sure he thinks he played enough drama to convince everyone the trial is on the up and up—that he actually cares about Sergeant Perkins.

"We read everyone their rights. It's a matter of office policy."

"But Mister Ryan, did you read Sergeant Perkins *his* rights? That's who we're concerned with here. Sergeant Perkins. The man sitting over there. You remember him, don't you?"

Sergeant Perkins looks at the floor.

"He seems familiar, sir."

The defender and the prosecutor look at each other. The colonel acting as judge raps his pencil on his desk.

For a moment I hear it as *boom, boom, snare. Boom, boom, snare.*

"So, Mister Ryan, did you, in fact, read Sergeant Perkins his rights?" the major asks after the colonel quits rapping.

"Well, as I said, it is our policy to read everyone his or her rights."

"But did you specifically read Sergeant Perkins his rights?"

"I see here that he initialed the part about being read his rights. It's right on the form." Then, as an afterthought, I add: "Sir."

The colonel acting as judge clears his throat.

"I think I've heard enough. I am going to dismiss this case. Sergeant Perkins you can go."

Sergeant Perkins stands up and looks around, as if he's waking up. He seems taller than I remembered. His defender snaps his briefcase closed.

"What kind of bullshit is this?" the colonel asks after they leave. "You're a disgrace to the US Army, Mister Ryan."

Maybe, though, just maybe I've done something good. Sergeant Perkins is a free man. I got him off.

✦ ✦ ✦

"Ryan, what kind of a cute, fucking performance was that," the major prosecuting the case asks as we walk out of the courtroom. "What's this 'We would usually read them their rights' stuff?"

"Well, I . . ." I begin.

He looks at me as if I were something stuck to the bottom of his shoe.

"You know, Ryan, it doesn't matter. Your stupid little try to wipe your hands clean of us doesn't matter. The fact is, we've got Sergeant Perkins cold. He's already in jail, he just doesn't know it yet."

"But the trial's over."

"But not the next trial, Sergeant Ryan, or the one after that. The army doesn't like these married men living with their girlfriends. It's bad for our image. Sergeant Perkins is going to Leavenworth."

"But . . ."

"The truth is what we say it is, Ryan. Never forget this, even after you leave the army. One more thing."

"Yessir."

"Just remember. We always win. Always."

"Boom, boom, snare," I mutter. "Boom, boom, snare."

"Dismissed, Mister Ryan. You're dismissed."

58.

In my dream, I call Walt Rostow again.

"Look, you little crumble ass, don't call me again. You don't have any real problems. You never felt the smack of a bullet. You got to sit on your ass in Germany and drink wine. Look at the faces on those boys wounded in Afghanistan. Look at them. Their eyes look like they've been boiled in blood."

"But."

"Don't but me nothing, buddy. Unless you've sucked at the tit of Mother Battle, you don't get to say a thing about war."

"Look."

"Look bullshit. You try to talk about war to someone who's been there—why, that's like finding out they have wild cards for all your aces."

"I worked for the empire, just like Joel Niederman."

"Oh, Joel Niederman—now that's a sad story."

"It's all about money and power."

"Of course it is. What did you think it was about?"

"I know that, but no one will listen to me. The wounded veterans are so caught up in their own pain that they're afraid to talk about it. So it just stays a secret, or sometimes a truth told by people who get demonized as Communists or stuff like that."

"Now you're getting it, Ryan. Let me tell you a secret: we've been practicing this stuff for years. Decades. Centuries.

It's the story Homer never told. War: it's the oldest business in the world."

And then he begins laughing. And laughing. He throws his head back, and Dwight Eisenhower, and Lyndon Johnson and General MacArthur and ranks of men whose faces I can't make out have their heads thrown back and laughter cascades and ripples back and forth as certain and powerful as the tides of the sea.

59.

On May 24th, the *Baader-Meinhof Gruppe* set off bombs at Campbell Barracks, the US Army facility in Heidelberg, killing three people. It was the front-page story in the *Stars and Stripes* I picked up at the snack bar on my way into work the next morning.

The attack really frightened me. I wondered if Angelika had anything to do with it. I was nervous as I came into the main hall of the Turley Barracks MP Station, but the door to her office was closed and I didn't have to deal with it. I was relieved.

"Ryan, did you see this?"

Lance B. Edwards was standing in the doorway to my office in our MP Customs suite a few minutes after I got to my desk. I thought he was talking about the bomb attack and went on studying the picture of the overturned Ford Capri in the parking lot at Campbell Barracks on the front page of *Stars and Stripes*. The car was blown up in the lot just outside of the main Twenty-Second MP Group Headquarters.

"Man, this is all a little close for me," I said to Lance B. Edwards and held up the front page of the paper.

"Ryan, I knew you were talented, but I didn't know that you were famous."

"What do you mean?"

I put down the paper.

"Here." He handed me a small poster with torn corners.

And there I was—or there's my customs police ID photograph, the one Angelika wanted—on an anarchist wanted poster.

GESUCHT, the poster said right over the top of my face. WANTED. *Wir suchen diesen Mann wegen krimineller Aktivitäten gegen das deutschen Volk. Verratsgesuch.*

We're searching for this man who's guilty of criminal activities against the German people. Traitor Wanted.

"You must have quite the night life, Sergeant Ryan," Lance B. Edwards said, for the first and only time using my actual army rank.

"Jesus," I said. "Jesus H. Christ."

What was it Angelika had said?

I fix you good. I will call my Baader-Meinhof friends.

"Where did you find this?" I asked Edwards.

"They're all over Heidelberg," Edwards said. "What's your rotation date?"

"June 15th. Jenny's leaving this Saturday. Most of our stuff has already been shipped."

"Look: I got a call from headquarters about a raid in the morning. You and Goldberg go on that one. Then I vote you pack your stuff and get your ass out of the Federal Republic of Germany next Monday. I'll get you some emergency orders, OK?"

I looked at the wanted poster of me, a little artifact that has me squarely on the wrong side of something. Is this, I wonder, what history looks like?

60.

I was even more nervous the next morning.

I had my wanted poster folded and inside the pocket of my green Harris Tweed jacket. I was wondering whether I should show it to the Germans, but Herr Diener had brought along his own copy.

"*Ach, ja,*" he said, holding up the wanted poster. "*Herr Ryan, der Freund von Albert Speer und berühmte Kriminelle.*" He chuckled.

Mr. Ryan, friend of Albert Speer and famous criminal. I tried to laugh, too, but my throat felt dry.

"*Ich hab' gehört, dass diese Leute, die wir heute sehen, etwas mit der Baader-Meinhof Gruppe zu tun haben.*"

The people we're seeing today have something to do with the Baader-Meinhof Gang.

"*Was?!?*" I say. I am getting more and more nervous. "*Was sagst Du?*" You must be crazy.

Herr Hellman furtively pulls the handle of his pistol out of his coat pocket and shows it to me as if that will cure my woes.

The apartment was on the top floor. Herr Diener and Goldberg and I, led by Herr Hellman, shuffled up the stairs after someone buzzed us into the building. When, out of breath, we got to the top floor, the door to the apartment was slightly ajar, and a skinny-faced man in a T-shirt leaned against it, looking at us.

"*Was geht?*" he asked, an American good at German slang. What do you want?

"Customs Police," I said and held up my credentials. "May we come inside?"

I was following the rule book. If you asked to come in and the people gave you permission, then you could search without a warrant. If you also had a warrant, Lance B. Edwards said we were double covered. No US court could throw out the case.

"Sure. Come on in. I been kinda missing the army. Be a chance to shoot the shit with my buddies."

"And you are . . . ?" Goldberg asked.

"Wilbur. Russell Wilbur. You know, the famous deserter. The famous accomplice of the Baader-Meinhof Gang. Known far and wide by the CID."

I glanced at Goldberg with a quizzical look. Could this be true?

"You got some kind of identification?" Goldberg asked him.

The door to the apartment opened on a cramped living room combined with both dining room and kitchen. A very pregnant woman was pacing back and forth.

"Russ, why'd you let them in? Fucking Nazis."

"We won't be here long," Goldberg said. "Just want to ask you a few questions, ma'am."

"Nazis," she said again and crossed her arms over her chest. "Goddamned Nazis."

Herr Hellman's head jerked every time he heard the word "Nazi."

"Filthy Nazis!"

Goldberg studied the green army ID card Wilbur handed him.

"I don't want to be rude," Goldberg said, "but this says you're fifty-one years old. You look like you're about twenty-five to me. This wouldn't be a forgery, would it?"

"Somebody made a mistake," Wilbur said. "Hey, it's the army—mistakes happen all the time. People die for no good reason at all."

"I mean it, Russell, why did you let these Nazis in here?" She turned to Herr Diener. "*Haben Sie öffentliche Papiere mitgebracht?*"

Did you bring official papers?

Herr Hellman was bringing jars out of the cupboards and setting them on a table. They were jars of Gerber baby food purchased at the PX. If Wilbur wasn't actually in the military, then these were black-market items.

Diener handed her the warrants. She studied them, but then Herr Hellman caught her attention. He had stacked thirty or forty jars of baby food on the table and was sitting there counting them.

"Hey, *was geht's hier ab*?" she yelled at Hellman. She stood in front of where he sat at the table, her enormous belly in his face. "Nazi, Nazi, Nazi!" she screamed.

"*Ich will Ihnen Nazis zeigen*," he said, and stood up. "*Es war überhaupt alles besser in der Nazi Zeit.*"

I'll show you a Nazi. It went a lot better in the time of the Nazis.

"You fuckers. She's right." Wilbur began moving away from Goldberg. "We're just poor people about to have a baby. That's food for a goddamned baby. What kind of creeps are you? You have no right to be here. You're stealing our food, motherfuckers."

Hellman swept the jars of baby food off the table. They clattered and crashed on the floor. Some exploded when they hit like glass artillery shells. I could smell the scent of peas.

I felt sick. I was finally ashamed of myself. I wanted to get out of there. Escape from the web of lies that had trapped me in that apartment.

The woman put her face up close to Hellman's.

"Nazi, Nazi, Nazi," she yelled.

Hellman began fumbling in his suit pocket.

"Ich will Ihnen Nazis zeigen."

I'll show you a Nazi.

I could see the outline of the pistol.

"No," I heard myself yell, as if I were another person.

"And what do we have here?" Goldberg held up a pile of my wanted posters. "Doing a little publicity work for the folks over at Baader-Meinhof?"

"They don't break in to the apartments of poor people. I can tell you that," Wilbur said and tried to grab the pile of papers. "Give me those. You have no right to my papers."

"So you do work with the Baader-Meinhof Gang," Goldberg said.

Then the woman started yelling again.

"Arschloch Nazis. Nazi. Nazi. Nazi."

Asshole Nazis.

Hellman finally jerked the pistol from the folds of the jacket fabric, pointing it first at the ceiling and then at the ground. I grabbed his arm, trying to stop him, but managing, perversely, to steady it as he fired toward the woman, who was only inches from the barrel.

Blam.

Everything seemed to stop, a frozen moment.

The woman's mouth formed an O and, in slow motion, she looked at Hellman, at me, and then down at her belly, where a red blotch began to appear.

"O O O O," she screamed.

The pressure of my hand on Hellman's arm made him point the gun toward the ceiling, and a couple of more rounds went off. Blam. Blam. I suddenly remembered the smell of gunpowder in the basement of my childhood. Blam. Blam.

The room smelled like gunpowder and peas.

"Hey da, hey da," Rudi yelled. He was standing at the door, looking like Oliver Hardy in the midst of chaos. He walked

over and put his enormous hand around the gun Hellman held. The gun vanished, as if Rudi had performed a magic trick.

The woman sank to the floor, moaning.

"You know what," Goldberg said. "I think you and I should get the hell out of here. I don't think this is our problem."

I knelt down beside the woman.

"Are you all right?"

She seemed to be breathing. I lifted her up. A section of her back stuck to the floor. Yellow and red viscera stretched like partially dried glue. I briefly thought of airplane models I'd glued together as a child. I remembered the doll the sergeant had shot at Fort Gordon during my MP training.

✦ ✦ ✦

"My God," Carol says. "You never told me this. Did she die? She must have."

"I don't know."

"You don't know?"

"I don't know."

"How can you not know?"

"I don't know."

✦ ✦ ✦

"I think we should get out of here," Goldberg says again. "I mean, I'm leaving, and I think you should come, too."

"What have I done?" I asked.

"Your job, Ryan, your job," Goldberg said. "Just remember that. You were just doing your job. None of this is your fault. You were just doing what they told you to do."

The man who wasn't there arrives.

Boom. Boom. Snare.
Boom. Boom. Snare.

61.

*A*ch, *ja,* Herr Ryan. So good to have you here.

Albert Speer bows at the front door, welcoming me.

We've been expecting you. Many of your friends are already here. Mr. Rostow has been asking after you. Come.

He holds out his hand, and I take it. It feels cold, ice cold, like death.

The head of Henry Kissinger is overhead, and in the distance the sound of the drums starts. I am afraid I will hear them forever.

Boom. Boom. Snare.

Boom. Boom. Snare.

62.

"OK, what they're saying is that you shot the woman."

It's a gruff voice on the phone.

"They're saying that you grabbed the gun and shot the woman."

It's the operations sergeant at headquarters. A wave of cold goes through my stomach.

"That's not true," I say. "I was trying to get the gun away from him. I was trying to save her life. I was just doing my job."

"The colonel's not happy."

I begin to shake. Maybe I did kill someone. Jesus. I'd never been in this kind of trouble before. The Man Who Wasn't There Arrives. It's all so perverse and wrong. I looked down at the bloodstain on my Harris Tweed sport coat. I got it when I leaned over the woman and haven't been able to get it off.

"They're saying your fingerprints are on the gun and that you fled the crime scene."

I don't know what to say.

"The German police want to talk with you."

I try to speak but can't form the words.

"What happened to the woman?"

I am shaking so much I can't hold the phone to my ear.

"Let me talk with Edwards."

Lance nods at me when I hand him the phone. He nods some more when he gets on the line.

"Uh huh, uh huh, uh huh," he keeps saying, holding the phone close and occasionally looking at me.

"What'd he say?" I ask when Lance hangs up.

"You gonna get your ass out of Deutschland and the army, Ryan. Once you get out of the army they can't touch your civilian ass. Don't worry. You're lucky. That German Badguy Group is messed up in this."

"Baader," I say. "*Baader-Meinhof Gruppe.*"

"Whatever. They'll save your ass. That couple—they're working for them. Bad-guy stuff all over the house. Posters, AK-47s, shit like that. The Germans will blame them."

"Saved by the sixties. How funny."

"But to be sure, you need to get your ass out of the army. Then they can't touch you. You'll be long gone."

"Oh."

"Got that Ryan? Long gone."

"How about the woman?"

"She's not your problem. The way I see it, she's German Customs's problem. And, by the way, here's this. No time like the present."

He hands me a large, white envelope.

"What is it?"

"Open it up."

It's an ARCOM—an Army Commendation Medal.

"Congratulations."

"This seems like kind of a funny time . . ."

"You deserve it, Ryan. You did what you were told. Congratulations. You've been a good soldier."

"What about the woman?"

"You've got other things to worry about."

"Under sometimes difficult circumstances, Sergeant Ryan faithfully executed his duties as a customs military policeman," reads the citation.

Boom, boom, snare.

Boom, boom, snare.

63.

In this dream, the light scours everything. It's blinding. It's so white it turns everything else into a shadow. Looking hurts my eyes, and I try to turn away, but I can't.

The shadow of the pregnant woman slowly rises from the floor. I can see the dark blood dripping from her back. She shakes her head, as if refusing something.

"Why?" she asks in a quiet voice.

The light feels like razor blades across my eyeballs.

"Why did you shoot me?"

I didn't, I want to say, but that's not true.

"Why?" she asks again.

"You called me a Nazi."

"Weren't you? Weren't you a Nazi?"

"Not a real Nazi."

"They didn't mean to hurt people either. Most of them were just doing their jobs."

"But they hurt people."

"And you didn't? Look at me."

She turns, and I can see the organs inside her body, make out the pulsing dark mass of her heart, which is slowing down. It's hardly beating at all.

"Look at me," she says again. "You did this to me. You. You. You."

I keep waiting for the next beat of her heart, but it never comes.

64.

On June 1, 1972, the sky over Germany is blue, and it would be hard to believe there's trouble anywhere in the world. I'm back in uniform. Good Sergeant Ryan, carrying my duffel bag with its silver-painted identification across the parade grounds at *Gutleut Kaserne*, where I'd once scrubbed the cobblestones with my toothbrush. I've got my ARCOM and a Good Conduct Medal they handed me at headquarters. Most importantly I've got my separation orders.

"Ryan, huh?" the clerk says. "I got a call this morning, and they want you out of this man's army pretty pronto. Here." He looks at a folder of plane schedules. "Is tonight soon enough?"

And then I'm going through the Twenty-Second MP Customs Unit line and getting on a plane and looking over my manila folders and seeing the picture of me and Jenny taking ski lessons at Berchtesgaden and then I'm getting on a bus at Fort Jackson, South Carolina, for the airport near Columbia.

✦ ✦ ✦

And then Carol and I are talking. It's decades later. Jenny and I divorced in 1977. I married Carol in 1979. She wasn't there, in my MP days.

"You really shot her didn't you?" Carol asks.

"Shot her?"

"The pregnant woman."

"Oh you're back to that."

"How could I forget?"

"This is just a story."

"But I want to know."

"I don't know."

"What do you mean, you don't know?"

"I don't know. This is just a story. I get lost in it myself."

"Let's start at the beginning. How about Mr. Niederman? Is he true?"

"That's not his real name, but the story is mostly true."

"But how about Sergeant Perkins and Mrs. Downy and *Minor Memories* and all that?"

"The Sergeant Perkins story is true, and so's Mrs. Downy, though her real name is Mrs. Davies, and we never had an Algebra Squad. The real name of my junior high yearbook is *Young 'Uns.* I never liked that title. I think *Minor Memories* is better."

"And the pregnant woman, Rick. What about the pregnant woman? The shooting? What about her?"

I didn't want to hear that question.

"And Grimes Poznik," I said. "Don't forget about him. The trumpet player. He's real. He became The Human Jukebox at Fisherman's Wharf in San Francisco. Dead on the streets of alcohol poisoning. Steve Unger's real, too. One of the most talented people I ever knew. They made him a door gunner in Vietnam."

Boom, boom, snare.

Boom, boom, snare.

65.

We've come a long way from eighth grade algebra and Mr. Niederman and Buddy Holly, haven't we?

Oh, Mr. Bauch, there are so many facts of the matter to consider.

This one, for instance, from Wikipedia:

> *George Stephen Morrison (January 7, 1919–November 17, 2008) was an admiral and naval aviator in the United States Navy. Morrison was commander of the US naval forces in the Gulf of Tonkin during the Gulf of Tonkin Incident of August 1964. He was the father of Doors lead singer Jim Morrison.*

Another fact might be some of Jim Morrison's lyrics:

> *This is the end, beautiful friend*
> *This is the end, my only friend*
> *The end of our elaborate plans*
> *The end of everything that stands*
> *The end*

And perhaps we could then finish with this paragraph from Robert McNamara's obituary in the *New York Times*:

> *Congress authorized the war after [President] Johnson contended that American warships had been attacked by North Vietnamese patrol boats in the Gulf of Tonkin*

on Aug. 4, 1964. The attack never happened, as a report declassified by the National Security Agency in 2005 made clear. The American ships had been firing at radar shadows on a dark night.

Did Fleet Commander Morrison know that the intelligence which escalated the war in Vietnam was at least suspect and maybe plain wrong? Did he know that millions would die for nothing? And what did Jim Morrison know?

Radar shadows on a dark night.

When asked, Jim Morrison often said that his family was dead.

Soon everyone from this little story will be dead, and even these few remaining pieces from the jigsaw puzzle will be lost in the dusty interstices of time.

66.

On my way out of Janesville, after touring the house at 863 East Memorial Drive with Patsy Apple, I drive downtown for a kind of last loop through my past. Many of the businesses of my childhood have vanished: Harrison Chevrolet, Wisconsin Bell, and Woolworth's are gone. The Clark gas station has been turned into a parking lot, though the little plaque is still there: *On this spot in 1898, Carrie Jacobs Bond wrote "I Love You Truly."* On Main Street, another store of my childhood is about to go. The inside of its display windows are papered over.

DREYHOUSE SHOES
GOING OUT OF BUSINESS SALE
EVERYTHING MUST GO

"You—you, why yes, I remember you! Of course I remember you!" the bent-over old man says when I walk into the store. The few hairs on the top of his head stand straight up, as if they've been electrified. "You were a boy here once. A boy, yes, who bought shoes from me."

He tries to make one of his conducting gestures, but his arms won't go that high anymore.

"A boy here, yes. What was your name?"

Still a salesman, I think. Not hard to guess that many of the men coming into his store were boys in Janesville once.

Probably every boy in Janesville of a certain age bought shoes from Mr. Dreyhouse.

"Rick," I say. "I was Rickie, then."

"Ah, of course. Yes, Mrs. Ryan's boy."

"You remember after all these years?"

"Please. It wasn't just money for me," he says. "It was a life I had. Such wonderful people I met."

"Do you remember, Mr. Dreyhouse, your shoe X-ray machine?"

"The Adrian. Yes, the lovely Adrian." He pauses and then lifts his shaky fingers and points toward the back of the store. "You come with me."

We part our way through some soiled beige curtains into a backroom lit by flickering fluorescent lights. Shelves filled with shoe boxes lean this way and that. The air smells of oil and leather and rubber.

"Back here." He kicks empty shoe boxes out of the way, and we go down some rough stairs to the basement. He reaches up and pulls the beaded chains connected to overhead bulbs as we walk through the musty smell.

"Voilà." He pulls a dusty canvas off, and there—with pieces of its aluminum trim hanging loose and what looks like the splintered dent of a kick mark in its side—is the old shoe fluoroscope.

"You put your feet in there!" he commands.

Without thinking, I step up and stick my feet in the hole. Waves of memory come back to me. I close my eyes and think, for the briefest second, I might see my mother standing there. When I open them, though, I see Mr. Dreyhouse putting the frayed cord of the machine into an equally frayed extension cord that dangles from the light switch.

"Do you think this is safe?" I ask.

"It is if I don't touch the exposed copper." He holds up the wire, and I can see the dark glitter of the exposed wires between shreds of old knit fabric.

"I come down here all the time to try on shoes. I love to see my toes wiggling there. It makes me feel young again." He smiles, sharing a secret with me. "You won't tell my daughter. She's the one who's selling the store. She doesn't understand. She thinks I'll get something from the radiation. What does she know?"

He plugs the cord in.

"Here we go," he says.

He flips the Bakelite switch. Nothing happens.

"This machine's like me. Sometimes you got to give us a little push to get us going."

He flips the switch back and forth and bangs the kick mark on the side of the machine with his foot. Suddenly the Adrian thunks. It snaps to attention. The familiar humming starts, but I hear crackles and then I feel the tingle of a little electric shock.

"Whoa . . ."

"Nothing to worry about. Just a tickle of electricity. Look at your feet, Mr. Reilley."

"Ryan."

Mr. Dreyhouse isn't listening; he's looking through one of the viewfinders on top of the machine. I look, too, and sure enough, there are the bones of my two feet in that wavery green light that now brightens and now darkens.

"Too tight, Reilley. See how those shoes squeeze your little toe?"

The Adrian begins to lift and drop, as if it's breathing, and the crackle of the electricity becomes louder and the tingle sharper. I step off the machine and see a slight halo of electricity around Mr. Dreyhouse's fingers.

"Science lets us see the truth inside," he says. He leans on the Adrian. Maybe the electricity locks him there.

I walk away through the must of the basement. I turn around. He's still back there, haloed in the light of the single overhead bulb, his thin hair standing straight up.

"You'll electrocute yourself," I yell at him.

"I'm used to it. Finding out the truth requires a little pain sometimes, Mr. Reilley."

67.

Sergeant Richard Ryan received a United States Army Commendation Medal from the Forty-Second MP Gp (Customs) for his work as a translator and black-market investigator in Germany during the early 1970s.

R. M. Ryan is the author of another novel and two books of poetry.

This novel is dedicated to Steven Unger, who died in November of 2011, late casualty of the war in Vietnam.